EMPIRE ᴏF CARNAGE

SANTANA KNOX

Editor: Karen Washo, Utterly Unashamed LLC.

Cover Design: Designs by LM

Interior art: Brianna Billiard, @FlashFryed

Author's Note

Here we are again, at the end of a deep dark tunnel. If you are new to my writing, please understand I do not write these stories in an attempt to romanticize anything, not violent and dangerous situations, not the cártel or gang life, or any of the things you may see in my writing. These are just stories that live deep in the trenches of my troubled mind.

Any of the kinks seen in this book are not meant to be used as educational material.

This book is the darkest in the series, please heed the trigger warning page (next page) seriously, if this book is not for you, please reach out to me and I can tell you how the story ends. Always prioritize your mental health above all.

Due to the nature of this book, there is no playlist.

Content Warnings:

Nonconsensual drug use, racism, sexual assault (not done by the love interests), torture, mutilation, decapitation, teeth removal, burning, cutting, suicidal ideology, human trafficking, guns, reckless behavior.

To every person who was forced to adapt to survive, and lost a piece of themselves in the process.

Glossary

Abre la boca - open your mouth

Amiga - friend

Carajo - damn

Cabrones - bastards

Cállate - shut up

Cállate idiota - shut up idiot

Cálmate - calm yourself

Claro – of course

Chingadera – fucking thing

Chisme - gossip

Cobarde - coward

Entidendiste? – do you understand

Corazón - heart

Cultura - culture

Desmadre – mess

Dios - god

El es familia - He is family

El pasado ser el pasado - the past be the past

Está bien – it's all right

Familia - family

Güera - blonde

Hermanito/a - brother/sister

Hijo de la chingada - bastard/motherfucker/insult

Jefa - boss

La Flaquita - in reference to Santa Muerte

La Madrina - in reference to Santa Muerte

Loca - crazy

Lo juro por dios - I swear to god

Mamá - mother

Mi vida – my life (term of affection)

Morena - term of affection for dark haired, Brown women

Muerte - death (Sometimes used in reference to the deity
of death Santa Muerte)

Papá - father

Payaso - clown

Payasada - ridiculous

Pendejo - dumbass

Pinche - fucking

Porque soy mejor - Because I'm better

Puta - bitch/whore

Puta madre - mother fucker

Presidente - president

Primo - cousin

Princesa (princesita) - princess

Querido - dear/darling

Que chingados? - what the fuck

Quiero ser tu todo – I want to be your everything

Reina - queen

Señorita - Miss

Sobrina - niece

Soy mas grande - I'm bigger

Te amo - i love you

Te quiero - i love you

Te acuerdas de mi? – remember me?

Tío - uncle

Todo es mio - everything is mine

Todo se fue a la verga - everything went to hell

Ven a mi - come to me
Vamos - lets go
Y quiero eso mas - And I want this more
Zorra - slut, insult

1

Celia

L o juro por Dios que this is the last time I end up in the fucking trunk of another sedan.

Fucking cocksucking hijo de la chingada.

Guillermo's lackeys had barely shut the trunk before they opened it again, this time to throw Santos in with me. I watched the needle slide into his neck, and the same medicine they used to immobilize me was now coursing through his veins as well. His gagged screams of protests turned into mumbles just as his tongue froze inside of his mouth.

There was nothing worse than staring into the face of someone you loved and seeing nothing but pain, knowing that there was nothing you could do to make it better. Restricted in our immobility, we laid there, staring into each other's eyes, crammed into that tiny, piece of shit trunk.

Seconds turned to minutes which became a lifetime, reliving the grief splintering me open. An awkward tear rolled down my cheeks every now and then, Santos was powerless to do more than ignore it. Time moved slowly and eventually my muscles tingled with an intense burn when sensation began to return to my body.

I wiggled myself closer to him, resting my forehead on his chest. He moaned a muffled sound that was filled with pain. He was hurting, physically, and in every other way possible. Mateo and Ronan were dead, and we were headed towards our end too.

The realization was a blade, dead center in my chest.

There could be no penance for this.

It was my fault.

I would have gladly met my demise a hundred—no a thousand times over if it meant they would have survived. But it was too late now to make those kinds of compromises and I had cost them their lives. I deserved this, they didn't. My sobs were an incoherent mess of sounds echoing off the trunk that caged us in together.

They were gone.

They were fucking gone.

My ocean, my fire. Both snuffed out from right in front of me and there was nothing I could do to stop it from happening. Nothing I could have done to save them.

I wanted to drown. I needed to burn. Instead, I was trapped inside my own body and locked in this trunk, forced to do nothing but feel and come to terms with my loss.

Our loss.

They'd been glued to each other for half their lives, and in a matter of weeks I destroyed it all. I wasn't the rain that mortals knelt for, I was the deluge that swept all of existence from the Earth.

The question of whether or not we'd be able to survive without them briefly crossed my mind before I realized we wouldn't be surviving at all. We were headed towards the inevitable muerte.

Death.

By the time the paralytic ran its course through my body, the car came to a stop, and we were forced to take an undignified piss break. Being groped and manhandled by Los Muertos grunts was the better alternative to peeing myself. Santos tried to fight, earning himself a few more sucker punches to the gut and two more syringes of muscle freezing bullshit before they tossed us back into the trunk.

I was sore, stiff, and every inch of my body burned by the time we made it to the West Coast. I could smell Ocean Valley before they'd even bothered to open the goddamn trunk. The salt in the breeze and sound of the waves crashing was undeniable. And then a surge of emptiness washed over me, where home just didn't feel like home anymore. That place you once had belonged to was now lost in the drawer of your mind and filled with the rest of your nostalgia.

Home went by a lot of different names in the last thirty years. México, Ocean Valley, my 2003 Ford Mercury.

I knew better now.

Home wasn't a place. It was a person, or rather, people.

And I'd never be home again.

I would never smell the scent of Ronan's cologne on his neck. I would never feel Mateo's strong fingers dancing over my flesh. Grief would drive me and Santos apart, I knew that. I could already feel my heart turning cold, feel myself losing the will to fight.

I'd let so many tears fall, by the time we finally came to a stop my skin burned, and my throat ached from dryness. Santos never looked away. His eyes stayed fixed on mine as if to prove that he could endure my pain. Afterall, it was also his pain. Those were his brothers, and he was mourning them too.

He looked defeated. Like all the fight had been taken from him with the sound of those two bullets hitting Ronan's stomach.

I couldn't get the vision of Mateo's lifeless body hitting the grass two stories below me out of my mind. I replayed the night in my head trying to figure out how it could have gone so wrong. The Russians, the cártel, they were more involved with each other than we were aware of.

And I brought nothing but death to the door of all of those who cared for me.

I was still completely immobilized when Guillermo's men slung me over their shoulders and carried me into the old house. It must have been right off the shore because I could feel the sea salt on my skin the minute the fresh air wafted into the trunk. I couldn't focus on anything in the present. My brain kept taking me back to the first moment I stepped into the Black Crow's building. Ruminating over every choice and decision I had made since the age of eighteen.

I spent so long running away. Maybe if I hadn't been such a cowardly pendeja, maybe if I would have just owned up to my duty, claimed what was mine, none of this would have happened.

Maybe I'd just already be dead with a few less casualties involved.

Whatever oversized brute was carrying me didn't bother to be gentle, forcing my head to bounce off his back with every step. We were in some sort of basement, and my limbs were starting to tingle, readying my body for movement again.

"Can you stand yet?" I heard a voice behind me I didn't recognize. They were talking to Santos. I couldn't make out his answer, but I heard the clinking of the metal chain and the unmistakable sound of handcuffs closing.

Funny how the sounds that correlated with trauma permeated deeper into our memories than the joyous ones.

A thousand happy memories couldn't wipe away the existence of one bad moment.

Then it was my turn. Multiple hands slung me about until I was chained to a metal pole, my arms up and joined together at the wrists, bound to a hook. Mirrored opposite to me was Santos, just two or three feet away. If we both reached hard enough, we could have touched our toes together.

A box was placed under my feet, taking the pressure off my arms and reducing some of my pain. A small kindness in this hell. My eyes met Santos' again, nothing but sadness staring back at me. But I had no tears left; I'd cried them all out during our journey.

Guillermo's henchmen left us without another word, the heavy sound of their boots marching up the stairs and the slam of the door confirmed we were alone. It was dark, only a single, dim lightbulb hung from its electrical cord and it was somewhere out in the distance, inside another room with its door wide open. It was too far away to make any difference for us, though it wasn't a very large basement.

Then again, it didn't need to be.

It held the two of us just fine.

A large metal table was positioned to our right, and a small sink was pushed against a wall, years of debris and dirt staining what must have once been white porcelain.

Between the two poles that kept Santos and I apart, was a drain.

I fucking *hated* the rooms with a drain.

Nothing good happened inside these rooms.

The chances of me coming out of this basement alive significantly reduced the minute I realized its presence.

"Morena," Santos grumbled, lifting his head up from his chest.

Fuck.

He looked like shit, reminding me that I probably looked no better.

His face was bruised and cut up to hell, but the pain he wore wasn't physical.

"I'm sorry, Morena," he mumbled. The dry well inside of me somehow found a way to pull from the reservoirs, my weakness cascaded down my cheeks once more.

Was he sorry that we were in this mess?

Or was he sorry that they were both dead, and we were now alone in this world?

Did I even want to survive this if there was no one waiting for us out there?

"We're gonna get out of here, okay? We'll kill him together," I lied, already deciding then and there I would do whatever it took to guarantee Santos' life.

2

Santos

My bullshit karma had finally caught up to me, except the trifling bitch didn't care who she hurt in the process as long as I got what was mine too. I practically killed our men, murdered my brothers, and there was a good chance Celia was only here so that Guillermo could force me to watch him kill her.

As a punishment.

Or maybe this was how I'd go too.

We weren't left alone long. Soon the basement door opened again, and the sound of high heels clicking delicately down the stairs followed heavy boots.

"Carajo, you weren't lying," a female voice spoke, and Celia's head jerked up, her eyes went wide like she recognized the speaker.

She yanked at her chains violently, turning abruptly with eyes jarred open and nostrils flared while she searched around the room for the voice.

"I didn't think we'd get the chance after Carlitos failed so horribly," the voice whispered.

"I was hoping this pendejo was gonna do it for me, but it looks like I'm gonna have to teach my primo a lesson, Lina." Guillermo stepped into the light, and behind him stood a woman.

One whose hair lacked shine, and whose aura seemed smudged and polluted by whatever hardships life had placed in her way. Her eyes were a chestnut brown, and her hair matched the color of the freckles on her skin. They didn't look much alike, but side by side you could see the similarities.

Impossible to deny that they were sisters. She was, in every way, so much like Celia, and yet somehow there wasn't a single shared trait I could pinpoint.

"Carolina?" Celia seethed, her voice raspy from the journey and the chains clanking loudly.

"Puta madre," she chuckled, stepping towards her sister. "You look like dog shit Celia. Here I've been hating you for half my life when maybe you did me a favor. Has it been a rough fifteen years hermanita?"

"What the fuck?" Celia screamed, throwing her body with no success as her chains barred her from much movement. "What the fuck?" she continued to repeat, thrashing against her restraints while her sister threw her head back and laughed.

Celia's expression briefly showed a glimpse of something that looked like pain before she masked it over with a steel hard gaze. She cocked her head back and spit a wad of saliva on her little sister's face. Carolina reached her hand up silently, and with no command needed, Guillermo placed a tissue in her hand.

It begged the question of who was in charge here.

"Is that any way to greet the sister you left for dead?"

"Left for dead? You were all buried by the time I left the hospital. Instead of finding me you've been hiding, conspiring against me? I can see Ignacio raised you. Una rata just like him." Celia yelled, not bothering to reign in her emotions.

"Tío said you'd say all those things. Told me you would try to poison my mind with Papá's sentimental lies." Carolina stepped closer to Celia; a sharp surgical tool was in her hand now.

He'd spent the last fifteen years brainwashing her.

Poisoning her against her family.

In a way, that almost meant he'd won.

"If you think I'd waste a second of my time letting you hear words Papá meant solely for my ears, you're delusional," Celia taunted her. "You did get one thing correct though, hermanita, Ignacio was right, you should have killed me when you had the chance. Because if I get out of here alive, I'm gonna rip you apart with my bare fucking teeth you ugly puta," Celia roared, thrashing against her restraints while her sister cackled like a mad woman.

The back of her hand slapped violently against Celia's cheek, the sound echoing throughout the basement.

I couldn't believe this was the sister I had heard so much about. The sister whose death broke Celia in half and even left a stain of sorrow on Ronan's life. This same fucking bitch was somehow behind my cousin's brutality, the murder of my brothers, and so many of our men.

"You still think you're better than me? Still think you're worthy of Papá's favor even though all it got you were scars? We'll see who's ugly, you spoiled bitch," Carolina shrieked, dragging the knife across the side of Celia's face, stopping just before reaching the corner of her lip.

Carolina's eyes widened like she couldn't believe what she'd just done, but Celia's expression remained cold and unchanged, like she hadn't even felt the pain of her skin splitting open from the sharp blade. The blood poured freely down her jaw, staining her chest and dripping down the black leather dress she still wore from the Black Crow Party. She lifted her chin up again, a sinister look filled with nothing but hate burned straight from her eyes into Carolina's.

Celia smirked.

She actually fucking smirked, pushing more blood out of the side of her face. Carolina retreated back with shock at first, but Celia's reaction only forced more anger from her. She lifted her hand as if to slice the other side of her face.

"Dame una sonrisa hermana."

"Stop. Wait," I shouted as loud as I could, getting their attention. "Don't hurt her, don't fucking hurt her… please. You can do whatever you want to me. Just don't hurt her," I begged.

"And what kind of satisfaction am I supposed to get from that?" She laughed and just as her arm came down to cut, Guillermo stopped her with his own hand.

"I can use this. I need to teach this pendejo a lesson anyway." He yanked her back by the forearm and she winced, rubbing the sore spot that he squeezed too tightly. "You want to take all her pain? All her punishment? I'm going to make you regret not killing her so badly that you'll ask me to do it yourself when the time comes to let her go, primo."

"You want to teach him a lesson, amor? Consider this the first one," Carolina declared, her accent heavier than I'd ever heard Celia's in the entirety of our friendship. "You can have the other half," she said sinisterly.

She walked over, standing directly in front of me before digging the knife slowly across the side of my face, mirroring Celia's new cut. I groaned from the pain, biting the inside of the opposite cheek to distract from the sharp pain of her blade.

"Stop it. Fucking stop it," Celia screamed, shaking in the chains.

But it wasn't enough, Carolina smiled proudly at herself and looked to Guillermo before sending the knife down the other side of my face, cutting my eyebrow and sending the blade down my cheek. The burn was intense, and the blood spilled out too fast, forcing me to squeeze my eye shut to keep it from dripping into my vision.

It only made the blood pour down faster.

"Fuck!" I cursed loudly and she cackled, the sound antagonizing Celia as she struggled against her restraints even harder.

"Honestly, this is a gift. Think how hot you're going to look when this is healed." She giggled. "Oops, you're probably not going to get to see it by the time we're done with you."

Blood ran down my face and my vision reddened. It dripped into my eyes, my mouth, down my chest, and didn't stop. She raised her arm to slice again and Celia shrieked, but Guillermo held her back.

"Corazón, they need time to heal, or they'll bleed out. They need time to learn their lessons, Entendiste?" he asked her, earning a bitter look from the youngest Flores sister before pulling her back and standing in front of me. "Ay primo, this could have been so easy. You were my best soldier. I still have hope for you though. Maybe once all of this is done, you'll come back to me. Once you've learned the real meaning of family."

"I'll let you teach him your lessons amor, but he's not yours anymore. Los Muertos is mine, and so is Santito here." She bared her teeth at him, confirming who was in charge.

But was it her, or was it his dick, following the tightest cunt it could find?

"Get the brand," she told him, a growl escaping from his chest that she ignored.

Guillermo disappeared into one of the back rooms behind a closed door. The clanking of metal tools falling on the ground only making Carolina more and more irritated. He came back into my line of vision, the brand almost as big as my face scorching red hot at the end of the rod. The five-petal flower glowing bright as it taunted me, promising me the pain of eternal damnation.

"No! Stop!" Celia begged and screamed repeatedly.

I bit my tongue to keep the scream from forcing its way out, tasting the liquid metal pooling in my mouth while the smell of my charred skin invaded my nostrils. I couldn't fight my body, and the warm stream of piss dripped down my legs as I convulsed from the pain of the brand blistering away at my skin.

The burning ache over my heart throbbed violently, the overwhelming nausea from the smell of my burnt flesh fought against the need to close my eyes and fade into the darkness.

"Now everyone will know who owns you." Carolina smiled with satisfaction as she pulled the brand back, revealing where it now burned into where my Los Muertos tattoos once was.

This said everything it needed to.

Los Muertos was part of the Flores Cártel now. Everything my primo had ever wanted. He wanted to rule it, and he found himself at the mercy of a woman. She didn't know it, but he'd never kneel for her.

They'd never work.

"I guess I don't have to take you to the bathroom now," my primo laughed.

Celia let out an unhinged cackle, the sound of her cold laughter shocking me to my core.

"Cállate! Did you already lose your mind?" Carolina spat the words out.

"The problem is you keep trying to take the things that are mine, in typical little sister fashion. But that isn't your brand hermanita, it's mine. And you just proved to the entire world that he belongs to me by putting *my* symbol on his flesh."

She wasn't wrong. Because I *would* kneel for *her*.

He sent his heavy fist into my stomach, stealing all the air out of my lungs with the sharp hit and forcing blood out of my mouth. I lifted my neck, tilting my chin back to try to keep the blood from obstructing my vision as I looked into my primo's face. I breathed noisily through flared nostrils, my anger consuming me in a way I never thought it was possible to feel.

Narrowing his eyes, he painted a sinister smile on his face, like he truly believed everything he was doing was for the good of our family. He turned on his heels and walked away, leading Carolina out of the basement with one hand on the small of her back. He knew nothing about family.

We were so fucking far from it.

My family consisted of two dead gringos and a dark haired beauty with half a Black Dahlia wound cut into her face now.

And I'd make sure we were all avenged before this was done.

"We'll kill 'em together, eh, morena?" I asked her, ignoring the agonizing pain in my mouth while tasting the blood making its way through my cheek and grazing over my tongue.

I forced myself to stay conscious by shifting my focus from the burn on my chest to the cuts on my face, each time the pain became too much to bear I tuned one out and surrendered to the other.

Her chin lifted up slowly before her eyes fluttered open to look at me.

The blood streaked down her face. The stream of red dripping much slower now from the cut on her cheek. She wore a lethal expression. There was nothing but the promise of death in her gaze, and she made her intentions known with just one look.

"I'm gonna do more than kill them," she rasped out, her teeth coated in crimson as she spoke her curse into the world. "I'm going to tear them apart until Death herself can't recognize them. I'm going to ruin their souls, so la Flaquita refuses to take them into the comfort of her embrace and usher them into the afterlife."

Her gaze hardened into a look I didn't recognize from her.

This wasn't the woman I knew.
I'd bow at her feet as well.

3

Mateo

Nothing made you want to die more than being stuck in that feeling between lucid and unconscious, then having it disturbed by relentless hospital machinery. The beeping piled on top of the nagging of a woman you didn't love, trying to wake you up from a heavy dream was more than any person on the verge of crossing over could tolerate.

"Kane. Wake up, Kane. Mateo, Mateo." She shook at my shoulders until I could no longer ignore her. "I really need you to come back to me buddy, you're scaring me."

"Ugh, let me fucking sleep, Emory." I pushed her hand off me only to feel a deep soreness pulling at my stomach. "Fuck," I wheezed, opening my eyes to the sterile white walls and fluorescent bulbs of one of the rooms in Saint Murphy's intensive care unit.

"Thank fuck," she said in that subtle Irish accent. "I've been trying to wake you up all day, Mateo. I thought you weren't coming back from that one."

"From what one? What happened?" I groaned out, trying to sit myself up but she stopped me.

"Don't move, you're still recovering from surgery. I pulled a bullet out of your stomach. You're lucky it didn't hit any organs, but they found you bleeding out on the grass, and you needed a lot of blood. I can't believe you're actually alive right now."

She couldn't hold back her emotions, the tears streaming down her face as she clasped her hands together, almost in prayer.

"We lost so many of you." She shook her head.

Then everything came back to me.

The party. Celia in that fucking sexy as hell dress, sandwiched between me and Ronan. Los fucking Muertos infiltrating the Black Crow headquarters and shooting down more than half our men.

"Fuck," I groaned, trying to sit up once again, but the Doc placed her hands heavy on my shoulders to stop me.

"I mean it Mateo, I will sedate you again now that I know you're not brain dead," she warned me.

"Where is everyone?" I said, my voice hoarse and dry. "How long have I been out?"

"It's been five days. Like I said, you lost a lot of blood. The Crows that are left made their way to the Diablos Locos compound." She looked apologetic, like she was trying to empathize but with something of this magnitude it was too hard.

"Where are Ronan and Santos? Where's Cecilia?"

"We didn't find her body or Santos'." She slipped a medical glove on her right hand before following suit with the left. "Ronan..." She wiped her eyes with the back of her forearms, trying to hide her tears from me.

"Where is he?" I asked her, panicking at the thought of our girl missing and the thought of Los Muertos having taken Santos home.

"Ronan is still sedated." She reassured me at the sight of me visibly unraveling from the possibilities. "Taylor found him with two bullets in his stomach, bleeding out. You lost more blood, but he was worse off. With his temperament, I knew better than to wake the giant up before he was healed enough to go out destroying the villages," she said.

She checked my vitals, running the cold stethoscope over my bare skin and jotting notes down onto her chart like she could so easily disregard my urgency.

"Unplug me Doc."

"You need more fluids Mateo. What do you think you're going to do if I let you out of here?"

"I'm gonna get my girl back." I gripped her wrist in my hand, tugging her towards me to let her know this wasn't negotiable.

"I thought she was Zerkos' girl?" she asked, a frown forming on her face while her confusion challenged me.

"Then you better wake him the fuck up too," I said, leaning close.

She pulled the IV's out of my arm, but before I could get up she placed her hand on my chest.

"I'm not stupid. I woke you up because I knew you were well enough to hopefully not kill yourself by going out there. I know they need help. But I can't turn down Zerkos' drugs yet. You and I both know he'll kill himself to save them. And that's just the thing Kane, he *will* kill himself if he wakes up now. He got shot... *twice*."

Shit. If I was lucky to be alive, then the sentiment doubled for Ronan. But all I could think about was her being out there again, surrounded by enemies.

"I can't help them alone," I told her.

"You're not alone," César Villalobos' voice called out from the corner.

I leaned my head around Dr. O'Connor's body to see his smug fucking self, sitting in the chair, ankle crossed over his knee with his motorcycle club vest on. He had the need to announce what gang he belonged to at any given time of the day—like anyone fucking cared.

"Fuck me," I groaned.

"Who the fuck do you think convinced the pretty Doctor here to wake your bitch ass up pendejo?" He smirked but it only lasted a second or two, like he quickly remembered the situation.

"You got enough men to help us get them back?" I asked as Emory finally gave in, helping me into a sitting position.

"Yeah, I got the men." The cocky bastard stood up putting a cigarette in his mouth and just as he was about to light it, Emory snagged it from his lips.

"You're insane if you think I'm going to let you light this in here." She stomped over to the trash and broke it in half before dumping it in.

"Are you?" He paused, tilting his chin. "Insane?" His eyes hooded over, and he wet his lips with the kind of audacity only someone like Villalobos had.

His tongue ran over the diamond glued to his canine.

She stared at his mouth unblinking, like she was stuck in a trance. I cleared my throat, breaking the hypnosis he had her under, and she shook her head, walking back in my direction and tucking her red hair behind her ear.

"Why are you helping her? You left her to die once, why's it any different this time?" I needed to know.

Otherwise, I wouldn't be able to trust him. Not with her life on the line.

"I didn't leave her to die, I left her with *him*. I left her to put this shit behind her and try to live a normal life, something I knew I'd never get a chance to do. I'm not sorry and she doesn't expect me to be." I could tell he was annoyed that I'd even say something about what he did to her.

How could I think anything but?

The things I'd seen him do to her, the things he *failed* to do for her.

Too many people had let Celia down, and I wasn't going to be one of them.

I ran my hand over my face before grabbing the hospital bed to pivot my legs onto the floor. Emory and César both rushed to me as if I was seconds away from breaking and if I was going to be honest with myself—I kind of fucking felt like it.

"We have to wake Ronan up." I looked past the doctor, my words meant for César alone.

He nodded like he agreed, and Emory tsked loudly.

"I swear to fucking God Mateo, I'll put all of you to sleep. If Ronan so much as moves the wrong way, his internal stitches could open, and he'll die. Do *not* make me wake him up."

"You don't understand Doc. If I go without him, *that'll* kill him. Ronan would rather die out there trying to save her, then spend one more second in this hospital, asleep, avoiding our problems. I know my brother," I reminded her.

"This is wrong." She shook her head. "At least give yourself time to get your legs back under you. You can't help him if you can't help yourself," she bit back at me.

"Fuck. Fine. Help me up then," I told her, but it was César who came to my aid first, though I wasn't sure it was a love for me that did it or a need to keep the Doc from touching me any more than she had to.

Something happened between them while I was dying. But the only thing I cared about was getting Santos and Celia back.

4

Celia

Carolina hadn't shown her face down here again.

After Guillermo had made the decision that all my punishment was to be given to Santos, she didn't bother to grace us with her presence anymore. As if it was only my misery she'd been interested in witnessing. It had taken me a full three seconds to wrap my mind around my sister's betrayal.

Grief, shock, and happiness, along with complete and utter rage filled its way into my body before I could process the truth.

Puta miserable.

Not only had she been alive the last fifteen years, but she had watched, maybe even had a part in our mother's death. She wasn't ignorant to the attacks Ignacio had attempted over the years or the lives he had taken to try to get to me.

My papá was right.

Power changes everyone. I could almost hear his voice in my ear.

"How are my two favorite lovebirds?" Guillermo chirped as he stomped down the stairs.

It was impossible to know how long we'd been here. I couldn't dissociate and wait for it to be over or for death, because it wasn't happening to me, it was happening to Santos. I was apparently on a fucked up journey, trying to figure out what the cruelest form of torture was.

Each time I found it, a worse version would show itself to me, letting me know it could *always* get worse.

Watching one of the men I loved with all of my heart, suffering and bleeding, was the most painful violence I'd ever endured. But my screams did nothing for Guillermo except urge him on. It showed him that his plan was working and by hurting Santos, he hurt me. And somehow that was worse than the physical pain itself.

Santos hadn't spoken a word to me in days.

I didn't want to be protected if it cost me his love.

Or worse yet, if it cost me him.

I screamed and begged every time Guillermo or one of his men came down here and sliced that knife over his flesh, again and again, until he went pale from losing blood. They burned him, scarred him, and pummeled him senselessly all in the name of loyalty and family, hoping this would bring him back to them.

Maybe it would.

Maybe every hit that was supposed to be mine forced him closer and closer back into Guillermo's poisonous reach.

"What do you think primo? You ready for me to cut you down and get back to work?" Guilermo teased, dangling the keys to his restraints in front of his face.

A dance they did every few days.

Santos raised his chin slowly, a large vertical scab began to form over his eyebrow and the top of his cheek, while another crossed from his ear to the corner of his lip. My own matching wound itched just from staring at it. His shirt had been cut off and every mark Los Muertos had put on his body was now on display.

The five petal Flores brand ruined his gang tattoo, the skin was angry and raised up, red all around and likely nearing infection.

"I'll never work for you again, Guillermo," he said through a crooked mouth. "You might as well kill me here and now."

Guillermo chuckled as if he noticed how Carolina's cut had deformed his speech.

"Oh 'cuz, that's where you're wrong. I won't kill you. I'll keep you both here, barely alive, for as long as it takes. Years if I have to. I'll feed you old bread and dirty water until you hate her almost as much as you hate yourself.

But I will prove my point, and you will do the job I've asked of you." He stepped closer to him. "Eventually, you'll be begging me to let you put a bullet in her brain to free you."

Santos snarled, yanking the chains that kept him bound to the pole across from me.

"I even heard my men talk about how loud she moans every time they wipe her cunt when they take her to the bathroom. How she begs them to let her get on her knees for them to be free." I clenched my jaw shut, looking away from Santos, hoping he didn't believe the lies.

I would do just about anything for his freedom.

Not for mine.

"Just let her go," he mumbled, forcing Guillermo to bark out a laugh.

"Primo you're not getting it. *She's* the reason you're here, sewn up with half-ass stitching." He plucked at a gash on his arm, forcing a pained moan from Santos. "Looks like this one needs to be closed up again," he said before slicing a knife over the old cut, tearing even deeper into his flesh this time.

Santos hissed, his eyes filled with a hatred I'd never seen before, all of it directed at Guillermo.

He grabbed a short blade, less than half an inch long and placed the handle between his fingers. Closing his fist so that nothing but the sharp edge of the knife stuck out from his knuckles he slammed it into Santos' stomach, once, twice—

"Please! Guillermo stop," I shrieked, seeing the blood pour down his waist.

He stopped striking, dropping his head back in a psychotic laugh and twirling the blade through his fingers.

"Little cártel princesses, begging me to make their lives better," he sighed. "There's really nothing that makes me quite so hard." He cut again, opening another old wound in his primo's arm.

My voice was scratchy and worn out from screaming, pleading with this monster to stop hurting Santos. I couldn't even remember the last time I'd even felt the urge to pee, my tears were taking everything from me.

"Please... Please," I chanted between sobs as he cut into Santos repeatedly, with such brutality, I thought for certain he had every intention of ending him this time. "I'm sorry... I'm sorry." I shook my head. "I'll do anything, please. Whatever you want. Please Guillermo, stop hurting him."

"Anything, now?" He turned to face me with a calculating look on his face while he seemed to weigh out his possibilities.

"Just stop hurting him, please," I begged again.

"You do realize that *he's* taking *your* punishment right now? How you gonna do me better than that?"

"Celia, *stop*," Santos growled, making Guillermo laugh.

"Celia, stop," he mocked. "You're right, maybe he's had enough of this for now. I can torture him in other ways. I'm ready for that anything now, morenita," he said before pulling at the chains that kept my arms hooked to the pole above my head.

I dropped to my knees on the cold concrete floor, my wrists were still cuffed together, and my body ached from hanging.

"Here's the rules zorra. You use your teeth; I'll fuck him up. You try anything funny; I'll fuck both of you up. You do a good job, make me come, make me feel like a special boy, and I'll let Santito here have a whole day without pain. How's that sound?" He brought his fingers under my jaw to lift my gaze up to him.

"Celia don't you fucking do it. Celia!"

Santos snarled and growled like a caged animal, his chains rattling while he screamed with ferocity for me to stop.

There wasn't a choice here.

Anyone who could even think there was, would be a fucking idiot.

I nodded my head, doing my best to avoid Santos' stare and his defeated pleas.

5

Guillermo

How many men could say they had not one, but both Flores sisters sucking at their cock? Rafael must have been rolling in his fucking grave the minute her cute little face nodded up at me, eyes filled with tears. She was still the prettier of the two, even if Lina had fucked her face up. It was scabbing up nicely, and at least she didn't cut all the way to her mouth or through her cheek like she had with Santos. That would have made what was about to happen a little less pleasant to tolerate.

I had spent years trying to get Los Muertos on Rafael Flores' radar. I was young, but I was smart and full of plans.

I knew the west better than anyone and I knew what it would take to thrive out here. Flores shut me down time after time, warning me to keep the cártel out of our little street gang's mouth.

His final message came in the form of a tape. I'd sent one of my boys over to him, to see if Flores could use him for a job. Instead, he sicked his little bitch of a daughter on him and dumped his body on his mamá's lawn with the video proof. The little bitch killed him before he'd even had the chance to attack.

Guess I had the last laugh now. Los Muertos and the cártel were one in the same.

Ignacio Flores wasn't a quarter of the man Rafael's ghost was. Which made him easy to manipulate and even easier to fool. Los Muertos was rebranding itself as the Flores cártel right under his nose and he didn't even know it.

Once we figured out a way to get Lina's money that her old man had hidden away, we'd be able to buy more men, more guns, and more drugs. Then once we had control of it all, we could kill Ignacio and any of his men who refused to follow us.

And then I could finally get rid of Carolina. She was fun at first. Ignacio dropped her at my door when she was fifteen, said she wasn't a kid anymore and that he didn't have time to keep raising his brother's orphan. She was a doe-eyed little thing, and I corrupted her to my needs.

But goddamn was she clingy, and sometimes I think she forgot which one of us was actually in charge. I kept her satisfied with money, sex, and the idea of power.

Everything a little princess bitch could want to stay happy, but enough was enough. Thirteen years with the same woman by my side was more than I'd granted my own mamá.

That wasn't to say I was monogamous. I smiled remembering the last time Carolina had found another woman in my bed and the bloody mess I had to clean up. An idea flashed through my mind for a second—the image of Carolina and Celia in a battle royale to the death, in bikinis, bloody and violent.

Yup, that did it.

I cupped my hard-on and gave it a good squeeze, my bulge already in front of her face and primed for her.

"Make it as good as you make it for him, okay baby?" I encouraged her before pulling myself out of my pants.

Santos' cursing and shouting was damn near killing the moment, and I found I could no longer ignore it.

"Hold on darling. Let's set the mood." I yanked my shirt off, shoving a wad of it into my cousin's mouth so that his obscene yelling became muffled.

The scab on his face stretched apart, threatening to bleed again.

Celia trembled, most likely because all she'd had to eat this week were a few pieces of stale bread, and even that had been shoved down her throat by force. Stubborn puta would have probably killed herself out of spite to not let us do it on our own terms. She was Rafa's daughter no doubt. Lina, not so much.

As if the coffee grounds were the same, but someone didn't brew it quite right.

Now that I was here, standing in front of the real thing, it was easy to see why Rafael had put all his energy into his oldest daughter. She would have made a fierce fucking jefa. The girl had an abyss of hate burning deep into her soul, and just one look at her eyes was enough to force you to reckon with your own sins.

And she was on her knees for me.

Her eyes searched over to my cousin, an expression on her face that told me she was desperate for him to look at her. To see the sacrifice she was making.

And the stupid idiot was looking away.

"Mira," I hissed at him, grabbing her jaw and shoving my dick in her mouth.

She gagged, closing her teeth around me and I pulled out, slapping her face with the back of my hand hard enough to knock her onto her side. She was so frail and pathetic; a couple hits would be enough to take her out. But what would be the fun in that? I stuffed myself into my pants again and pulled up the zipper.

I pulled the microblade out again and jammed my fist into Santos' stomach two more times.

"NO! Stop," she cried. I stomped over to her and grabbed a fistful of hair, yanking her up to my eye level.

"Then quit fucking around, or I'll kill *him* just to prove a point to you, zorra." I sent my fist into her stomach before dropping my hold on her hair.

She doubled over in pain, coughing and whimpering while Santos muffled protests through my shirt. I grabbed her chains and lifted her up onto the hook once again, keeping her dangling just above the ground. I walked over to the table of tools and picked up the pliers.

"Abre la boca pendejo." I forced open his mouth, pulling the fabric out before shoving the dirty tool into his mouth and clamping it over one of his back molars. "Hold still and it'll hurt less." Celia thrashed and screamed, calling me an animal, getting my cock hard once again.

Santos stood still like a good boy, exhaling heavily through his nostrils and moaning in despair as I yanked the tooth out with nothing but brute force. It came free with a sharp tug, and I threw the bloody thing at the cártel princess' feet before shoving my shirt back inside my primo's mouth to clot the bleeding.

"Let's try this again. For every tooth I feel, there will be a tooth I pull. Got it?" I dropped the rusty pliers onto the ground before lifting her off the hook and letting her fall to the ground again.

A V formed heavily between her brows. "With finesse, okay? I don't want some high school blowjob bullshit, show some enthusiasm." She looked up at me with disdain. "Well?" I asked, drawing a smirk. "Pull me back out." I crossed my arms over my chest, satisfied with myself while waiting for her to comply.

I could practically see the steam rolling out of her nostrils. I bet she was biting her tongue so hard right now to keep herself from spitting venom at me. I let out another provocative chuckle, pushing them both over the edge. She knew any wrong move would just be a punishment for him instead.

This was the best form of torture.

"*Now* Celia," I harshened my tone. "Show my primo how little it takes for you to get on your knees for another man." She got into position, a disgusted look on her face like she was determined to sour my mood. "I would have taken C minus work before corazón, but you wanted to act like a brat. Now I expect a B plus at the minimum."

Santos was still breathing loudly through his pain, but I'd be able to tune it out once she started choking on my cock. I grabbed a fistful of her hair and brought her closer, her fingers shook as she unbuckled my jeans.

"No need to be nervous little Flores, it's just like any other cock. Except bigger." I laughed, grabbing it at the base and helping it find its way into her mouth.

"That's it, nice and big. Wrap those teeth up good for me. Show Santos what he's missing out on." But my primo was still looking away, refusing to acknowledge that I could so easily take anything he cared about and ruin it for him forever.

He'd learn soon. As much as Lina hated her sister, this wasn't about her. This was about teaching Santos a lesson. And I'd teach it over and over again until it stuck in his mind. It wasn't the worst blow job I'd ever gotten, but I was having to work twice as hard to get myself off with her lack of enthusiasm.

I slammed her head back and forth, ignoring the gagging sound she made every time my cock touched the back of her throat. Tears trailed down the side of her face, but with a bitch as cold as Celia Flores had been trained to be, I could proudly say it was the sheer size of my cock doing it.

Back and forth, using her gargled breaths as motivation to get me where I needed to be until my orgasm broke through me. My cum shooting straight into her mouth while I held her head in place to make sure she got every single drop.

"Now swallow like a good girl." I tilted her head back to force her eyes up at me.

She spat my cum at me and it landed on my abdomen. I pulled the shirt out of Santos' mouth and wiped myself clean before shoving it back through his lips again. His disgusted gagging fuelled my laughter.

With one hand I grabbed Celia's chains and dragged her back over to her post, lifting her up and dropping her onto the hook again to keep her dangling in place.

"I think I'll like this new routine after all," I declared, giving her cheek a few firm slaps before walking my way back up the stairs and turning off the lights.

6

Mateo

T hanks to the miracle that was strong painkillers, I was now mobile again. A full twenty-four hours awake with hospital monitoring and I convinced the Doc to let me go with César and his men out west. Her only caveat was, Zerkos could only come if she did.

Watching Ronan wake up from a medically induced coma was like seeing a bear get its head stuck in a trap. Emory wanted to sedate him again because his wild trashing in the room was enough to make her think he'd open all his stitches.

"Zerkos, if you can't settle down, I *will* put you back to sleep and you *will* stay back," she threatened.

"Stay back?" His nostrils flared, and I could see his brain begin to piece together the memories of the party before the attack. "Celia. Shit. Fuck!"

He swung his legs as if he was just going to magically jump out of the bed and be healed but immediately yelled out in pain.

"Fuck." he roared.

"Yup, that's what two bullets in your gut feels like big guy. Settle down or you *will* fucking die Ronan. Do you understand?" Emory chastised. "I'm letting you go. I'm not letting you be stupid about it. This entire thing is already idiotic to begin with." Her emotions began to rise, and her voice squeaked. "None of you have even talked about the possibility that they're already dead."

The room went quiet, and regret covered her face.

"I'm sorry… I just mean, it's been ten days. What are the odds you aren't sending yourselves off to die?" The redheaded doctor couldn't keep it together any longer and her tears started to fall.

"I'm grateful for the tears doll, but we both know none of us are worth your sadness," Ronan told her, and I watched her eyes dart over to César. "But if you ever fucking say some shit like that again, I'll put you under myself, okay Doc?"

César growled under his breath.

"She's not fucking dead. Her tracker is still active, still showing her location," I said.

"Has she moved?" César asked.

"That doesn't mean fucking shit. We're doing this Lobo." I used his road name as a way to trigger his ego.

"I've got sixteen chapters of Diablos Locos ready to ride west. Get yourself together Zerkos." He nodded at him before tilting his chin at the doctor. "A word, Doc?"

The two of them left the room, the silence between Zerkos and I said far too many of the things we couldn't voice out loud. What if she *was* dead? What if they both were? What if we'd lost everything we had, and every chance of happiness was out the door now?

We stared at each other as if we could read our thoughts but neither of us had the answers we were looking for. I could hear César's voice booming in the hall just outside Ronan's room.

"It's too fucking dangerous Emory. I got my own doctor. I'm not letting you risk yourself."

"He's a *medical student*, they deserve better than that. What if someone gets seriously hurt? I'm a grown woman, *papi.* I make my decisions."

Emory pushed back into the room, the door slamming against the wall before bouncing back closed.

"Give yourself a few hours to get moving again, then we can head out. It's at least four days driving with the stops we'll have to make to keep you comfortable," she said before walking back out again and giving César a cold set of side eyes.

"Taylor has rounded up our uninjured who are willing to come too," I caught Ronan up.

"This isn't Black Crow business. They shouldn't be risking their lives like this." He shook his head.

"They made it Black Crow business when they broke into our home and shot our people during a celebration, brother. Our men have a right to retribution."

"You're right," he said, stunning the shit out of me.

"What the fuck was that?" I said with a laugh.

"I'm learning I can be wrong too. It's not too late to change." He tried and failed to move, so I helped him into a sitting position.

"Well shit, remind me that your reset button is just two bullets to the gut then."

He elbowed me in the side, forcing a pained grunt out of both our mouths from the excess motion.

"Let's go get our girl then, Kane," he rasped out with a smirk.

7

Celia

"Oh, fuck Celia, you're getting so good at this. You'd be so fucking proud primo. She's using tongue and everything." The pig couldn't help himself but lie to try to hurt his family.

There was no way anything I was doing felt good. At this point, I was barely drinking enough water to survive as my own form of self-harm. My tongue must have felt like rough sandpaper. But he played this game, once a day coming down and forcing me on my knees in order to kill a piece of Santos.

It was working.

Every day Santos seemed closer and closer to taking that gun and putting a bullet in my head. Maybe not for the reasons Guillermo expected but out of mercy. Six times he'd come down here now, which meant it had been six days of this. Impossible to tell how much longer we'd been here before that. There was no method of telling time before he put his filthy cock in my mouth.

But today was the day I was done.

There was something in the air, something tangible I could almost feel.

A warning from La Flaquita.

Either I'd die trying to get us out of here or I'd actually do it. But I wasn't going to let this be our lives. I couldn't allow Guillermo to dictate how my end would be written. I was determined to go out fighting, despite being stuck here with a mouthful of the short end of my luck.

I'd played nice long enough, through these little visits, he'd quickly begun letting his guard down. So typical of a man. As soon as blood rushed to their cocks, they lost all sense and logic. I wasn't stupid. I'd wait until he was close, head so dizzy and filled with pleasure that it would take him a while to register what was happening.

He always let me know when he was getting there too. He gripped my hair tighter and egged Santos on, encouraging him to glance my way.

"Come on primo, she's begging you to look at her. Do you guys talk about it when I leave you alone to yourself?" he asked, thrusting deeper into my mouth.

He didn't need to gag him to keep him from shouting anymore. We'd all resigned to our fates and accepted it.

And there his fingers went, gripping the back of my head and yanking tight like he was on the verge of total bliss. I relaxed my throat and let him as far back as I could before I bit down. And I clamped my teeth shut like there was nothing that would stop me from having his manhood as my next meal.

He screamed a bloody screech, making me fearful someone would come down here. Guillermo yanked at my hair, but I didn't let up, ignoring the pain and biting down until I could taste blood and feel his flesh ripping under my teeth. He went flaccid in my mouth while I relentlessly chewed through his dick. Finally ripped at my hair hard enough to take a fistful from my scalp.

I screamed, my mouth full of blood, when he sent his fist flying at my face. Santos was screaming at me to let him down and his cousin flailed wildly on the floor with his mangled cock still out. I positioned myself under Santos to give him just the leverage he needed to get his chain off the hook and get down on the ground. Guillermo was still crying and screaming, but his eyes went wide once Santos' feet touched the ground.

"Morena, stand back," he said before throwing his neck to the side and cracking it without the use of his hands.

"Primo help me. Fucking puta loca," he screamed. "My fucking cock!"

Santos kicked his foot down into his cousin's stomach with no hesitation and no impression that he'd been starved and beaten for days on end. He swung the chain across Guillermo's face, ripping a chunk of flesh as the heavy metal slapped against his skin. It knocked him back, forcing his head to hit the ground again. In a cat-like move, Santos swung his leg around the floor, positioning himself behind his primo and using the chains keeping his wrists bound to choke the ugly bastard.

"If you kill me, my men will just come down and kill you too."

"They can try," Santos hissed.

"Where is she? Where is Carolina?" I yelled, stepping over his fucked-up remainder of a dick and he yelled out again, making me wonder why his men had yet to descend on his behalf.

It almost seemed like his brain was hashing out the same thought, and I watched a look of worry spread across his face as the sound of machine guns went off upstairs. Santos' eyes met mine and he tightened the chain against Guillermo's neck.

Either our salvation was upstairs, or it was someone who wanted Guillermo dead just as much, and there was a good chance we'd die in the process too.

"Hold him still," I told Santos, crawling over to the table and grabbing the same rusty pliers he used on Santos nearly a week ago.

I shoved my chain into his mouth, to force it open while he flailed and thrashed. He was bigger than Santos and I combined, but the damage we'd already done to him was enough to give us the advantage. I sat on his chest and forced the pliers in and with all the effort in my body, I heaved upward until a tooth came loose from his mouth.

Blood pooled in his mouth and he choked on it, but I just reached back in and pulled another canine out, this time with a bit more ease now that I had an idea of what I was doing. I was low on energy though, and it was almost enough to make me lightheaded.

"I think I'll make a necklace," I told Santos, throwing him the teeth. "Finish him." I stood up and grabbed a seven-inch knife off the table of tools. Then it got quiet upstairs. I eyed Santos, but he didn't hesitate. He ripped through his cousin's throat with the knife, not stopping as he serrated past his vocal cords and then through his spine. Blood covered his face, his chest, his lap and it took me a while to realize that the feral scream wasn't coming from our victim but from Santos' mouth instead. I stood there, unmoving as I watched until finally, he sliced through the last bit of flesh that kept his primo's head attached to his body before holding it up like a trophy. Blood flooded down fast. There was a lot more than you'd expect for something as small as a head.

Santos' chest heaved up and down with heavy, labored breaths before he dropped the head to the ground. I pushed away Guillermo's corpse with my foot and climbed onto Santos' lap, wrapping my arms around his neck. He buried his face into my neck and broke down into a hearty, woeful sob. We rocked back and forth, holding each other for comfort for what felt like a moment frozen in time.

Then the basement door swung open and light spilled down the stairs. My heart rose up to the top of my throat, or maybe it was bile I was holding back from flashes of Guillermo's head getting ripped off before my very eyes.

It took everything to breathe through the nausea, but my nerves only skyrocketed at the sound of heavy boots slowly stepping down the basement stairs. Santos pulled me behind him, kicking his cousin's corpse even further away as if he could hide it from whatever enemy would be coming down for us.

"Sunshine?"

My heart nearly exploded.

I must have been hungrier than I thought because I was hallucinating a dead man's voice. Santos looked up too and then, there he was, coming down the stairs, blood splattered onto his face and his clothes.

"Mateo?" I blurted out, tears flowing down my face as my heart made sense of what was happening before my brain could.

He took large strides to get to me, cradling my face in his hands and disregarding all the fresh blood covering me. He pressed his forehead to mine, and I let out a banshee cry as I allowed myself to feel the nameless kind of emotion that came with knowing that someone would always be there to rescue you.

I was a miserable bitch, and I did not deserve this kind of loyalty.

"I thought you were dead," I finally blurted through hysterical sobs.

"It would take a lot more than that to rip me away from you, beautiful," he said, pulling back to take a look at my face.

He brushed my hair behind my ear, shaking his head in disapproval, as he ran his gaze over my features, his thumb traced over the scar on my cheek softly. And then his eyes shifted to Santos picking up his primo's head off the ground, and he let out a long exhale. He looked better now that some of his wounds were starting to heal, but the brand on his chest was still a bright scorched up mark. He had so many poorly stitched cuts he looked like a Mexican version of Frankenstein's monster.

"Shit, brother, you look fucked up. Let's get you both out of here." He heaved Santos up, propping himself under his shoulder on one side and I followed suit on the other.

Mateo frowned like he didn't need my help but before he could utter a word of disapproval, the basement steps squeaked, and a shadow lingered at the top of the stairs.

"Thank fucking fuck," Santos said and I turned my gaze to the doorway to find Ronan standing there, jaw sharp and flexed with worry as he stared down at the three of us.

My knees gave out at the sight of him. I dropped to my hands and knees and scrambled up the stairs on all fours before I found myself at his feet. Collapsed and crying, my entire chest ripped open, heart bleeding in offering at his altar.

"You came for me," I barely whispered as he swooped me into his heavy embrace.

"Every time flower, every time."

I shook violently in his hold, his arms wrapped around me, squeezing me tight in his embrace. For a few seconds I forgot where I was, because I was home. Ronan groaned, it sounded like agony, and I looked up to finally see how pale and drained of life he was. Looking back, Mateo didn't look much better, and Santos was worse off than both of them.

"Los Muertos?" I asked, wiping the tears off my face.

"You got your big brother to thank for that," Mateo grunted while he and Santos used each other for support to make their way up the stairs.

I frowned, shaking my head and looking at Ronan.

"I don't understand."

"There's some wingless Black Crows up there too, but he brought a hundred and fifty Diablos to Guillermo's door. A few Los Muertos escaped, but it looks like we got all the ones that mattered." Ronan shifted his gaze, and I followed it to see Santos was holding Guillermo's head in his hand like a bowling ball. Fingers hooked into his eye sockets.

We made our way out of the basement to find bodies scattered all over the house. Bikers clad in leather vests were dragging them into a corner making a neat pile of corpses. The sun shone brightly through the windows, but even so, I wasn't prepared for the shock of the daylight once we crossed the threshold.

I shielded my eyes from it until l could make out César's shape in the distance, leaning against a van with a cigarette in his mouth. He frowned seeing the state I was in, but

I couldn't help but smile to see him here for me, risking himself and his men for my sake.

"You do love me," I said as we collectively made our way towards the van.

He chuckled, flicking his cigarette to the ground.

"Familia eh? Don't say I never did anything for you, princesita." He grinned, bringing me into his chest and placing a kiss on the top of my head.

"I thought I knew what family was supposed to be, now I'm not so sure anymore."

"What's that supposed to mean?" César asked.

"Carolina. She's alive. This was all her," I said, hating the words as they came out of my mouth.

"That was the woman we saw leaving then. Fuck!" César cursed, kicking the side of the van.

The joy that came with being reunited was short. Everything felt cold. I should have been exploding with happy emotions at the sight of Ronan and Mateo, but between the weakness and thoughts of my sister, I felt like I was crashing. There truly was nothing that could have prepared my heart for the overwhelming joy that came with seeing both of them alive. But instead I was frozen.

Mi corazón. Broken and full at the same time.

Alone, surrounded by people who loved me. I felt nothing. My heart, draped with a layer of ice, and every time I looked at Santos and found his gaze awkwardly shifting away it cemented the feeling deeper into my soul.

"We're gonna get both of you better okay, sunshine? Fuck, I'm so glad to see you." He was crying, he was actually fucking crying and maybe if my soul hadn't shriveled up and died inside of me I'd still be crying too.

He looked to Santos and found the same empty shell of a stare coming from him. Mateo pressed his lips into a fine line and nodded his head like he understood we'd need time to sort ourselves out from this.

"They're mostly all dead now, except your sister," César explained.

"I'm sure she scurried off to Ignacio to warn him. Her time is coming too," I said as he helped me into the backseat of the van.

Mateo climbed into the front with César while I sat between Santos and Ronan, staring out the window as the car slowly began to move. Ronan's head dropped back onto the headrest of the seat, and he winced from pain with every bump the tires hit.

"You doin' alright?" Mateo asked, looking back.

It was meant for Ronan, but his eyes scanned all three of us. Ronan's hand on my lap squeezed, and I placed my palm over his for comfort.

"Emory and the cavalry are waiting to know where to meet. Then she'll be able to give the three of you medical attention," César announced from the driver's seat.

"Emory is here?" I asked, not feigning my surprise.

"She said the Diablos' doctor wasn't qualified for the level of damage Ronan was risking." He shook his head. "So where to, sister?"

"Send your men south," I told him. "We're crossing the border tonight."

The conversation ended there, and we rode in silence for nearly another hour. I stared out at the scenery. It wasn't until I felt Santos' finger lacing through mine and the gentle squeeze of his hand that I realized I was crying again. I broke free of both of their hands in order to wipe my face dry. Ronan didn't miss it. He took my chin between his index and thumb.

"Tell me what happened in there, flower," he whispered. "Let me help make it better."

I wanted to tell him that just by coming, he already had, but instead Santos spoke.

"Nothing happened," he bit out, like lying was somehow going to save me the shame of what had already happened.

I wasn't embarrassed.

It wasn't me who got taken advantage of.

It was the stupid pendejo who thought he could trust to shove his dick into the open mouth of a piraña with the expectation that it was somehow going to come out still whole.

I turned to face him, hardening my stare and dropping my voice down to a cold octave. "Nothing happened?"

"That's not what I meant," he said in a hushed tone, and César turned the radio off completely, the silence in the car becoming damn near unbearable.

"Then what did you mean? Because you couldn't even stomach looking at me Santos. You looked away every single time. Why couldn't you look at me?" I raised my voice to a yell.

He sighed, looking out to the road again, like he couldn't voice out his reasons.

"Santos?" I shouted and César cleared his throat uncomfortably.

"I couldn't stand to see you that way. That's not who you are. I didn't want to see you like that." His voice broke and a tear fell down his fucked-up cheek.

He turned completely away from me once he noticed my gaze fixed on the scarring flesh.

"I needed you to see," I said desperately, and he whipped his head back at me.

Ronan's grip squeezed around my thigh. His head was still dropped back, eyes closed, but his face was wet.Mateo looked out the window and I couldn't hear a single breath in the car.

I'd broken all my men.

César's gaze met mine in the rearview mirror, and with a single look he gave me back the strength of our family. He nodded like he understood the entirety of my experience, and for some reason I felt it in that moment. All of our pain and suffering, it was always unified even when we were far apart.

"I needed you to see that it was my choice. That he wasn't making me into a victim because I was doing it of my own volition. I was saving *us*. I don't regret it, and I'm not ashamed. I'd do it a million times over if it kept his blade away from you," I spat out, crossing my arms over my chest.

"I'm sorry." he said, regret being the flavor of his sorrow.

"I did it because I love you, Santos. And I would have done the same for any of you fuckers in this car." I attempted to keep the bitterness from my tone, but I was tired of being looked at like I was some poor thing who'd been beaten.

I was a fucking survivor. I'd proved it over and over again.

There wasn't shame in that.

"So what's the plan, reina?" César asked, changing the mood in the car.

"Guadalajara. If we're gonna do this, we're gonna do it right. First we get what's mine, then we go home hermanito."

I leaned into Ronan. He let out a low, pained sound and wrapped his arm around me, bringing me into his chest. He dropped his head over mine and I let the comfort of his embrace soothe me for the rest of the ride.

8

Ronan

We were exhausted, broken, and beaten.

But I'd never felt more whole in my life, and in that van, I promised myself I would do whatever it took to make sure that we stayed this way. I wasted too much time before I realized it. She was right. Together we were complete. There was no way out of this without any of them. Well, maybe without fucking Villabolos, but even that pain in the ass was starting to grow on me again.

He was the only family she had left, even with Carolina rising from the fucking dead. She somehow managed to end up a major cunt, which probably meant she was better off dead.

We ended up stopping at a hotel for the night so Celia and Santos could clean themselves up, and Emory could properly look at everyone's injuries. The Doc insisted on sharing a room with Celia and forced me to stay with César and Santos with Mateo. I wanted nothing more than to sleep with my arms wrapped around my girl again, but she denied the opportunity immediately, and told Celia just how bad the extent of my gunshot wounds were.

She sided with the fucking Doc.

But now it was a new day, and we were in the car ready for whatever would come next. Celia was showered and her hair was brushed silky straight, so black it looked hot to the touch from the sun scorching above us. The scar on the side of her face was red and bright. It looked painful but it wasn't as deep as Santos'. She untucked her hair from behind her ear to cover it up once she noticed me staring.

I grabbed her chin with one hand and tucked her hair back again. She challenged me with a look, exaggerating those damn lines in the middle of her brows. I placed a gentle kiss on the scar.

"So what will this key open?" I asked while César pulled into a small bank outside the city.

"All of the secrets Jamila refused to take to the grave with her," he answered.

Celia was tired of secrets; I could see it on her face. The fact that her mother likely had a million more hidden somewhere only that little key would open was infuriating. How long had Celia been carrying that thing around her neck, too afraid to find out on her own? Or better yet, why had her mother kept this from her?

The thought briefly occurred to me that maybe Jamila had somehow been the better parent out of the two. Doing what she could to keep her daughter away from the violence even if it meant keeping her away from the money.

No matter how you looked at it, it was blood money.

And accepting it meant also accepting her father's sins as her own.

"How do you know this?" she asked him.

"I've been here before, when I was just a kid, before Ignacio burned down the villa. Your mamá wasn't a secretive person, but the few times she brought me here, something was just off. I'm betting my life that key opens up a box here. I saw it too many times in her hand to think otherwise."

It was just a bank, nothing out of the ordinary and nothing suspicious about it. It smelled like old paint, and there was a single teller behind the counter.

"Nombre?" the clerk asked.

"Jamila Gomez." She gave her the alias that belonged to her mother.

She shook her head and denied her request, so Celia tried once again with the Flores name instead, along with the rest of her identifying information she still knew by memory. The teller searched and searched until finally her face lit up with a match.

We walked through metal detectors, all of us setting it off and relinquishing our guns into plastic tubs. The clerk led us down a hallway filled with lockers and took out her own set of keys, opening up a small door with a 131 on the front. There was a single box inside, made of metal, big enough to hold a few letters.

We followed the clerk again, past the lockers, to another door which she unlocked with an electronic keycard before pushing open and guiding us inside. She told us in Spanish to take our time and to shut the door once we retrieved everything we needed from the box.

"I'm really fucking anxious." She exhaled, holding the key between her index finger and her thumb, tapping it against the key slot on the small metal box the clerk placed on the table.

"Do you want to be alone?" I asked her, and she responded with a hard glare.

"Never again, I'm just… nervous." She looked down at the box before looking back at me again. "What if there's nothing there?"

César laughed. "I wouldn't put it past Jamila."

She stuck the key in the box, shaking out the last bit of her nerves with a little dance before she put her hand back on the key and turned it. She opened the lid and the four of us crowded around her, waiting to discover what should have been seen fifteen years ago.

There was an envelope and a torn piece of paper. Nothing else.

"Puta madre. She's really going to kick me down one more time even in death, isn't she?" She exhaled deeply before picking up the little piece of paper.

"What is it?" Mateo asked.

"It's coordinates," César said, reaching over his shoulder and grabbing it from her.

He plugged the numbers into his phone while her hands trembled with the envelope in her hand.

"I don't want a letter. Someone else open it. There is nothing she could possibly say to me that I would want to hear right now." She tossed it on the table, shaking her hands frantically like she was drying the water off of them.

Mateo picked it up, ripping the envelope open to reveal what looked to just be a bunch of documents. Santos picked one up and looked it over before handing it to her.

"It's just birth certificates," he told her. "This one is yours."

She took it from his hand and set it on the table without a single glance.

"Whose is that?" she asked about the one in Mateo's hand.

"Carolina's. This one belongs to big brother here. I thought your last name was Villalobos?" he asked him, shuffling the papers around.

"It is," he said, his annoyance obvious.

"No, this says César Ortíz. Your mom was Maria Villalobos, but your father was Diego Ortíz," Mateo said as César ripped the document from his hand.

"What the fuck?" Celia looked pissed. "Did you fucking know?" She stepped up to her brother and I flipped over her own birth certificate, her mom's name bright and clear.

"You've said a lot of dumb shit before princesita, but this one takes the cake." He shoved her shoulder, and Mateo and I both shifted towards him.

He eyed both of us, raising his hands up in defeat, before he'd even gotten a point across.

"None of this makes sense. Diego was my tío's name, he was my mamá's brother. Her last name was Gomez." She ran her fingers through her hair, like she was trying to make sense of all this new information.

I picked up her birth certificate again.

"No." I shook my head, handing it over to her. "This says her name was Jamila Ortíz."

"No." She shook her head in disbelief. "That would mean—"

"We're cousins," César finished, but Celia continued to shake her head.

"It means that it's technically, *his* cártel. No?" Mateo asked.

César wrapped his hands around Mateo's neck and slammed him into the wall. His nostrils flared widely for a few moments before he decided to finally speak.

"Listen here pendejo, I'm only ever going to say this once. You ever repeat those fucking words again, I don't care what you mean to her, I'll gut your gringo ass alive. Entendiste?"

"Roger that, hermano." Mateo said with an exaggerated American accent, pushing him away.

"I was four when they took me in, I kind of always knew I was Diego's son. I think you knew it too. We knew we were already family, but it always felt like brother and sister, so why mess with that? There was no way I was a random stray, Rafa? He was too cold to just take in some pup from the street. I knew there was no chance I was his bastard either, she would have hated me if that was the case, Jamila was good to me. They never talked about Diego, and she always sent me those sad eyes if someone brought him up." He scratched the back of his head.

"Why so testy about it?" Mateo asked.

"Something deep in my gut tells me my dad didn't want to be a part of this shit. I don't either. I just wanna finish this war for her, go home to my club and live the rest of my miserable life. Is that too much to ask?" He turned back to her. "He raised you for this shit. You've bled for this chingadera princesa. This isn't my empire, it's yours. And I'll kill anyone who says otherwise."

"Tia Larissa wanted as far away from this desmadre as physically possible. That's why she moved to Ocean Valley. Now it's clear it wasn't just because she was protecting my mamá, but because she'd seen the carnage of it all first hand. She grew up with this too." She lamented, piecing together her family's history.

César simply nodded.

"How many times did we hear Diego's name but nothing about him? No memories, no stories. They buried him just like they buried all the lies and secrets they thought we weren't old enough to handle." Celia's voice shook with anger.

"Age had nothing to do with it princesa, it was about the fact that no one wants to be the person who shares the painful truth. They'd rather absolve themselves from the burden and leave it up to the universe, or some higher power to bring you to find it yourself." César said with a sneer.

"God didn't bring me here. Revenge did." She peeled her upper lip and he nodded in agreement.

César pulled a lighter out of his pants, flicking the flame on and touching the corner of the paper to it. It quickly lit, and he dropped it to the ground, letting it burn to completion on top of the stained concrete floor. The flames triggered the smoke detector and an alarm went off, causing the sprinklers to pour down on us in a heavy torrent.

We ran out of the room, leaving the empty box on the table before collecting our weapons and running out of the bank at rapid speed. We piled back into the car in a rush to avoid the angry bank teller cursing us down.

Celia stared blankly at the piece of paper that had her birth name written on it after we left the building. Her eyes didn't unglue from it the entire ride out to the middle of nowhere.

Because of course the GPS took us to the fucking desert.

The mystery coordinates, on the random piece of paper in a fifteen plus year old safety deposit box, took us to the middle of nowhere.

Why the fuck would it not have?

And of course we all fucking followed it, with the insane hope that none of this was a trap or a terrible idea. When we arrived it was practically dark already. We left the headlights on to provide us with a fraction of visibility to find the exact location we needed.

Celia and César took turns digging at the precise location where X marked the spot—figuratively of course. Celia insisted that the three of us were far too injured to be exerting ourselves that way and refused to risk us opening any stitches. Villalobos grumbled something about not wanting to deal with the Doc's wrath.

She hadn't come out unscathed though, her scars weren't so visible this time, at least not all of them. But they were still very much real.

Santos could barely stand straight. His entire upper body was draped in markings of all textures, shapes, and sizes and for this very reason he was now wearing a long sleeve turtleneck in ninety degree weather.

We were coming apart at the seams, just as we were figuring out how to become whole.

"Fucking finally. Carajo," César shouted from the bottom of the hole.

The sound of the shovel hitting metal over and over again rang out until finally the two of them were able to get it loosened from the soil. The box was big enough to hold a body, though I wasn't sure if it said more about me or them that it was my go-to measuring format. There was at least a sixty percent chance there was a body in there.

"Put it in the car so we can get the fuck out of here. Let's go home," Celia said.

Her face changed when she said home.

"You don't want to open it now, jefa?" César asked.

"It doesn't matter. Now, later—I already know what's inside." She shrugged, walking back to the car.

9

Celia

I don't know why I called it home. Statistically speaking I lived less of my life in the Guadalajara villa than I did in Ocean Valley, but that sure as fuck wasn't home. I was feeling a million ways out of sorts. Coming back to the land that made me caused a magnitude of feelings that couldn't be described. Feelings of knowing, in my heart of hearts, that la patria was the center of who I truly was at my core.

The urge to sink my roots down into the soil to reconnect was immense.

And then came the shattering feeling of inadequacy. I was an imposter. A pretender, and they would all see it. Not damn near Mexican enough. They would all know just by looking at me. Would they hear it in my voice too? I tilted my chin up to force the tears to be reabsorbed into my eyes. I was fed up with letting them fall.

"Wait, we should open it first." Mateo said.

"Whatever's inside will still be there when we get to the villa. I've had enough of my family's secrets for one day." I tried helping him lift the chest into the car with little success, finally allowing the boys to tag in for this one.

I looked over to César as he shut the trunk. "What's that little favor gonna cost me?" He knew I was referring to him burning his documents, I didn't have to specify.

"I didn't do it for you, reina. I did it for me. When Rafa died, I felt *relieved*. I was a shit brother because I wanted my freedom so bad that it didn't matter what it would cost me. I don't care what some stupid piece of paper says, you're my sister. The throne was always yours. I have everything I want in Grimm's Reach. I just want to be free to go home when this is all over." I swung my arms over his neck and squeezed him tight.

He lifted me off the ground into his embrace and it was the first time in fifteen years I felt the loss of my papá as sharply as the first. Cousin, brother, it didn't fucking matter. He was the only family I had left willing to go to bat for me. And we were going up against our own blood.

"You're supposed to be my number two though."

"You don't need me for a number two guy, you've got three of them." He gestured over to my men, standing back and letting us have our moment.

Maybe he wasn't wrong about that.

The question was, did they want to be?

The drive back was filled with silence, so many what ifs and what nows still unspoken as we followed what seemed to be the path that was laid out for me. Or maybe I was still fucking delusional and leading us to our deaths.

There was a strange familiarity in going back to your childhood home. The only bad memory I had of this place was of my last night here. The air felt thicker as we drove through the gates and past the gardens. A row of cars followed behind us into the Flores property and I turned my head nervously before Ronan reassured me.

"They're Crows and Diablos."

"They were waiting for us?" I asked, scrunching my face together.

"César told everyone you were supposed to be the first person to walk inside," Mateo explained from the front.

Great. No fucking pressure or anything. Not momentous at all.

They all stood outside, some a hundred and fifty men, while I walked through the villa doors. There were plenty of bedrooms and accommodations here for all of them until we went to war. Between this and the guest house there were at least fifty rooms and most of them had multiple beds.

"Now what?" Calaveras' gravelly voice rang high over my head.

"Now we recoup. We lick our wounds, we plan well, and I get my papá's men on my side. Then we kill the hijo de la chingada." He and the Diablos who'd overheard all nodded in agreement as we walked through my family's villa.

Flashes of celebrations, meals, even weddings for cártel families that were held in this property ran through my memory. My papá made this a home, but looking back this was no place for a kid to grow up in. None of us were sheltered from the violence or the blood. Even Carolina knew it well, but we were desensitized early on. He was my papá, I would always love him. But now that I had grown up, I could acknowledge that he made plenty of mistakes. There were some I was determined to never repeat.

Bringing children into this world was one of them.

I sat with my arms crossed on a metal bench while César and Santos used the shovel to attempt and pry the box open. It was three in the morning and far too late for this bullshit, but they refused to end the day without knowing what all of this was for.

I couldn't blame them.

But I showed no trace of surprise when they finally forced the lid open, the smell of the past seeping out first before the contents became visible.

"What's this?" Santos pulled the leather journal out of the metal box first, a wave of nostalgia hitting me as memories of my papa with that thing stuck under his arm filled my head.

"Secrets. Blackmail. Currency of the cártel," I explained.

The Ortíz ledger was the reason why Augustin Ortíz was able to take the cártel in one fell swoop. He knew every dirty secret, every sellable crime any family had committed. And he used it like a leash to control his grunts, his own people. Following suit my papá had no choice but to continue in tradition. After all, why risk something new when you knew the old and tried way worked best?

No, this was what paid for their loyalty. Protection from their past.

"Jesus H. Christ," Mateo said in disbelief as he stuck his hand into the box, hundreds of diamonds slipping through his fingers and falling back into the heaping pile they came from.

"This is the kind of money that's gonna fuck with the economy when you put it back in circulation." Santos scratched the back of his head.

"That's the point. Then she'll own the fucking country."

It was easy to make this place feel the way it used to again, despite the fact my rat of a tío had tainted it with his presence not too long ago. I was here with the three men that I loved the most despite their aversion to me.

I knew the problem. I wasn't a fucking idiot.

Between them thinking I was some fragile little fucking paper doll, and them trying to distinguish the boundaries between the four of us, everything was a mess. At least they'd now finally come to realize that there wasn't a choice between the three of them. It was all or nothing. I meant it when I told them that, before the attack on the highrise.

Three weeks had gone by and all of our scars had begun to fade. Ronan was still in terrible shape which meant Emory was constantly on his ass to make sure he wasn't overdoing it. "No sex for six weeks," she reminded him. "Unless you want it to be your last time," she said like the evil Irish witch she was.

Which meant Santos and Mateo weren't touching me. I guess that was my own fault when I said all or nothing, but that was definitely not what I had meant. Things were just different now, and something told me they were waiting for Ronan to make the first move.

Which left me sexually frustrated and constantly on edge.

How was I supposed to concentrate on a war when there was so much sexual tension and testosterone just fucking floating around in the air at all times? I finally put my foot down and kicked Emory out of my room. I needed space to decompress and process all the fucking trauma I'd been trying to put behind me since it clearly wasn't going to leave me alone until I went through it.

And man did I need to go through it.

Dark humor was starting to become a dangerous coping mechanism, and no one was laughing at my suicide jokes anymore. It didn't matter. I learned long ago the only person who was capable of putting me six feet under would likely share the last name Flores. And now there was a good chance that Flores wouldn't be me.

"Why is Emory telling me I have to share a room with Santos and Mateo now?" Ronan rumbled into my ear from behind, sending goosebumps down my neck.

I was folding newly purchased clothes and tucking them into the dresser.

"Well, I was hoping she would have taken the hint and boarded up with César, but it looks like she's really making him work for it," I said, turning around and placing a kiss on his cheek. "You can sleep with me. If you promise to be good."

"How do you expect me to sleep next to you and not fuck you until my guts split open again?" He pressed me against the dresser, the hard steel of his erection strained against his pants.

I looked up through my eyelashes and bit my lip. Ronan was fucking massive. And now that I couldn't find a single reason to hate him anymore, all I wanted to do was let him crush me under him and suffocate me until I saw stars.

"Well, you best be a good boy, or I'll have you swap rooms with one of the others." I smirked and he pressed into me harder. His fingers wrapped around the back of my neck, and he forced my gaze up at him.

"You might be their queen, but I'm here to remind you that my hand around your neck has always been your favorite collar," he said, stroking my throat gently with his thumb.

"What do you call a man who owns a queen?" I asked.

"One lucky motherfucker," Mateo answered from the doorway, breaking the staring contest.

The disappointment from Mateo interrupting our moment was brief. Reality checked me hard, even with Ronan's undeniable sex appeal, and my cunt practically dripping just from the idea of being touched.

Ronan was lucky to be alive, and I wasn't stupid enough to risk his recovery.

As if my letdown was obvious, Ronan chuckled again, this time moving his hand to the front of my neck while the other roamed the waistband of my jeans. He turned us both to face Mateo. Santos stood behind him.

Had they been there the whole time? Had he brought them with him?

"You're telling me you fought this hard for both of them, and neither have taken care of you? You deserve to be fucked within an inch of your life. But I'll settle for mine if I have to. Tell the Doc to get a blood donor ready." His hand traveled south, reaching into my thong and stroking against my center.

"Oh fuck," I whispered, dropping my head back against his chest.

He continued his teasing, making circles on my clit before dipping inside of me, two knuckles deep. He groaned in my ear.

"You're so fucking wet." He thrusted two fingers all the way inside before pulling them out, forcing my eyes open at the shock of him leaving me desperate and needy.

By the time I turned around he was already sitting on a velvet chair in the corner of the room, forearms on his knees as he settled in. Mateo and Santos still hesitated at the door.

"I'm so tired of you all treating me like I'm made of glass. You didn't break me, and neither did he. If somebody doesn't fuck me soon, I'm going to go insane." Mateo was first, behind me all too suddenly before his hands traveled up my body, under the fabric of my shirt. His coarse hands massaged my breasts, kneading them softly before turning his attention to my nipples.

My eyes were still stuck on Ronan, sitting in the chair.

"Close the door or get out," Ronan told Santos in a commanding tone.

"I thought you didn't want to watch me with anyone else," I antagonized while immediately regretting my inability to hold my tongue even when it benefited me.

"I was wrong." His gaze hardened my way. "I want to watch them split you open. Then once I've heard you scream enough, I'll clean you up with my tongue."

He leaned forward in the chair and nodded to Mateo, who began to move his hands once again at Ronan's instructions.

Puta madre.

I felt like I was going to combust from every small touch. The sound of the door closing made its way to me, but before I could look over Mateo's shoulder to see if he'd come in or not, Santos was already there, pressed to my other side and pulling my jaw in his direction for a kiss.

I opened my mouth, parting my lips and letting his tongue dance its way in before reciprocating the movements myself. He swallowed my moans just as Mateo's fingers flicked around my nipples.

"Take her clothes off," Ronan said.

Santos didn't delay, he broke our kiss, pulling my shirt off and throwing it on the ground while Mateo worked to undo the buttons on my jeans. I helped him, stepping out of each leg as he rolled them down my calves. I reached for Mateo's shirt, taking it off of him and turning to Santos to do the same.

He grabbed my wrist in his hand to stop me and pinned my arm to my chest before forcing my back against him.

"Where do you want her?" He asked into my ear but the question wasn't for me.

"Bring her to the bed." Ronan leaned back and crossed his ankle over his knee.

I didn't miss the bulge in his pants and his refusal to adjust it.

We made our way to the bed, where Ronan had the perfect view. Mateo's fingers danced up my spine, forcing a shiver from my body. Once he got to the band of my bra he unclasped it, exposing me to all three of them. I heard the faintest growl coming from the corner but it was hard to tell if it hadn't come from the other two men.

"Take your shirt off," I told Santos, but he ignored me.

"Lay her on the bed. Head towards the edge." Ronan was in charge, and I had no problem with that. I couldn't look away from him. He was hungry, in every sense of the word, and somehow he was going to make do with what I gave him.

I was on my back. Mateo had me boxed between his arms as he hovered over me, and Santos stood above my head.

"I want to hear her choking on her screams," he told them.

Santos pulled me by the shoulders, letting my head dangle off the edge of the bed and before I could figure out what was going on I felt Mateo's hot, wet mouth on my center, lapping up all of my anticipation.

Santos chuckled like he knew exactly how to fulfill Ronan's demands. I heard the unzipping of his pants and shifted my focus from the vortex of pleasure that Mateo was drawing out from between my legs. His tongue fucked me continuously, only stopping to provide more attention to my clit every now and again.

"Open your eyes," Ronan commanded, but it wasn't him I saw once I did.

It was Santos' engorged and overly pierced cock, throbbing as it waited to enter my mouth. I moaned, parting my lips to let him in. I barely had time to inhale, and with this position he slid all the way down my throat with ease, filling up my airways and blocking all possibility of me breathing. I felt each bar of his Jacob's ladder against my tongue, the cold steel making it impossible for me to not try to wrap my tongue over each one as he sheathed himself inside of me.

A tear dripped from my eye, rolling down onto my forehead and soaking into my scalp. Santos wiped it before pulling himself out from my mouth.

"What are you doing?" Ronan asked before I could.

He didn't answer, he just scratched the back of his head anxiously before shaking his head and locking his gaze onto mine.

"I want this," I told him, lifting up and turning onto my elbows, turning back to look at him.

Mateo had come to a full stop, seeing the tension between Ronan and Santos and completely clueless on how to fix it.

"I promise, I want this," I told him, turning towards him.

10

Santos

I t was as if I was constantly being punished.

I wasn't ignorant enough to say things like, "I didn't know for what". The list was endless. I had sins that had expired by basic statute of limitations, but that didn't mean I didn't need to repent for them.

Her mouth open, my cock deep in her throat.

All I could see was Guillermo.

Her sacrifice.

My fucking shame.

Not being able to do enough to keep her from his brutality.

It had been eating me alive, and though she'd left me to commiserate without pushing, I knew I'd eventually have to face her, face myself, face my regrets.

She turned fully, folding her legs under her and sitting on her heels on the bed. She didn't look back to see what Mateo was doing, she stayed focused on me.

"What is it you see when you look at me Santos?" she asked, her voice not wavering.

I scanned over her body, from the scar on her face, to the small brand below her breast. Both scars matched mine. That meant something.

It had to.

"I see the strongest, most beautiful woman I've ever known," I answered with the truth.

"What else do you see?" she asked, knowing I was holding back.

"I see my failures. I see all the ways I should have protected you but wasn't able to." I cupped her face, thumbing the scar on her cheek.

I would have taken both of them if I could have.

"Take your shirt off," she told me again, this time her voice rang with authority.

"Celia," I warned her.

They'd seen the extent of my injuries, but now that they were healed it was different.

I didn't look so much like a victim as I did a monster.

Not even a monster but a monster's plaything, covered in holes and crooked stitching.

"Take your shirt off," she gritted out, her fingers gripping the hem of the fabric.

I inhaled, wrapping my fingers over hers and letting her guide the shirt over my head. I held that exhale at the bottom of my lungs and waited for any of them to say something, anything, to confirm how disgusting I knew I now looked.

"Fuck man." Mateo was the first to break the silence.

She ran her fingers over the areas where skin was puckered and raised up, scar tissue doing its best to heal wounds that had been ignored.

"Ask me what I see when I look at you," she said quietly.

"Morena." I sighed again, wishing I could make her understand that it wasn't about how I looked, but how I felt.

And I felt like a monstrous failure. Her fingers lingered over the raised up scar in the shape of the five petal flower.

"I see a man that belongs to me. A man who selflessly sacrificed himself for me. A man who gave me everything, including the courage to keep going. Their hatred and their insecurities may have left a permanent mark on you Santos, but all I see is a declaration of love. That scar on your face is the same as that brand on your chest and both of them say 'property of Celia Flores to me."

This woman was a titan, and I was a mere mortal, searching for a place to worship her even if just in evanescence. I would let her have me for as long as she considered me worthy.

"All of this is my fault," I reminded her before looking up at the rest of them.

Ronan ran his fingers over his face like I was ruining the moment, but she seemed unphased by it all.

"I'm so tired of figuring out who's to blame. We've all fucked up tremendously. Isn't that enough?" she asked.

"I haven't." Mateo smirked and she actually laughed, cracking the serious mask she wore and making my heart flutter with nostalgia.

I used to be able to do that to her.

"I guess that settles it, you can both get out," she said, turning back towards Mateo, locking her arms around his neck, and pressing her lips to his.

"Sorry sunshine, you're not calling the shots on this." He spun her around, one hand gripping one of her perfect tits and the other traveling down to her hip.

He shoved his knees between her legs, spreading them apart from behind and putting her on display for both Ronan and me.

She moaned loudly, dropping her head against his chest and grinding her pussy against his thigh.

"Somebody touch me, please." Her eyes found Ronan's who then found mine.

How we had gone from him wanting to punch my lights out for loving her, to asking me to fuck her was beyond me. It was time I dropped all my insecurities. I could do it if Zerkos could too.

I climbed up onto the bed and on my knees I made my way towards her. She was dripping all over his thigh, a look of need glimmering through those black eyes of hers.

"Please," she whimpered again.

I turned my face to Zerkos.

He gave me a crooked smile.

"Fuck her so good she doesn't know whose name to cry out."

I pinched her chin between my thumb and the side of my index finger.

"Is that what you want morena?"

"Please."

11

Celia

It was nearly unbearable, having all of them watching me, craving their touch, and not getting it. Mateo sensed my need and rolled my nipples between his fingers again, flooding me with an aching desire for more.

"Puta madre. Please," I begged.

Ronan chuckled louder. "I regret not doing this sooner."

Mateo sat, bringing me down on his lap with his erection pressed at my ass.

"I'm going to fuck you here, Sunshine," he whispered in my ear.

He wasn't quiet about it though, and Ronan tossed a bottle of lube his way with a smirk. Santos peppered kisses down my neck, his fingers dancing their way down my belly until they found the slick folds of my pussy right against Mateo's thigh. He moved his leg out of the way, getting ready for what was going to come next.

Santos' fingers made contact with my clit just as Mateo's lubed up fingers skirted the entrance of my puckered hole. First one finger slid through, eliciting a full body shudder from me while Santos sparked bursts of pleasure from me.

I moaned again and heard a wheezed grunt coming from Ronan.

Mateo inserted one more finger just as Santos speared himself inside my pussy, fingers scissoring their way in and rubbing against my walls. I cried out, an unexpected orgasm bursting its way out of me before I was ready.

"You weren't supposed to come yet, Sunshine," Mateo whispered in my ear.

I clutched his thighs, digging my nails into his flesh as I rode the last of that wave and forced him to hold me up from behind. He gave me the courtesy of letting me catch my breath before he hitched my legs up, wrapping my knees over his elbow and splaying me open for Santos and Ronan.

"Do you want him to fuck your ass, baby?" Ronan asked me.

"Yes." I nodded at him first before turning my head back to Mateo.

He shoved his tongue into my mouth, a passionate sloppy kiss to distract me from the burning sting of his way too thick of a monster cock pressing against my puckered hole.

"Fuck!" I bit out, breaking our kiss as the head pushed its way through the tight barrier before sliding in. "Shit. Shit. Shit." I breathed, recognizing how long it had been since the last time.

Santos dropped his head down my center, licking this way through my most sensitive area while Mateo continued to work his way inside me. With a few more thrusts he had bottomed out, and the confusing sensation of fullness paired with the emptiness I still felt with my pussy unoccupied was too much to bear.

"I need both of you, please," I gasped, yanking my fingers through Santos' hair to pull him up to my face level.

He wet his bottom lip. Any reservation he may have had before was now gone. I could see it clearly. We'd wasted too much time holding back before, and all it got us was regrets and scars. It was time to claim what we wanted and burn anyone and everything that stood in the way of it.

I practically screamed once Santos pushed himself inside. Each bar of his piercing drug along my walls with every inch he sunk deeper inside me. He knew exactly the type of madness that thing caused, and he knew how to use it well. He pulled out completely before he'd had a chance to go more than one or two bars in, and with a violent thrust of his hips, he impaled me.

The noise I made wasn't human.

It didn't stop them from continuing their torture.

Mateo still held my legs under the knees, and Santos' hands roamed everywhere they could find within reach. Thrusting back and forth once they'd found a rhythm that worked for them both.

"I can feel your dick piercings," Mateo groaned, making me wonder what that felt like for him, if it felt this good for me.

"Fuck," Santos breathed out, picking up speed.

"Wrap your hands around her neck." Ronan gave one last command and I waited to see which one of them would oblige.

Mateo froze, but I knew it was in hesitation. I gave Santos my most seductive stare, challenging him to dare to disobey. He didn't have it in him. His hand found its way to my throat, pressing at the side to restrict my blood flow. Mateo did the rest of the work, moving my hips in sync with his thrusts so that each time my hip came down I would come down onto Santos as well.

The position had his dick hitting my g-spot every time he skewered into me, but with his grip around my neck I wasn't able to moan, to cry, or scream. My breathing was shallow but the winding in my core grew tighter as my body got closer and closer to release. One hand still on Mateo's thigh, the other gripped Santos' forearm, and I squeezed, knowing an earth shattering climax was just around the corner.

My vision went hazy from the pressure around my throat, and I closed my eyes to lose myself to the colorful bright spots in my eyes, feeling the next climax tear through me like an avalanche.

"Not yet." I heard Ronan's muted voice telling Santos when he tried loosening his grip on me.

Another thrust. There was no distinction between the end of one orgasm or another. I couldn't keep my eyes open. I didn't know what any part of my body was doing at any point in time. I was simply in pleasure, like diving into the bottomless ocean. A moment where all that mattered was how good I felt and how good they could make me feel.

And we were all in it together.

I exploded again, this time hearing Ronan's approval and Santos moving his hands just in time for a guttural cry to rip its way out of me. He pulled out in a single move, his piercings rubbing every right spot along the way, prolonging an orgasm that felt like it would never end. A flood of liquid poured its way out from between my legs and onto the sheets, my body convulsing with tremors as I collapsed onto Mateo.

"We're not done," Mateo spoke from behind, forcing my eyes to flutter back open.

He was right, they weren't.

Santos looked determined, cock hard in his hand as he stroked up and down, playing with the bars of his piercings every time his fingers grazed over them.

"Fuck, that thing is so hot." I let my brain vomit voice itself out loud through my mouth.

I was panting hard, but I was a puddle of cummed out mess, unsure if I even had it in me to satisfy the two of them. I was already three deep and they hadn't even come once yet. Mateo let my legs go, dropping me to my knees on the bed while he stayed inside me. He placed his hands between my shoulder blades, letting me know he wanted me to drop down.

I obliged, lifting my ass up into the air as I pressed my chest to the mattress, turning my head to continue watching Santos pleasuring himself. Precum gathered at the tip, and he rubbed his thumb along it, spreading it around and coating his length in it. He didn't need it. He was still plenty wet from being inside of me.

Before I knew it, my mouth was watering. Watching his hand work his manhood in a way that had his eyes burning into mine as he chased his own pleasure was riveting. With every thrust of Mateo's hip against my ass I felt myself creeping closer to unraveling all over again. No time to get my bearings or recover, I was shaking at the first contact Mateo's fingers made with my clit, giving me the friction I needed to find my release again.

This time I took him with me, feeling the way his cock pumped inside of me while his cum filled my ass. He pulled out slowly, aftershocks surging through my body and forcing an awkward twitch from me as I wriggled against him. As if my pleasure was enough, Santos took two more pumps of his fist before ropes of his cum were landing on the bed, warm droplets landing on my face while he moaned through his climax.

The three of us breathed heavily, taking our time to come down from our high as gently as possible.

"Spread her legs," Ronan demanded and Santos was there in an instant, flipping me on my back while Mateo held me open like a buffet.

I raised up onto my elbows, watching Ronan struggle to get off the chair on his own before slowly making his way towards us. Mateo stood, giving him his arm to help him down onto his knees.

"Fuck me," Ronan whispered before his head disappeared between my legs.

He was making good on that promise.

The flat of his tongue raked against my swollen, abused clit but he didn't care. He licked up every drop of arousal that coated me before shoving his tongue deep inside, doing the same to all of the liquid heat that threatened to spill its way out of me again.

"Oh God," I cried, every nerve ending on my body was still too sensitive, but he didn't seem to care.

His tongue moved in and out of me as he cleaned every inch of my ass and pussy with his mouth. It was too much. I shook my head back and forth, whispering obscenities in Spanish until there was nothing left but for me to come once more, violently shaking in his hold while Mateo kept me spread apart.

"Fuck!" I cried out, clawing the sheets below me desperately.

Once I could finally stop hearing the blood pumping through my ears, I rose back up to a seated position and looked at Mateo and Santos.

"Help me undress him," I told them. "Get him in the shower." I nudged my head towards the en suite bathroom.

Santos was up first, lifting Ronan from his knees while Mateo did his best to remove his shirt without putting him through too much pain. He was healing well, the Doc said so herself, but he was still supposed to be receiving assistance with day to day things like this.

I headed over to the bathroom, stepping on the cold tile floor before walking through the glass doors of the shower and turning it on. Hot water sprayed from the showerhead, instantly filling the room with a plethora of steam.

"Sit." I gestured to the concrete stool across from the showerhead.

All three followed but only Ronan took a seat, knowing my words were just for him. I filled a loofah with soap before dragging it across his body, starting with his shoulders and being mindful to not put pressure on his stomach. He leaned against the tile wall, closing his eyes and seeming unbothered by how cold it must have felt. I bent over and turned to scrub his massively muscular legs.

"Will you tell me what happened? When Guillermo had you both?" he asked, his eyes remaining shut.

"I got on my knees for him," I told him. "To keep him from hurting Santos any more than he already had." His eyes jarred open and looked past me.

He was looking at his brother's scars again.

"How can I make it better?" It was so Ronan of him to ask me that.

Ever since we were children, he was always looking for a way to make things better, to fix whatever it was that was keeping a smile from my face. But it wasn't up to him or Santos or Mateo to make it better. It was only up to me. I was the one who decided how damaged I was going to be from this, not them, and certainly not Guillermo.

"By letting me get on my knees for you," I told him, not wavering my gaze from that emerald forest that burned so brightly in his stare.

I lowered down in front of him, the water hammering into my back like a hot massage that pressed against my muscles. He was hard and ready for me, and there was no way I wasn't going to be savoring all the best dick of my life in one day. I wrapped my lips over my teeth and lowered my mouth onto his erection, licking the shiny head of his length before sending it further into my mouth.

He groaned, grabbing a fistful of my hair and pulling.

"Fuck flower, I forgot just how good that mouth of yours feels." He let out a desperate grunt and I looked up to find him watching me intently, not a care in the world about the two other men enjoying the show behind me.

He pulled at my hair, letting me know he was going to take control and I relaxed my throat, readying myself for it. He thrust deep down my throat before pulling all the way out to slam again. I closed my eyes, but a picture of Guillermo's sick smile flashed over my vision in the dark.

"Look at me," he said, as if he knew exactly where I'd gone.

I choked out an inhale, opening my eyes to find him looking down at me with nothing but admiration.

"I love you," he said, pulling out of my mouth.

"No, stop. We're not done, you're not done." I shook my head, but Santos pulled me up from behind and began washing me with the same loofah before I'd had a proper chance to fight about it.

Mateo helped Ronan up, but he walked out of the bathroom on his own. The two of them stayed, closing in on me while Santos continued to lather me up.

"It's okay to not be okay, sunshine." Mateo cupped my cheek. "No one expects you to pretend like you're fine."

"I *am* fine," I said through clenched teeth, my nostrils flaring widely before I pushed through them, dripping wet with no towel as I made my way out of the bathroom.

"Fuck!" Santos cursed just loud enough for me to hear.

Ronan stood there, as naked as I was, but seeming ten times less bothered than me.

"Let me try again," I said nervously.

He shook his head.

"Another time, I just want to sleep next to you again. I want to hold you in my arms."

"I love you Ronan," I said the words that had taken too long to come out of my mouth again.

"I love you too, Cecilia. Celia. Whatever the fuck you want to be called these days."

"I'll settle for your majesty." I smirked, grabbing a towel that hung from a chair and using it to dry myself.

"Then come sleep with me, your majesty." He reached out and I accepted his hand, letting him pull me closer.

I helped him onto the bed, thankful that all the wet spots were at the bottom towards our feet and making a mental note to change them in the morning when I wasn't completely fucked out of energy. He laid on his back, and I propped the pillows up just slightly for him, making sure he was comfortable and settled in.

I nudged myself into a nook at his side, draping one leg of mine over his and laying my arm over his chest. My head found a comfortable place on his arm, and I closed my eyes to appreciate this moment, wondering for a second what the fuck was taking the other two so long to shower.

Ronan ran the tips of his fingers up and down the side of my arm, the gentle touch sending a wave of goosebumps down my spine.

Guadalajara was quickly becoming home again, because home wasn't a set place.

I didn't know that I'd ever get tired of saying so.

12

Celia

To be queen I needed more than just a throne, I needed an empire. Which meant I desperately needed people I could trust. As of right now that list was small. I required more men, my father's men, more importantly. The ones that went into hiding when my tío betrayed my papá.

The metal chest we'd dug up in the desert contained the Ortíz ledger along with millions of dollars in gold and diamonds. Blood money certainly, but my hands were far from clean. I could play differently, but I couldn't change the game. My skin was thick, I was primed for this.

If I had any uncertainties about it, then I should have passed the torch to Carolina.

We'd been settled into Guadalajara long enough now that I'd made contact with a damn good lawyer and paid him everything it took to get Celia Flores out of her grave and back in tip top health. Apparently not such a difficult task. I'd also found out that since I was the only living heir of the Flores and Ortíz families, that I was filthy fucking rich.

Like puta madre rich.

César didn't want my money.

Apparently he *was* too good for my blood money. A laughable thought if you took into consideration that he ran a one percent biker gang.

Club. Whatever. Los Diablos Locos weren't to be fucked with, and I was happy to be making allies this early in the game.

I'd procrastinated long enough. We'd been here for weeks and for the most part we had healed. It was time to see who'd stand at my side. Time to see who'd give me a chance to prove myself to be better than both the men who came before me.

The Ortíz ledger was thicker than my thighs. An old leather cover sealed the documents, but the binding was four metal rings, allowing the holder to add to it over time. This is what secured the cártel for the Ortíz family long ago, and this is what my papá gained by marrying my mamá. She was an Ortíz, and everything I'd known about how the Flores family took control was a lie. She was a pawn, as women often were, moved across the board to further the interest of men.

Weak.

Diego was the oldest, but he died before I'd ever been born. Which meant there was a good chance my abuelo arranged to marry my mamá off to the Flores family as his only option for not losing everything upon the death of his line.

As if women ruling was so out of the question.

Their errors would be my gain.

Now I had all of the Ortíz money, the Flores name, and my papá's cojones hanging from my legs. And that ledger, I had that ledger, and it was probably my most powerful weapon.

The cártel was successful because it was a well-oiled machine built on lies, secrets and the never ending struggle for control turning the gears day by day to function. Every blackmail, every dirty skeleton in a closet, every confidential piece of information that might only be privy to the military? It was in that ledger.

It was why my tío wasn't able to make nice with the politicians down here. He had nothing on them. This ledger had generations of crimes with statute of limitations that didn't run out. One secret outed, and that family's name would be tarnished for good.

I had a lot of stops to make, but I was starting with papá's arms dealer.

"Celia. This is a surprise. I had heard rumors but..."

"Yes, quite a surprise, I'm sure." I walked right into his kitchen. It was about the size of Mateo's closet. Tiles were missing from the floor where dirt rested in its place instead. The walls were concrete and stained, and a simple calendar was nailed to the wall above the tiny old oven. Time had not been kind to the Riveras, or maybe it was my uncle.

Dominico's daughter, Gabriella, stood just past the hallway, she must have been in her early twenties now. I vaguely remembered her as a baby when I was just a young girl. She had blonde hair, and her eyes were blue even though both her parents had dark hair and dark eyes.

I pulled out a wooden chair and sat down, gesturing to both of them with my hand to sit. They made their way across the table from me. Dominico looked behind me, eyeing the men directly on my six, guarding my back. I chuckled. "Don't worry Dom, they're harmless, unless you give them a reason to shoot. Sit, let's talk like old friends."

"Like old friends?" He raised an eyebrow up.

They both took a seat. Gabriella looked at me from underneath her eyelashes as she kept her head tucked down. I didn't mean to be intimidating, I just knew that acting like the biggest fish in the room was the only thing that actually made it true.

"I'm going to cut the pleasantries. I'm here to tell you I've come into possession of Rafa's ledger, the Ortíz ledger. I am not here to offer you the option of death or generations of indentured servitude to me. I am not my papá. I am better than him, and I intend to *be* better than him. I will not blackmail you into my corner."

"What is it you offer then, if not blood?" He looked into my eyes, his wrinkling hands fell heavy on the table. He must have been in his late sixties now. In his prime he was a feared and respected officer in my papá's army. Not to say he couldn't be feared now, but I'm sure he was a much easier kill these days then back then.

But he had all the knowledge and connections I lacked.

"What my papá didn't give you, a choice." With my words he looked to his daughter and squeezed her hand. "If you stick with me, I will provide for you better than Rafa ever could. You will feel my protection twice over and my loyalty. My papá ruled through fear, I plan to rule by earning your respect. If you decide not to back me, I won't press you, I won't come back for you, and I won't kill you. I will leave you and all of your descendants to live or die in peace." I looked at Gabriella and tilted my chin down at her in recognition.

"That simple?" He eyed me suspiciously.

"That simple. However, this ledger, as you can imagine, is very precious to me. It stays in my possession at all times. If I were to be a casualty in this war that will *no doubt* come to fruition… Well, it would be a shame if Ignacio were to claim what isn't his. Wouldn't it?" My gaze at Gabriella turned into a menacing one so that my message could ring loud and clear.

It wasn't a threat; it was a promise.

If my tío got ahold of this ledger he would use it to trap every single one of my father's soldiers permanently, through as many generations as he could until he was dead and gone. I was offering freedom. I was offering a life where I wouldn't hang the threat of revealing their dirtiest secrets out into the world if the opportunity struck.

Because there were many. You didn't sign yourself over to the cártel if a life of clean money was something you could easily attain.

"If you help me through this fight, you can retire, without worrying whether or not your daughter is going to be stuck under my heel. That's a promise. Your secrets die with me." I stuck my hand out in an offering and raised an eyebrow at him. "Maybe this ledger even ends up falling into a fire at some point. Maybe we can rebuild on a truer loyalty."

"Rule with respect, huh?" he said as he clapped his hand against mine in agreement. "You've got yourself a deal reina."

"No offense Dom, I'll take you by my side any day. You're as fierce as they come. But you're an old man these days, and aside from your connections, I just need your voice." He scowled, taking offense at my bluntness. "What I mean to say is, Gabriella over here looks mighty hungry." I smirked at her, and she returned a matching smile that let me know I was reading her right. "She's all grown up now. Maybe she wants to fight too?" She didn't look to her papá for approval and right then I knew she was my type of girl.

"I do," she confirmed with a steady voice.

"Good girl." I shook her hand as well and stood from the table. "Then we're in agreement. Contact the men under you, and I'll send over more information in regards to finances and where we'll be meeting soon."

"I look forward to it. My men will be ready as soon as I give them the go ahead."

I nodded my approval and made my way out of his home without looking back, my men surrounding me as we walked through the threshold and made our way to the next name on the list.

Every conversation went the same. Old men, tired of hiding their families from my tío, hoping for something to come along and end their bad luck streak. I was just that thing. Soon my papá's entire council was behind me, and every connection he had was ready to back me. Well, at least those who hadn't betrayed him for Ignacio or gone running to him the minute todo se fue a la verga.

There was only one place left to go, the place that still lived in the back porch of my mind. Where I tucked away the little girl I had once been and became the woman I was today.

13

Mateo

A retinal scan and a digital fingerprint of all five fingers were needed before the main doors opened. We were in the absolute middle of nowhere. It was as empty as it got out here in the desert, aside for the five by five metal barrack with steel reinforced doors sticking out of the ground. The doors opened with a mechanical hiss, sliding inside their compartments and allowing us to enter.

She looked calm, comfortable. Like she was in her element. But I'd watched enough of those videos to know that behind those doors was also the place where her monsters tried to eat her. She of course had ended up eating them instead, but nonetheless, no child should have faced the burdens Celia Flores had been made to bear.

It was a tiny steel room with a trap door on the floor, we turned on our phone flashlights and the stairs presented themselves.

"There are many entrances, but to unlock them I have to open the main door and turn the system on then send power to all the other doors," she explained.

The stairs went down into another room, and there an elevator, with far too many digital screens on it, waited for us. First another retinal scan, another fingerprint on one of the glass screens on the wall. Then a device came out of the wall holding a piece of glass that reminded me a lot of a microscope slide. She reached her hand out to us.

"Who's got a knife?"

Santos was the quickest, placing the blade in her hand. She gripped it tight, pressing the sharp edge against the pad of her index finger until blood pooled around the blade. She squeezed, the droplets of blood straight onto the glass. She pressed a button, and the device withdrew back into the wall, the lights turning green and the elevator opening up.

"No fucking wonder he couldn't steal this from you," Zerkos snorted out.

"He is just a pretender, playing at being the boss. My papá worked hard to make sure that his empire would only be accessible to me." Her eyes seemed to darken as she turned toward him. "Now he will feel the full force of my fury. He's going to pay for what he did to my family, for turning my sister against me, and for all the lives he's taken."

The elevator opened, and the screen read negative fourteen, which meant we were a long way down. Far below civilization—where no one could hear your screams. It opened up to a massive room, the walls lined with large stones and a cold concrete slab floor. Several hallways split off in different directions letting me know this place was bigger than it seemed. This wasn't somewhere you wanted to get lost.

She seemed to know exactly where she was going, head held high like none of the trauma she suffered here had been anything but a stepping stone on the way to becoming who she was always meant to be.

She even looked like she fit the part. She wore a black two piece suit, fitted to her curves from every angle. She wore her long black hair slicked back into a low ponytail and her lips were painted a captivating black.

Battle colors.

"How soon can you get Taylor down here working?" she asked Ronan.

"She's just waiting for you to give her the word." He had no problem deferring to her, it was an odd thing to see because Ronan Zerkos didn't defer to anyone.

"We should be able to track him down within the week," she said confidently.

"How do you figure?" I asked.

"This dungeon is the central hub. There's sixteen total throughout México. Four of them never got locked down when my papá died, that's what he's been working with this entire time. The other twelve I can open through the command station with Taylor's help." She walked over to a large table dusting it off to show a map. "Every dungeon is connected to this one, through a tunnel system. Once I open up all the doors, he'll know I'm here. Either he'll go scurrying like a rat and go into hiding, or he'll take the bait and come straight to me."

"Is that what you want?" Santos asked her, the scar on his face was finally starting to lose its shine.

"I'm not afraid of him anymore. Let him come, less work for me."

Ronan's phone rang, breaking the intensity of the moment. He stepped away to take the call and I turned back to her. She looked as beautiful as ever, radiant. *My sun*. She wore her makeup heavier than usual, to cover the scar on her face.

The scar didn't take away from her beauty.

It enhanced it.

It told the story of her strength and her refusal to die in a world that wanted nothing more than to bleed her out. Fuck. She was a goddamn reckoning, and she was coming for them all. It was an honor to be considered worthy enough to stand at her side and watch it happen.

But all I wanted to do was reach out and touch her. Slide my hands between her legs and bend her over one of the desks and fuck her senseless. She was so wound up from the stress and the crushing weight of all the expectations that came with being her father's daughter.

I couldn't do that.

Not in front of her men, her soldiers.

I knew she played a calculated game and that to be respected she needed space.

But I hadn't touched her in days, and I was ready to die because of it, I was sure. She cocked an eyebrow at me like she could read my thoughts. She shook her head and turned abruptly to say something to César in Spanish. Then Ronan stepped back into our circle with a pissed off look on his face, his jaw muscles ticking hard like the whole world pissed him off.

"Something's happening in Cove City," he said to me before looking over to gauge Celia's reaction.

She didn't have one. She wasn't just damn good at the game, she was a prodigy, carefully cultivated by a monster of a man who genuinely thought he was doing the right thing. The life was a wicked game, and we are all just pieces on a chess board, waiting to be knocked over.

"You're leaving then?" César spoke for her as if he could sense her lack of words was due to anxiety.

"I gotta sort some things out. I'm surprised your men haven't called you. The Bratvas are sending threats, and the Crows are spread thin in multiple directions and with no purpose. I gotta figure out the future for my men." He looked at both me and Santos, the question was there in his eyes, but he couldn't ask it.

I shook my head.

"It's you brother, it's always been you. Go handle it and come back to us." I tilted my head before slapping my hand on his shoulder, giving him my vote of confidence.

"You won't go with him?" she asked, concern spread over her face.

"He doesn't need us, morena," Santos said from a chair, his arms resting comfortably on his thighs with his shoulders hunched forward.

"And I do?" Shit, she was offended. "Fuck that," she spat out. "All three of you can fucking go. Deal with your Crows desmadre and then come back together." She waved her fingers between the three of us angrily.

César choked out a laugh like the asshole he was. Santos huffed out a response, and Zerkos smirked, seeming happy enough to not be on the biting side of her anger for once.

"If you're opening up these dungeons, you'll be exposed, vulnerable for your uncle to try something. I'd feel better if at least one of us stayed," I told her, finding myself with a shovel in hand, ready to dig my own grave.

"You don't think the hoard of bikers can protect me from the big bad wannabe cártel jefe but you can?" She pouted her lips seductively and stepped closer to me, running her index finger from the center of my sternum and slowly dragging it down.

My breath hitched as she got lower. I could hear César pretending to suck something out of his teeth to distract himself from the moment.

She was dangerous as fuck when she wanted to prove a point.

"Or that the men I've collected who've sworn their allegiance to me, who've dropped to their knees for me, they aren't capable of keeping me safe like you can?"

"That's not it, sunshine," I said with an exhale, feeling frustrated that her past had shaped her to believe that having people who cared for you somehow made you seem weaker. "It's that there are three men in this room who would likely eat a bullet if they found out something *else* happened to you while we were gone."

Her jaw clenched hard, a familiar mannerism of Ronan's. Little moments like this always reminded me that they'd grown up together. Now I saw it for what it really was. It was her behavior not his. He had been mirroring *her* all this time. It made me wonder if she'd learned it from her father.

She was calculating her options.

Damn, I loved a smart woman.

"Everybody out." She didn't even have to say it loud, and the room cleared out fast. All the little techie nerds that were already working to reinstate all of the built-in systems promptly stood and vacated to God knows the fuck where.

César stood as well, and she stood with her arms crossed, waiting for the room to empty completely.

"Are you not going to say anything?" I asked Santos, who still sat on a foldout chair, ankle over his knees and hands behind his head.

"Nah." He chewed on the toothpick pressed between his back teeth.

Of course he wouldn't, so I would be the only insane one who wanted to suffocate her because I couldn't handle the idea of her being on her own without her. Even though history would prove...

Either way. That wasn't fucking fair. Ronan wouldn't disagree because he was never going to be saying no to Celia ever again. And Santos, well... I didn't really know what his fucking deal was. I figured he was just handling the post torture shit poorly. Wouldn't blame him. He didn't talk much about it, but she did. She'd told me in confidence. Every day Guillermo would ask him if he still wanted to protect her, still wanted to take her pain for himself. Every day he gave him the option to swear himself back to Los Muertos, to kill her instead.

Every day he took what was meant for her, and they'd hurt him instead. And every day she watched. I hated that she had to do what she did, but I respected her for it. But Santos, he was still haunted by it and having a hard time looking past anything but his own failures.

14

Celia

Things were different between me and Santos now because we were different now. We no longer saw the need to keep putting on the mask we did with everyone else. We saw each other at our worst, we saw all of each other's flaws. I knew exactly who he was inside, and he knew the same about me.

It was comforting in a way, to have someone you could be your truest self with.

It was like letting go of a breath you'd been holding your entire life.

When you wore a mask at all times, you kind of forgot what your real face looked like. If I took too much time to think about it, it always sent me into a spiral of panic. An identity crisis that never resolved itself. I'd spent my entire life pretending to be whoever it took to get me through the next chapter, and I ended up forgetting who I was underneath the mask.

Santos saw through it now.

And he couldn't hide from me either.

The problem was that at my core, I wasn't sure who was behind the mask anymore. I felt like an insecure little girl with no personality and a watered down version of her culture that'd been forgotten through years of Americanization. *Assimilate or die.* It was a rough game, but by the time I realized what a good job I'd done blending into the crowd, it was too late. I was a thirty year old orphan with a second-grade education level in the country I'd impulsively moved 'home' to.

Oh, fuck. It was happening again.

I lowered down to a squat on the ground, hovering my ass just an inch from the floor while my head dropped between my knees. I took deep breaths, but the room just closed in on me faster with each exhale, and all I could hear was the high-pitched electronic sound coming from the computers.

And then Ronan's shoes appeared on the ground right in front of my face. I lifted my gaze up to find him there, head tilted as he waited for my eyes to follow all the way up to his. His hand extended out as he reached and caressed the side of my face, his Bleu de Chanel scent reminding me that it didn't matter who I was because he'd find a way to love all those versions of me.

Maybe they all would.

"Let me leave the goldendoodle with you, flower. I'll sleep better knowing you won't be alone in that big house." He smirked, navigating through my ego in a way that only he knew how to do in order to get me to acquiesce to his needs.

My heart slowed down with each stroke of his thumb against my cheek, and I used it as a guide to steady my breathing.

"You'll take Santos with you, to keep you safe?" I asked and he huffed out a laugh.

"Yeah, yeah. I'll take Álvarez to keep me safe." Their eyes met, but neither one showed any expression.

They still weren't seeing eye to eye, which was insane because at this point I thought we'd chalked everything up to water under the bridge. Maybe I was the only one standing on the bridge though. Poor Mateo wasn't even aware there was water to go over, he was so faultless in everything.

"Then yes, I'll keep the goldendoodle." I smiled back at Ronan.

"Did we get a dog?" Mateo asked and finally Santos cracked a smile.

It was just going to be a couple days, but it also just felt like we'd just all gotten each other back. How was I supposed to cope when they would be so far away? Yeah,

I *would* have told them all to go too, because I was a stubborn puta and every time I cut myself I ended up pouring salt in the wound, and then I followed it with tequila and lime.

Ronan and Santos got on a plane the next day and left for Cove City. César was tempted to follow, a threat to the Crows right now might as well have been a threat on the Diablos Locos compound. But he'd also told me about the trust he had in his VP and that he knew he could hold down the fort.

I wanted that kind of faith in my own men.

I was just getting to know them though; it would come with time. I needed to be patient. I was building an entire fucking empire from the cremated ashes of what once was. It was an impossible expectation to think I would have all my pieces on the board this soon.

I sighed. I would take borrowed soldiers until then.

"Why don't you take a breather," Mateo rasped into my ear right as I reached for my phone to shut off the alarm. "Just a day or two off from being the big bad queen of Mexico and let me work on unwinding you for forty-eight hours." He pulled my back into his chest and dropped his nose to my neck.

"If I was a man, and you were a woman. I would have assumed you were conspiring against me, and I'd be awfully suspicious of you trying to distract me for so long." I stretched my neck out, giving him the space he needed to pepper kisses down my throat.

I arched my back, pressing my ass to his morning wood.

It was only six in the morning. I could give him a few hours, maybe not the forty-eight he asked for, but I could give him some of me. His hand caressed down my ribs and trickled their way down.

"The guys…" I breathed out just as his fingers traveled down to the waistband of my pajama shorts.

"They're in Cove City. I can promise you I can make it so good you won't even remember they aren't here," he said seductively, his fingers dancing over my underwear and giving me the softest friction.

Just enough to drive me crazy.

"That's not what I meant. It's just. It's…" I couldn't put my finger on it.

"It's what, sunshine?" he asked, like he didn't understand.

But his hands were moving with a mind of their own, and though my brain was struggling to figure it out, my body said, cállate idiota!

"It feels like cheating if they aren't here. I don't know, we got to this place where it felt like there was understanding, but with both of them gone. I don't know. It just feels off."

He hummed into my ear like he was thinking about it, his fingers sliding inside my panties through the side and with zero hesitation he plunged them in. Finding me already soaked for him.

"I can fix that." I could hear the amusement in his voice, like he was really proud of his problem-solving abilities.

I gasped as he pulled out and used my arousal to coat my clit. He rubbed back and forth with the gentlest touch, like he already knew it wasn't about how fast or hard he did it in just the few times we'd been together.

This one took notes.

He was a good boy.

He moved in circles, my head spinning with his fingers and just as I closed my eyes to relish in the moment, I heard the loud dialing of his phone blasting on speaker.

"What?" Ronan answered.

My entire body temperature skyrocketed.

"What are you doing?" I hissed, trying to turn.

"Our girl needs to get off," Mateo said bluntly, and Ronan made a grunting sound on the phone.

"So why are you calling *me*?" Ronan said in his classic annoyed tone.

Mateo was unphased, plunging his fingers back inside of me and forcing a moan straight out of the depths of my chest.

"She's concerned about the ethics of it all," he said, pulling his fingers from inside me in order to assist me in fully removing my clothing.

"Get out," Ronan barked over the phone.

"He's busy. He's with people," I yelled at Mateo, who only chuckled.

"He's never too busy for you, sunshine. Tell her you're never too busy for her Zerkos."

"The dog's right, flower. I'm never too busy for you. Now turn on the camera and show me my girl," he growled out.

Mateo barked out a laugh, hitting a button on his phone as he propped himself up on the bed, running it over my body like he was showing Ronan everything he was missing out on.

"Where's Álvarez?" Mateo asked.

"He's here. Maybe if you make her scream, I'll let him come watch."

"Oh fuck," I gasped, the torment of his words building a heat inside of me from just the thought of the two of them watching while Mateo had his way with me.

It was so incredibly wrong.

So why did it feel so fucking right?

15

Ronan

"Hold the phone between her legs, I want to see how wet she is," I told Kane.

"Aye, aye," he chimed before lowering it from her face.

He thrusted his fingers inside her. I could hear her mewling in the distance, but the way she thrusted her hips told the bigger story.

"Slow down," I said, leaning back into the chair.

I looked up to find Santos still sitting at the end of the table, his eyes awkwardly averting mine. He didn't need my fucking permission to be with Celia. It wasn't about that anymore. It was about the fact that he was supposed to have been the one person I could have trusted with her life.

I never wanted to be wrong about it.

Now I was stuck here with him, because I trusted Mateo with her more than I trusted him. And that was saying a lot. Mateo Kane couldn't even keep a fish alive.

There were a thousand unspoken things between us. Most of them absolute bullshit that I would have rather just resolved with our fists.

But the guy was ugly enough now as it was. A visual reminder that he had been punished plenty for his sins.

I couldn't tell if his appearance was actually bothering him. He was going to be wearing his mistake for the rest of his life on his skin. Then suddenly it didn't feel so fair that I was here, asking him to feel remorse when Celia had somehow found it inside her to forgive me for the hell I put her through.

"Santos can't hear her brother," I chuckled, giving him a smirk.

He looked even more nervous.

Suspicious of me.

Untrusting bastard.

She cried louder the minute he lowered his face to her cunt, his tongue lapping at her clit and just as he covered it up he raised the phone to show me her face.

Fucking radiant.

She had one arm raised up high, her fist wrapped around the bar on the headboard of the bed. The other hand squeezed her breast and her teeth dug deep into her bottom lip from whatever it was Mateo was doing to her.

She was holding it back.

"Come on, don't make me say it." Her eyes sprung open, and she looked straight into the camera, even though she couldn't see me.

She bit her lip even harder.

"Fine. But I want you to cry out Álvarez's name for me when you come for me, flower."

"Fuck! Santos! Shit!" she cried.

Her body convulsed in violent quakes and the bastard finally turned his head my way.

He was fighting a smile so badly It was probably going to constipate him.

"I hope you didn't call me just to waste my time with one?" I egged Mateo on.

He flipped the camera to selfie mode to show me his face, glistening from her juices just as he rose up from between her legs. I would have given a million dollars to be there right now, in his place.

It was all I'd been able to do since I'd gotten shot. Emory had a million rules in place to make sure I didn't drop dead from internal bleeding or post-surgery complications. Gun to my head, dying while fucking Celia Flores didn't sound like the worst way to go. I couldn't fuck her for another two weeks and the doc had strictly prohibited me from getting off in general. Something about not getting my heart rate up too high. So I feasted on her pussy every night that I could.

And oh how I missed my favorite meal.

He was gloating.

Rubbing it in my face because he knew.

I would have done the fucking same.

He flipped the camera back and pointed it down just in time to let me see his cock slowly filling her up. It was the perfect fucking view and I had to clench my jaw tight in order to keep it from going slack.

We didn't have that much time, our men needed answers soon, and I'd just kicked them out to watch my best friend fuck my woman.

He was fully sheathed inside of her, his free hand roaming up and down her body, paying extra attention to her breasts and tracing gently around her nipples.

"Oh fuck," she moaned through the speaker.

"Does that feel good baby?" I asked her, getting her eyes to open for me again.

They somehow looked darker when she was drunk with lust.

"Yes," she hissed, her head bouncing up and down with each slam of his hips against hers.

Then his hand lowered to her clit, and she shook her head.

"No-no… I'm too sensitive still," she pleaded.

He listened, like the obedient little soldier he was and moved his hand away.

"No. Go back," I commanded.

Santos' shadow loomed over me, and I felt his stare behind my shoulder as he watched my phone.

He made a circle on her clit, and she whined and thrashed. Mateo thrusted harder and she sobbed something unintelligible that wasn't English or Spanish until she came down from her climax.

I shut the call off.

I didn't feel good about lying to her, but if I had told her the truth, she would have tried to stop me. Santos smelled my bullshit the minute I opened my mouth to tell her there was an issue that needed dealing with out here, but he didn't call me out. Instead he hopped along for the ride, probably hoping to catch a glimpse of the shitshow that was coming. I had one reason and one reason only for coming here.

"Let them back in," I told Santos, crossing my hands over the table and cracking my knuckles anxiously.

I did not want to fucking be dealing with this, but I had to. What was meant to be a trip to Cove City, ended up being a stay at the Diablos Locos compound in Grimm's Reach. This was where all of our members were taking residence ever since the Los Muertos attack on the high-rise.

No one felt safe going back.

I didn't blame them.

So here I was, using César's church room to conduct a half-ass Black Crow Brotherhood meeting with our members. They filed back in slowly, too many bodies in the small room and these were only the members who were privy to decisions we made, not just any soldier

I was anxious.

But this had been coming, I knew it from the moment she walked back into my life. I'd just been pretending like there wasn't a countdown above my head the entire time. It was now flashing zero.

Time was up.

"Berserk!" Ethan yelled, hair still wet from a shower.

He greeted Santos with a bear hug, not giving much notice to the change in his face. I embraced Ethan, slapping him hard on the back and Fletcher followed behind, hooting and making animal noises as he bounced on his toes and pushed his way into the room.

"It's good to see you both." I nodded as they made their way in the room.

The rest of our men gathered in, taking seats where they found them. The remainder stood shoulder to shoulder as they waited for me to address them. The last four months had been nothing short of a fuckstorm, but the Black Crows could rebuild from the ruins, they deserved that. I just wasn't sure if I was the one who could stack those bricks anymore.

"This compound is cozy and all boss, but people are ready to go home. Wherever that is. We've been in limbo for too long now and we need a purpose. We need to take out the assholes who hurt our families," Fletcher spoke first, nodding to Santos when he said family.

He was just now back at a hundred percent, and if I were him, I'd want blood too. We needed more than that if we were going to go after the Bratvas. We'd need everything we had and more.

"Everything's wrong right now. I know that," I started, getting the attention of all the men in the room. "I'm gonna do whatever it takes to make sure every ounce of blood gets paid back in double."

"Dez has turned some Crows against you. They don't whisper loud enough for us to know who they are, but we've all heard the whispers, Berserk." He used the nickname the city knew me by.

The name of the man I was before she came back to me.

Men began to talk over each other, but they were all practically saying the same thing.

They were worried. They had more than enough proof that Dezmond Archer Junior was now working with the Bratvas to get payback for Sokolov's daughter's face. We also never gave the other daughter back. Not our fault for lack of trying though, apparently she didn't want to go home.

Daddy had done enough damage that the Diablo's compound was cozier than a Bratva penthouse with all the fixins.

And now we had a major target on our back. Our rat problem became a traitor problem and we were down quite a few soldiers. Permanently. The attack on the high-rise killed too many of our people. Out of those who came out unscathed, quite a few decided to leave the life.

Who could blame them?

Not knowing which day was going to be your last and learning to be fine with that was a skill in itself.

Not something either nature or nurture could prepare you for. It was something that was burned into you with the flames of time. For Celia that was a cattle brand in her father's hand. For me it was a black dog tag and all the men I once watched die in the name of freedom.

"We're not ready to attack them head on right now." The second the words left my mouth a chorus of disappointment rang out from half the room while the other chimed in louder to my defense.

We were already divided.

What was I holding on for?

Like a kid who wouldn't share a toy even though he was done playing with it.

Except the Crows weren't a toy and these were people's lives at stake.

Santos stuck his index and middle finger in his mouth and whistled loudly, quieting the room.

"We wiped the floor with Los Muertos, why can't we do the same with the Bratvas?" Bruno, one of our heavier hitters asked.

"It's not that simple. Los Muertos wasn't even half the amount of soldiers as I would expect the Russians to have. They were distracted, the Russian's are waiting for us. Not to mention, we had over a hundred Diablos holding our hands on that fight."

"They won't help us again?" he asked.

Santos scoffed out a laugh.

"No. Los Muertos was a mutual problem. I'm not in any position to ask anything of any Diablo. They didn't fight that battle for us, they fought it for Celia."

Most of them still didn't know the full weight of the truth. They'd heard bits and pieces about how Celia wasn't just some random bitch in the trials, how we'd had history. They deserved the full weight of the truth, but they needed to prove they could be trusted. I could count the men in this room that deserved my unrequited loyalty with less than four fingers.

"Didn't we bleed enough for her?" It was Hughes who spoke next.

His face had the kind of coldness I hadn't seen from him in a long time. It made me realize I hadn't thought to ask what everyone had lost that day yet.

"It can't be now," I told them again. "Sokolov will have to wait. Until Celia has the full force of her army behind her, until she's the only person alive who can challenge the cártel throne, I can't—"

"I think you're too cunt-struck to see clearly Zerkos. Ever since you brought that bitch into our lives, it's been nothing but bloodshed. Either you do right by your people and use her to eliminate our target, or you lose the right to call yourself our leader." He stood up, nostrils flaring, and fists clenched tight.

Yeah.

There was a good chance he was working with Dezmond Rat Junior.

Fletcher stood, chest to chest against Hughes like he would have jumped to defend my honor. I didn't need that from him.

"Sit down Fletch." I stood myself. "He's not wrong."

Some voices gasped, the ones who had already been privy to the history between me and my girl. The ones who had overheard too much about just how deep the root of our problems stretched out.

"I *can't* be your leader anymore. The more I think about it, the more I realize it isn't right. How am I supposed to lead you when I'm following her?"

"You are?" Ethan asked.

"I am," I said without blinking. "She knows the game better than any of us, and I'd give my life for hers a million times over. I won't rush a revenge that I know she's calculating." I hardened my eyes at Hughes, knowing the fucker was going to take that juicy tidbit of information back to Dezmond.

Voices rang out over each other once again in confusion as my men tried to make sense of the news I'd just dumped on them.

"What does that mean for us? What about you?" Fletcher asked Santos.

"I go where she goes," he said, his eyes barely shifting to me. "Wherever he fucking goes too."

"Fuck," Ethan barked, taking in the seriousness of the situation.

The room dropped into complete silence.

"Me too." Fletcher looked up, brushing his red hair out of his face.

A few voices rang out with confusion, and he waved them off.

"I owe her my life, and if she's someone you consider following then I don't see why I can't do the same." He seemed so sure of himself.

"You don't even fucking speak spanish," Hughes shouted but Fletcher just shrugged.

"I'll learn. It's better than sticking around a lost cause with a rat for a boss." He was insinuating that if I wasn't the leader, Dezmond would certainly reap the opportunity.

He would, and he'd lead them all down a dangerous path, aligning them with our enemies who were really just waiting for the right opportunity to knock us down, wipe us all from the map. The idiots didn't see that. The Black Crows had taken money, power and opportunities from every major syndicate in Cove City. The thought that they'd align themselves back with us now that we were broken instead of using it as an opportunity to kill us off for good was laughable.

Then all hell broke loose, and the room suddenly became divided. They were choosing sides. Something I'd never asked them to do. Hughes stepped up to me, his chest pressed to mine and his nostrils flaring wildly. He was pissed, and I'd been so far up in my own bullshit I couldn't even figure out what it was that I'd done to piss him off.

It was a good thing I was stepping down.

Maybe I *wasn't* cut out for this shit.

Life was simpler when I was the one taking orders.

Ethan spread us apart before spit went flying every-where from how hard the man was seething.

"Get the fuck out of here." Santos pointed to the door, with his gun in hand once the distinction of who would be aligning themselves with Hughes and Dez, and who would be coming to Mexico was decided.

To join the fucking cártel.

16

Santos

"**F**aster," I shouted at the remnants of traitors who scurried out of the compound.

It would be a game of speed now between us to recruit soldiers to our side, see how many men Ronan would want to take back home. Saying it was weird, not saying it was... well, wrong for one. It *was* home.

Because she was there.

I wasn't sure if the surreal part was that it was with her, or that I was finally getting to live in the place where my family came from. Reconnecting made you feel like an imposter somehow, like an outsider intruding in.

Which meant Kane and Zerkos were feeling a thousand times more weird about it, poor gringo-ass motherfuckers. I made a mental note to put some effort into checking in with them about all of these changes. Culture shock was a real fucking thing, and I wasn't even sure the last time I'd seen Mateo eat anything not seasoned with mayonaise.

"We should end this thing with Archer Jr. before it gets out of hand," I told Zerkos without even looking back at him, gun still pointed at absolutely nothing since the last of the Crow traitors had evacuated.

"Killing him won't end this beef with the Russians," he said, his jaw clenching tight, making me realize Archer was just a fly on his food.

He wasn't threatened.

That was a mistake. It was always the smallest bugs that left the worst bites.

"Killing him will stop it from getting worse. Stop the men that up until five minutes ago were considered our family for the last seven years from getting killed in the process too." I scowled, my anger rising to the surface.

"Do you all feel that way?" Ronan asked the room.

"He needs to die brother," Fletcher said plainly.

"Traitors don't get to live," was my only contribution.

The rest of the men in the room all gave their silent agreement.

"How do we find him?" Ronan asked, accepting the fact he couldn't declare he wasn't the boss anymore while still trying to hold authority over our men.

We were all equals now.

"If he's cozying up to the Bratvas then he's hiding out in all their spots too, he wouldn't stray far from their protection," Ethan answered.

"Is Sokolov's daughter still here?" I asked.

"Yup. Looks like she's real comfy too." He smirked.

"I'll go find her," I announced before turning on my heels and exiting the room.

She wasn't in the main area with the bar and all the pool tables. I took the stairs up, skipping one or two at a time until I got to the top before I realized I had no idea which room she'd be in. I wasn't gonna be barging in on any of these fuckers' privacy. I didn't have a death wish.

Well, I did. But being pulverized by a biker wasn't how I intended to go.

A prospect tumbled out of his room with one of the little club bunnies in tow. He practically jumped when he saw me, distancing himself from her and scratching his head suspiciously. I could use a dumbass right about now.

"Hey kid," I beckoned him over and his eyes jarred open anxiously.

"Uh… What's up?"

"You know where and who everyone is around here?" I asked him and he beamed with pride.

"You know it."

"I'm looking for a Russian, blonde hair, all legs. Where's her room?" I asked.

"I don't think I'm supposed to tell that kind of information to just anyone dude." He scratched the back of his head.

"I'm not just anyone, and that's *my* prisoner." I clutched his shirt in my fist and twisted it pulling him closer to me.

He scoffed.

The fucking kid scoffed in my goddamn face.

"Tell that shit to Ladrón cuz he's already pissed all over her." He freed himself from my grasp, and I wrapped my hand around his arm,

"Where the fuck is the girl?" I pulled my Glock out of my pants and pressed the barrel to his chin.

He was green as fuck.

He trembled, stuttering nonsense about how he didn't mean to offend me or some bullshit.

"I just need to know where the fucking Russian is. Point. Now." My patience was wearing thin and if I didn't come back with her, Ronan would be coming for her instead.

For everyone's sake it was probably better I handled interactions with other humans.

Ronan only had a soft spot for one person, and even his soft spot was full of spikes when it came to Celia Flores.

His finger shook as he raised it up and pointed to a shut door. I shoved him off of me, he stumbled back and fell before scurrying away on all fours and running down the stairs. Whatever, if the kid couldn't handle conflict, he definitely wasn't cut out for a motorcycle club.

I made my way to the door and tapped my knuckles.

"Yes?" she called from inside.

I sighed. I didn't like dealing with this bitch.

Maybe I was holding a grudge but she stabbed my girl with a fucking fork, not to mention the tracker on her arm was the entire reason Papa Sokolov was able to find the high-rise in the first place.

My jaw ticked at the thought, and I pushed the door open.

"Güera." She looked up from her book and scowled when she saw my face.

"I thought I was a free woman now." She had that look on her face like my presence was a bother to her.

I chuckled.

"You're a free woman when we tell you so. Your prison's changed, but not your circumstances. Maybe you give us a little more of what we need and we can consider your crimes paid for, Susana." I gestured my chin towards the hall, and she stood up with a dramatic sigh.

"From one entitled cock-bearer to the next." She clucked her tongue and walked in front of me as if she knew where she was going.

"Maybe it's the company you keep, you ever think about that?" I asked and she stopped in her tracks to look back at me.

"When you're born into this life as a woman, you don't get to choose your company. You go where the man with the most power points you to." She turned forward again and walked down the steps.

"And now that man is telling you to go that way." I pointed to the closed door where Ronan sat with our men.

"You're an irritating one, but you already know that don't you? Irritating men always do." She swung in and out of her accent so often I couldn't figure out if it was an act.

Like she knew it made her sound less innocent.

Innocence could be perceived as weakness.

It made sense.

I didn't change my expression, and I didn't acknowledge her little attempt to disarm me.

I wasn't the same man who entered that basement wondering how my own flesh and blood could stomach to hurt me. I was the man who came out of it.

And at my core, I knew it wasn't a me problem.

But maybe if I'd been stronger I could have saved Celia from all of the pain that was born in that basement.

Maybe the real torture would be living with that knowledge forever.

I opened the door and shoved her in. Ronan was leaning back on what was obviously César's chair, his feet propped up on the table. He was laughing about something with the guys who were still at his side, but the laughter cut short once Susana walked in.

"Bratva Princess," Ronan chided.

"Not anymore." She raised her eyebrows at him, but he just looked at her with disbelief. "You don't believe people can want to change?" she asked.

"I think violent people keep breeding violence," he told her.

"Was your father a violent man, Ronan Zerkos?" She crossed her arms over her chest with interest.

"No. He was a weak man. Cheated on his second wife too and ended up dying of cancer. Got what he deserved."

"Hmm." She sauntered over to him crossing one leg over the other. "So where does your violence breed from then, I wonder?" She leaned her elbows on the table and stuck her ass up too high in the air. She was wearing jean shorts and a tank top with the MC's logo on it. Maybe her goal was to try to seduce Zerkos into leaving her the fuck alone.

"None of your fucking business," he grit through his teeth leaning forward on the desk so that his face was just an inch away from hers. "Where do your people play?"

She slumped into the nearest chair, looking around the room and taking in the rest of the men who sat waiting for information with blank stares on their faces.

"You're signing my death warrant," she said, a bit of anger rising to the surface.

"Heard you were getting real comfy out here in Grimm fuck nowhere," he challenged her back. "Would be a shame if our enemies found out you were hiding here."

"What do you want, you son of a bitch?

"I want to kill my rat, that's it. But if a few Bratvas get in the way, they might have to go as well."

She let out a defeated sigh once she looked around the room.

"If he's under my father's protection you'll find him at Club Moscow, if he's just clutching his coat tails you'll find him with the lower crowd, at Vosk. I can't help you otherwise. I wasn't privy to every safehouse he kept."

Zerkos nodded over to Liam, one of Taylor's henchmen in the tech lab. He wrote down all the information and made his way out of the room to start researching.

"Now, forget me. Haven't we had enough of each other? Unless you mean to fuck me, please, get a hobby Ronan." She chuckled and stood from the seat, getting up without permission.

She was a gutsy bitch and it worked in her favor. Ronan let her leave, and no one seemed to mind.

"You're good with this?" I asked him.

"I think we milked Sokolov's daughter for all we could, let her live her miserable life in peace. If she's happy in the Diablos compound let's wash our hands of this mess and call it a win."

"And Dezmond?"

"Let's go into the city. Tonight." Zerkos rubbed the blond scruff growing on his chin before he pushed up from the chair and left the room.

Another night in the Diablos Locos compound, meant another night drinking to forget we were away from our girl. I would have rather killed a man instead of getting belligerent and coming into my hands to forget the only thing I cared about was south of the border, probably still getting railed by Mateo Kane.

Did she miss me like I missed her?

Doubtful.

All I ever did was say the wrong things, all I ever did was underestimate her.

I still couldn't figure out why she wanted me around. The more I dwelled on it the more I went down a dark spiral of self-loathing. Fuck I needed out of it. I kept bouncing around from desperately wanting to be worthy of her to hating myself because I knew I could never be.

"You good?" Zerkos asked and I stopped in my tracks, realizing I was anxiously pacing back and forth in the small conference room.

"Yeah, I…Uh…I need some air." I nodded at him and pulled my phone out, dialing the number and holding my breath while I waited with a heart full of hope.

The video-call connected on the first ring.

"Hey," she said, all breathy like she was just now finishing up the little scene we'd watched her and Mateo entwined in.

"Hey," I said shakily as I walked out of the farmhouse and sat down on the porch swing.

She wrapped herself up in a blanket and found a chair to cocoon herself in.

"Weird being away from each other, right?" she asked like she knew exactly what I was feeling.

I didn't care what anyone else said.

There was no trauma like shared trauma.

And there was no shared trauma like watching the person you loved go through something you wished you could prevent.

We were the same side of the coin printed on both ends.

Her and I…

We'd always have violent images of each other's pain painted on the back of our eyelids every time we closed our eyes to go to sleep.

Was I grateful?

No, I wasn't fucking grateful.

But had Guillermo turned me into mincemeat any further, I didn't think she'd be looking at me the way she was right now. I was ugly now, but I was, at least, still within the threshold of "ugly enough to feel sorry for."

"Ronan quit the Crows." I wasn't sure why I told her instead of letting him tell her.

I just wanted to talk to her, and I didn't want to deal with the silence. Sometimes I called her and just stared at her face. She was okay with that too. She would just breathe and awkwardly laugh every now and then while waiting for me to say anything at all.

"What?" Her eyebrows furrowed harder than I'd ever seen before.

"I probably should have let him tell you that. I guess that was my way of telling you that I did too."

"Wait, what the fuck are you talking about?"

"I mean, I guess it's not that we quit the Crows, I guess really the Crows are done. We'll be bringing some men back with us." I corrected myself.

"This is crazy, what happened?"

I tried giving her as much clarification as I could, going over the meeting and explaining in detail everything that had happened the last few days while we'd been in Grimm's Reach.

"I never intended for either of you to have to pick between me and the Crows," she said, seeming deflated.

"You didn't. We made choices on our own. This wasn't on you. Okay?"

"Okay," she whispered.

"Morena," I started. "When we come home. I want to do things differently. I want to give you the love you deserve." I forced the words out before I turned into a chickenshit and took them back.

"No," she said, piercing through my heart. "I don't believe in starting over. We're fine building from what we already have. I just wish you could see that too."

"I wish I had your perspective on things," I told her, and she shrugged.

"Doin' anything dangerous tonight?" she asked with a teasing tone.

"On the Diablos compound? Babe you must be out of your mind," I joked, keeping our plans from Dezmond off of a recorded line.

We'd tell her when we got home.

Prison was worse than death for a relationship.

People could say whatever they wanted but at the end of the day, nobody waited. I'd seen plenty of my tío's lose their families in a cell for Los Muertos.

Time was a fickle bitch.

"Be good. Come home in one piece, okay Santito?" She sounded sweet but I knew it was a command.

"Yes, reina." I smirked, hanging up the video chat and sighing out loud.

17

Mateo

"**C**lose your fucking eyes pendejo," she chastised, pushing my back and forcing me to stumble forward.

"I don't like surprises, sunshine," I warned her.

"It's a good one, I promise."

I sighed and closed my eyes, letting her guide me through the villa.

"It better not be a fucking dog. I'm not letting the three of you rope me into taking care of some puppy."

She laughed so abruptly it came out as a snort and I couldn't help but turn towards her to admire how cute she could fucking be.

"A dog? I'm not much of a dog person," she confessed, still finding amusement in it all.

I raised my eyebrow suspiciously at her, unsure if I was buying whatever she was trying to sell me here. And then I took in the room we were standing in. A beautiful white grand piano stood in the center, all its glory on display. Different types of guitars hung on the wall and an assortment of string instruments were propped on their stands.

The cello grabbed my attention. It wasn't my ancient relic but it looked like she did a damn good job of finding something that was as close to it as possible. I could still smell the wood polish on its face, letting me know it was likely something custom made.

"Was I out of line?" she asked, the concern in her voice brought me back to reality, letting me know I had yet to even give her a reaction.

"This is all for me?" I asked, my mouth still agape and my shock clearly evident.

"No, I'm hiring a mariachi band and giving them all the wrong instruments to see how it goes, and I wanted your feedback." She gave me a sarcastic smirk and nudged me on the side with her elbow.

"It's too much," I told her, knowing damn well we'd be using whatever funds were left of the Black Crow

Brotherhood to pay for funerals and medical costs. She was in every way, providing for us here.

Her smile deflated.

"I just mean, you didn't have to." I rushed to defend my words, realizing I was hurting her more by not just being grateful like I should have been. "No one's ever given me a gift like this, sunshine."

"I want to give you everything," she said with a hurt look on her face.

"I think it's supposed to be me that gives you everything," I told her.

"Why? Because you're a man and I'm a weak little woman who can't provide for you? Surprise Mateo, I have more money than I'll ever be able to spend in this lifetime, and the next five lifetimes. Let me take care of us." She was all sincerity, even her sharp edges had softened somehow.

It filled me up with a sense of pride that I could get this side of her when no one else could.

I smiled, making her frown. "That's not it at all, Celia," I said, rubbing my hands up and down her bare arms.

She rarely wore sleeves down here, and I was a fan of how easy it was to feel her flesh under mine.

"You think I feel emasculated by the thought of you giving me things?" I scoffed, alarming her with my reaction. "Sunshine, I'd lick the dirt off your feet if it were the only meal you'd allow me to have, and I'd still say thank you. There is absolutely nothing that I or you could do that would make me feel like less of a man because, at the end of the day, I got you. But I'm still allowed to want to give you everything you deserve."

She reached her hand up and cupped my face. "You've already given me everything I deserve."

I shook my head at her.

"We've done nothing but cause you pain. I worry once the shock of everything fades, you'll snap back to reality and catch on to what a huge mistake all of this was. You'll pick Ronan once and for all and tell the rest of us to fuck off." I hadn't meant to blurt it out, I hadn't meant to be so honest, but every time she said shit like that it just felt like a lie.

Waste of space. My mother's words still rang out loudly in my mind.

"I wish you saw yourself as clearly as I see you." She shook her head, moving her hands to my chest where she flattened her palms against me. "You ever wonder if this pain is maybe part of what I deserve as well? I've done a lot of bad things in my life, there's only so many protection candles a bitch can light. Santa Muerte's waiting for me too, you know?"

"Don't fucking say that shit, because I'll fight her to keep you with me," I gritted out, pulling her against me tight.

"You can't fight Death, mi amor. She comes for us all." She caressed her skin against mine, but I gripped her wrist in my hand and kept it from moving.

"Stop it," I told her, not fighting the anger bubbling in my chest.

"Then don't say stupid things about me choosing Ronan." She frowned, but even without her smile she was so fucking stunning I had to remind myself to breathe.

"Can you blame a guy for being insecure? You've known him practically your whole life. And Santos has a fifteen year head start on me. Sometimes I wonder why I'm even around."

"Really?" she asked, sounding surprised. "You're the fucking glue Mateo. You keep us all together. Our family, it wouldn't feel right without you. I wouldn't feel right without you," she told me with a sobering expression on her face.

"And why's that sunshine?" I asked.

"Because you showed me that love doesn't have to be painful." She leaned close and pressed her lips against mine.

I groaned, throwing my head back.

"Don't do this to me. I can't keep calling those fuckers every time I wanna hear you scream just because they decided to leave." I whined and she smiled.

"Technically, you should have gone too but I agreed to keep you."

"Wait…" I pieced together all the fucking clues. "Am I the fucking goldendoodle?" I asked her, and she choked out a laugh.

"Leave me out of this." She pressed her lips against mine once again, but I pulled her back by the shoulders.

"Sunshine," I warned her, and she pulled her lips between her teeth and bit them like she was holding back a smile.

"How about we do something that doesn't involve the others?"

Her hands traveled down to my dick and her small hands gripped firmly around the fabric of my pants. Just the light touch of her fingers forced my cock to awaken under her control.

I groaned again and she lowered down to her knees.

This was shaky territory.

"Celia," I warned as she pulled me from my pants, already hard and precum glistening at the tip of my cock.

She took a breath to prepare herself, but she was trembling at just the proximity. It wasn't right. I picked her up and brought her to my chest before sitting us both down onto the chair in her bedroom, wrapping my arms around her and pulling her into my chest.

She shook silently while I ran my fingers through her hair.

"I'm not broken!" she cried out like she was trying to prove it to herself.

"I never said you were."

"Then why does it feel like I am?" A pitiful noise left the depths of her chest as she poured her soul out into salty droplets over me.

"Because whether or not you want to admit it, he took something from you that you wouldn't have given freely.

Regardless of your reason for doing it. Regardless of the fact that it might have been your decision to do it at all."

"It's okay to not be okay, Celia. Perfection isn't expected of you at all times."

"He expected it," she said, a bit of nervousness peeking out from behind the curtain.

She meant her father, I wasn't stupid.

"He's dead now," I reminded her.

A few moments passed before she nodded.

"Thank you," she said, looking up at me and blinking the droplets of tears from her eyelashes.

"I love you, sunshine." I caressed her face.

"It helps when you remind me." She smiled and it stretched up into the scar across her cheek.

I felt so much anger when I looked at it, but I was learning to not blame myself for the things I couldn't prevent. Wallowing in guilt over pain that was dealt to her wasn't fair of me. All she was asking of me was to love her, that I could do.

"I'll keep doing it at every chance I get."

18

Ronan

Dezmond Archer Junior would die tonight. Preferably with my bare hands, but if I had to use a weapon, I'd consider that a solid kill too. There was no way around it, the fates had pulled his cards and they'd announced his end. My brothers had called it, and I had agreed.

There was a part of me that still felt the aching pain of killing someone I considered my own family. Maybe I owed him the decency of a fair fight because of our shared history. Because he was once my brother too. But the stupid fucker's ambition was the very reason we had to bury some of our best men this year.

There was no going back anymore.

The Crows were done but vengeance went further than just a name. We were reaping because he had sowed.

We'd hounded Susana enough to get a few names from her. We paid off some girls she knew to help us get some intel, so we could figure out exactly where we could find Dezmond tonight. It wasn't hard. Just like she said, the fucker was there at Vosk, sitting in a VIP booth with some paid escorts pretending to enjoy his company while drinking some top shelf alcohol that was likely being put on Sokolov's tab.

"Hey sweetheart, go ask your friends to clear the booth out." I slipped some cash into the hand of a nearby girl and nodded over to Dezmond's booth.

She squeezed into the booth and whispered into the closest girl's ear. A game of telephone passed around and soon every girl was looking at each other with wide eyes and scurrying from the table.

Dezmond was too drunk to notice.

Santos shuffled into the booth next to him and Fletcher came in from the other side. I squeezed in, sitting across from the bastard who dared break bread with me while he was plotting to take me down. I pulled my gun out and placed the Glock directly in front of me, the barrel pointed his way but the piece itself was still laying on its side on the table.

He could have reached for it.

I wasn't afraid of him.

"S-shit," he stuttered out, his eyes blinking in an unco-ordinated way that let me know he was shitcanned.

"That's the problem about thinking you've got friends in high places isn't it brother? They can't seem to see you from where they're perched."

I could nearly taste his fear, it was delectable, but this place was too full. We needed to get him out of here and we needed to do it without making a scene.

"Zerkos, let's talk this out like men," he slurred, trying to make peace far too late in the game.

"Where's Hughes?" I asked him, wondering if we need-ed to be on the lookout.

A few of our men were lurking in the corners trying to prevent some sort of surprise or sneak attack.

"Waiting for me to give the signal to report the Di-ablos Locos compound for some serious illegal activity to the FBI. The raid would go down within the next twenty-four hours, maybe just enough time for you all to scatter the fuck out of here and leave Cove City to the people who really own it." He sneered and I couldn't contain my laughter.

"You think you fucking own Cove City?" I asked, my amusement irritating him further.

"You think *you* do?" he asked, a bitter tone to his voice.

"No, Cove City is a goddess. She can't be tamed by men like us. The sooner you learn that, the better off you'll be, rat."

"I thought you came here to kill me," he snarled.

"*They* would love that." I nodded to my brothers who didn't hide the bloodthirsty look from their faces. "So give me a fucking reason you dirty fucking traitor." I picked the gun up and slid it under the table, switching the safety off.

His eyes widened further than I thought possible.

"Berserk, you don't wanna do this. We're in public. They'll put you in prison for life." He raised his hands up defensively, his face glistened with sweat as he tried to reason with me by tossing out some legal bullshit that definitely didn't apply to me.

You either lived within the boundaries of the law or you didn't.

I didn't.

He'd somehow forgotten that.

"Then make it easy on me, *brother*." My nostrils flared. "Get the fuck up." I moved the gun under the table, pressing the barrel to his thigh as Santos slid out of the booth.

In a dark alley behind the club we each took turns letting our fists pay back all the pain he'd brought the Crows. Blow after blow of our hands and feet, crunching his bones felt better than I had expected. He didn't fight it, he knew he was a prisoner to the game. He thrashed and fought back even as we stuffed him into the trunk. Then we drove back to the Diablos Locos compound. There was a special entrance we were supposed to use so that the lower tiered members didn't see us dragging someone off to their untimely death.

Best not to have witnesses we couldn't fully trust.

"Zerkos I'm telling you, if there's a single drop of blood stained on my nice oak floors when I get home you're gonna be paying for the remodel from your own pocket. Not my sister's pocket…yours," César declared from the phone as I tried to get instructions on how to get inside his goddamn torture cellar.

This motorcycle compound was a labyrinth and apparently the guy was set on putting up a few more buildings like some sort of fucking commune.

"This seems like a lot of fucking work just to get a prisoner locked up, you need a better system, Villalobos." I'm pretty sure he growled into the phone but then turned to someone near him to bark out an order before returning to the line.

"Why is Ladrón not helping you with this shit?" he asked.

"He's *indisposed*." I cleared my throat, not mentioning the Bratva heir shacking up with one of his officers.

César sighed like he knew his men well enough to not need an explanation.

"I'm gonna need you to leave my wine cellar as you found it, Entendiste?"

"Yeah, yeah." I answered before hanging up the phone and tucking it back into my pockets.

I wasn't dressed for this.

But were you ever dressed for slow and painful murder?

The image of my girl, dirty and covered in blood in that leather dress climbing out of that basement flashed through my mind.

She was always dressed for murder. I wanted to give her my protection but the reality was, my girl looked good dripping in the blood of her enemies, she looked even better when she was the one bleeding them out.

I got the code right on the third try and the room opened up, bright fluorescent lights shone down a concrete wall covered with chains and just next to it was a table full of torture devices. I yanked Dez's ankle dragging him into the room behind me, he groaned, still delirious from the beating he received outside the nightclub from us.

I stretched my fingers out, feeling the burn on the torn skin of my knuckles and smiling and recollecting the satisfying crunching sound of his cheek against my fist.

"Get him hooked up to the wall," I commanded Santos and Fletcher before doubling back with the realization I wasn't anyone's leader anymore.

"Never mind, I got it."

"It's all good boss," Fletcher said, shaking his head like he understood.

The two of them worked quickly, getting Dezmond chained to the wall while he was still wavering back and forth out of consciousness from the multiple head injuries he was now suffering.

"Where's Ethan?" I asked.

"He went with Isaac and Smith to debrief the rest of our men, draw the line in the sand, and figure out who's going where," Fletcher explained.

"I didn't want it to come to this." I scratched the back of my head with a sigh.

"It's a good thing, you'll see that," Santos said, turning towards me. "Our people were already divided, if it was this easy to split off."

"They're split because… they weren't yours to begin with," Dezmond slurred, his head lifting up as he fought his way back to lucidity.

I swung my fist against his face, and it smacked against the concrete wall before ricocheting back down.

"Lights out!" Fletcher whooped.

Santos pulled the smelling salts from his pocket and stuck them in front of his face to wake him back up. Blood was pouring out of his nose violently and there was barely any light left in his eyes.

It wasn't fun when they'd already mentally checked out.

"What's the matter Dez? Is this not how Daddy's plan was supposed to go?" I tilted my chin and hardened my eyes at him waiting for the light of recognition to hit his face.

It didn't.

He was too out of it.

"My father knew you were all unraveling over the Mexican whore—" He didn't get a chance to finish.

I threw my fist again. The impact from the collision of his head against the concrete wall behind him made a deafening sound. Santos rolled his eyes at me and pulled out the smelling salts again to wake the bastard up.

"Good thing we don't need intel from him. You've practically beat him stupid."

I gave him a fraction of a smile. He nodded, and it tore through my heart. I missed our friendship. I spent a lot of time wondering how we'd ever get back to how things were, and it made me wonder if he did too.

She was right, she wasn't supposed to choose. Choosing would have been something she did to us, and this right here, this was the product of my own issues, my insecurities. She loved all three of us... and my problem was that he had loved her back the entire time?

Fuck. Was I the asshole here?

Was it up to me to repair the damage?

We bonded best through violence, maybe this was the closest thing to an olive branch we could get between us.

Dezmond woke up again, moaning a pained sound.

"I'm sorry, you were saying something?" I chuckled, cracking my neck on both sides.

Our captive spit a bloody wad onto the ground.

"He drew up the blueprint for the Crows, they were *his* men first. This should have all been his. It should have been mine," Dezmond yelled, the true source of his rage showing its ugly head and letting us know jealousy was her name.

"Maybe so, and then he opened his mouth about *our* Mexican whore and found himself on the wrong side of my barrel. Then I fucked her with said barrel while he bled out and his corpse went cold." Santos pulled his Glock out of his pants and shoved it under Dez's chin, forcing his head into an uncomfortable position. "Actually, I think it was this one right here."

He pulled the gun back and licked the rim of it before pressing it back onto his flesh.

"Your traitor piece of shit of a father is dead and gone, but my gun still tastes like her."

I laughed, remembering just how unhinged Santos could get when he was the one holding our enemies down.

"Quit playin' with your food Álvarez, if we got all we need from him, let's end this and go home to our woman." I clapped him on the shoulder.

"Yeah, run back south of the border to your little bitch. You think he doesn't know who she is? Why do you think he sold her twice? Why risk killing her when he can just keep selling her and hope someone else will?" He had the audacity to fucking laugh.

Santos smacked his jaw with the butt end of the Glock and his jaw broke, staying lodged on the left side of his face. He wailed, unable to open his mouth to actually speak again.

"Actually, I like him this way," I said, extending my hand for the gun.

I fired one in each kneecap without waiting.

His scream became a feral plea, nonsensical and completely unintelligible.

"I wonder if we can make him scream so hard it'll pop back into place?" Santos asked and Fletcher laughed.

"Y'all are sick motherfuckers."

"I'm not gonna lie, I forgot you were here brother. If this is too much for you…" Santos warned him, but he waved him off, crossing his arms to show he'd be staying put and watching the show till its end. "Let's cut his toes off and mail them to Sokolov," Santos said, turning back to me.

I hadn't seen a grin that big on his face in the last decade.

I wondered if it had something to do with me saying *our* woman.

I nodded my approval and while he stepped over to the table to pick out which tools were the right one for the job, I approached Dezmond Archer Junior. With a quick jab I knocked the end of my gun onto the dislodged side of his jaw, forcing it back in place with a crunch. The feral, animalistic type of scream that came from the depths of his soul tugged at the little bit of love I still had left for the man standing in front of me as I watched the piss drip down his legs.

"What did he promise you? How long had the two of you been working with the Bratvas?" I needed to know, needed to understand how long I'd had rats scurrying under me while feeding them the same food I fed my family at the same goddamn table.

"You better… kill me…I'm not telling you… shit." He struggled to get the words out.

I guess the guy didn't quite grasp the concept of torture. There was nothing threatening about a man that had already been tied up and beaten beyond recognition.

"Did he promise you the Crows? That everything would go back to the way it was before the three of us took over the city your father once thought would be his?"

He didn't answer.

"Oh shit, Santos. I think he promised him more." I laughed, rubbing my hands together and stepping back to let Álvarez get to work.

He snapped the scissor-like pliers open and shut in front of Archer Junior's face. He flinched, trying to keep a hardened face but it was evident that he wasn't brought up to tolerate this life, even if his father had raised him adjacent to it.

"Did he promise you his ugly daughter?" Santos asked with a hushed voice.

His eyes widened, giving him away before he fixed his expression into a pained scowl once more.

"Oof, that's a rough one. You'll need a paper bag to stomach giving it to her after what Celia did to her face." He laughed at our captive, a man we still called brother by habit.

"Not as ugly... as you," he said through labored breaths, reminding Santos that his face was different now too.

I pulled my tactical blade from its sheath in the holster and plunged it straight into his cheek, pulling it out and doing the same to his other side. He shrieked a louder sound than I had ever heard coming from a Prisoner of

War. What we were doing to Archer didn't even compare to what we put those fuckers through.

But even though my rage was driving the wheel, in the back of my mind all I could see were the flashes of memories, the last seven years fighting side by side with him and his father. The bridges we built together, the army we raised out of nothing to fight for our cause.

Maybe I owed him a better death.

Santos saw the look in my eyes and exhaled in defeat like he knew I was about to cut the fun short.

I pulled my own Glock out and pressed it to his head.

"Wait, hold on. It's not right." Santos stepped forward before I went in for the final blow.

"What?

"He hurt her too," he said before walking to the table and switching the pliers he was going to use to cut his toes off for some smaller ones. "He owes her too."

I raised my eyebrows at him suspiciously while he squeezed Archer Junior's jaw until it pried open and he sobbed out from pain, blood dripping out with his drool.

"I just gotta get something real quick."

Archer shook violently while sobbing unintelligible sounds, screeching an awful noise every time Santos yanked a tooth out from his mouth. After collecting a handful, he stuck the bones in his back pocket.

Bloody saliva dripped onto the floor from his mouth, and he mumbled painfully.

"We had some good times didn't we, brother?" Santos gave him a crooked grin, tapping his cheek a few times with the palm of his hand before he stepped back to let me put him out of his misery.

"Here's the bigger secret I want to let you in on before I put you under." I leaned in real close and whispered in his ear, "If you had just waited, you would have had it all. I would have stepped down and given it all to you without any bloodshed. Now our family is divided and at least half of them will die fighting for what they think is right." It was a sad realization, but it was just the way things went.

Blood had been spilled and now it would continue to do so until one side stopped fighting back or died.

That's the way war went.

19

Celia

I wanted to drive to the airport myself to pick up my guys, but none of my officers would allow it. Here I was, a supposed queen, somehow still fucking being told what to do by men. I hated admitting it but they weren't wrong. It was a matter of security and I couldn't make impulsive and risky decisions now that my tío knew I was readying for war.

The man was brash enough to try to execute a half-cocked attack just to have the element of surprise over me.

It wouldn't matter. What he didn't realize was that he'd already prepared me for this.

I was always expecting him. I had been for the last twelve years. Always looking over my shoulders, paying attention to my surroundings, and memorizing stranger's faces. Who had I seen before, and where.

It was easy to fall into paranoid thinking, but at the end of the day my tío never let me down, he always came for me. It was almost comforting every time it happened.

This would be the last time.

So I caved and let Mateo ride with me to the airport, along with the security detail car that followed behind. All capable and trustworthy soldiers hand-picked by Dominico himself and then vetted extensively by Santos before sending them over to Taylor for probing. She'd dug up more information on each of them than I thought was even possible, from ex-girlfriends to which toys they preferred on the playground in primary school.

Overkill, but apparently necessary.

I opened the door of the car but before I could fully step out I felt a hand on my shoulder.

"Jefa, please get b—"

"Rodrigo, right?" Mateo cut in, peeling one of my guard's fingers off my shoulder. "You seem like a nice guy, but if you ever put your hands on her again it'll be the last time you use them."

Down boy, but he *was* cute when he went into rottweiler mode.

"I-I'm just trying to do my job. I was told to keep her s—"

"Rodrigo, I'm an ex-Navy Seal. I think she's pretty safe with me, don't you?" He spoke with the smooth, calculated tone he got before he went borderline psychotic.

I smirked, some weird primal part of me enjoyed the dick measuring contest Mateo was starting.

My guy however looked uncomfortable and anxious, and I didn't need any rumors about me being hard to work for. Being a woman was a disadvantage on its own.

"Está bien Rodrigo." I waved him off and gave him a look that was enough to tell him to get back to his own car. "Don't scare my men," I told Mateo playfully.

He shut the door behind me before pressing me against it, running his hand up the back of my leg, he let out a throaty growl.

"I liked you in my T-shirts, but I like you even better in these clothes, sunshine," he whispered into my ear, goosebumps raising along the back of my neck as his fingers trailed along the hem of my mid-thigh length pencil skirt.

It was definitely more of Emory's style, but I needed to figure out a way to present myself in public if I was going to be taken seriously. The raggedy band T-shirts and ripped jeans weren't going to cut it anymore.

My papá always donned the finest suits.

I would do the same.

"I said, don't scare my men, Mateo," I repeated myself, giving him my coldest look.

"They don't get to touch you," he warned me.

"I thought you said you liked watching me come?" I challenged, knowing damn well that wasn't what he had meant.

His hands pressed against the car, boxing me in with his arms as he pushed himself closer to me, one foot planted between my legs.

"I'm suddenly finding we may need to reestablish some boundaries, sunshine."

"Oh?" I asked, biting my lip in an attempt to seem seductive knowing it probably looked nothing like I pictured it in my head.

"Yes." He lowered his forehead to mine.

"Name your terms, crazy boy." I batted my eyelashes, looking up at him through them.

"No one else touches you but us."

"And in return, I get?" I teased.

His nostrils flared.

"No one else touches you but us," he repeated as if it was also the answer to my own question.

"Fine. And if I break your rules?" I was having too much fun and since I wasn't allowed to go inside the airport this was the best entertainment I'd be getting.

"Then I'll punish them, cut their fingers off and hang them around their necks. Keep them around as an example so everyone else knows that you are untouchable in every goddamn way." He was speaking so close to my ear that every word pebbled my skin on contact.

"What about me?" I breathed out.

"It's me who'll punish you, flower." His voice came from behind Mateo, who freed me from the cage of his arms at the sound of Ronan's threat.

"Hi," I said with my best sheepish impression.

"Don't 'hi' me when I just heard you say what I think you said." Mateo moved out of the way to let Ronan take his place.

Santos rolled his eyes and walked towards the trunk, throwing all of their bags into it. Ronan gripped my chin between his fingers and pulled my gaze back towards him.

"Care to repeat yourself?" There was no amusement in his expression, but I wanted to poke the bear further, see how wild I could really make him.

"I think not." I shook my head with a smile, knowing that Ronan Zerkos was truly the only man alive who could challenge me like this.

Maybe Santos when he got into that mood.

He scoffed, pulling my chin up higher to give me a kiss.

I moaned into his mouth, missing the way we could wrap around each other so perfectly.

"I'm no longer an injured man. Behave or I'll make you regret it," he threatened before pulling me away from the car and opening the door to the back for me to get in.

Santos grabbed me by the wrist and pulled me into an embrace, stamping a kiss to the side of my face before letting me go. He climbed into the back, and I followed, seeing Mateo already comfortably settled into the passenger seat.

How had I been alone for so long when now I felt so incomplete anytime I was apart from one of them? I'd done so well for myself as a solitary creature, caring for nothing and no one with only a goal to survive until the next day.

That wasn't living, and my tío would pay for wasting so much of my life forcing me to live that way.

"So?" I asked, my eyes meeting Ronan's in the rearview mirror before I looked over to Santos. "Did you deal with... whatever it was you were dealing with?" I asked them, playing along like Santos hadn't already told me the truth.

Their eyes met; Ronan grunted.

I looked back over to Santos who gave me a look that said he was grateful.

"Tell me everything," I insisted.

"The Crows have absolved." Santos spoke and Ronan exhaled loudly.

"Ronan, what the fuck?" I yelled, and he moved a hand from the wheel to scratch the back of his head.

"It's more complicated than what Álvarez is saying," he tried justifying.

"Then explain it better, payaso."

"We stepped down. The crows split in two... maybe three actually," Ronan explained some more without giving me any details.

"Ronan!" I slapped the back of his seat. "Que chingados, pendejo? What the fuck are you doing?"

"I can't very well lead a criminal organization when I'm here with you, can I?" he asked.

It was a good point, one I hadn't stopped to think about yet which was exactly why he hadn't mentioned it until now, when he had already done it.

"Why didn't you let me in on this? Why wasn't this a decision you thought we could make together, between all of us?" I asked loudly, feeling myself getting angrier the more I thought about him throwing away everything he built for himself because of me.

He fucking laughed.

Laughed.

Mateo pinched the bridge of his nose, and it took everything to not crawl through the middle console to make my point clearer.

"Como?" I asked.

"I'm sorry darling, I just think it's funny that you'd think I'd let you in on a major decision regarding me spending the rest of my life with you, when the last time you had the chance you dropped the ball." His eyes met mine again with a coldness to them. "Completely," he added.

"Fuck." The memory of me leaving a suitcase full of money in our two-bedroom apartment while I drove away with a trunk full of cártel weapons haunted me still.

When you hurt the person you loved the most, you hurt yourself too.

I was plagued with nightmares of Santos' voice calling out to me from the dark telling me that I was going to destroy Ronan. I imagined his reaction for years, how he must have felt and looked when he read my note.

But I never actually asked.

I was afraid of actually knowing just the size of the damage I'd left behind.

"It was the right move, morena." Santos came to his defense, letting me know I was likely going to be fighting this one on my own if I wanted to ride into battle. "Our men were in limbo. Now they are free to choose where to go. Many will follow, soon Crows will be flying south to work for *you*."

"And the ones that don't?" I asked.

"That depends, quite a few have chosen to stay within the comforts of your brother's motorcycle club in Grimm's Reach. They'll make decent prospects out of them. Some are now floating in the abyss, ready to look for revenge over Dezmond Archer Junior," Ronan explained.

"You killed him," Mateo said, not a question so much as he was just confirming it.

"He was in deeper with the Bratvas than we thought," Ronan told him. "Leaving him alive wasn't a possibility. I weighed out all my options."

There was the faintest hint of regret in his tone. Killing someone you thought was family had to be hard, I was lucky to have gone thirty years as a Flores without experiencing it yet.

"That reminds me," Santos said, reaching down to the floorboard and grabbing his backpack. He fumbled around inside before pulling out a velvet pouch with a drawstring. "It's for you." He tossed it my way and I caught it just in time for it to look mildly cool.

I opened the velvet pouch, seeing the yellowish teeth clinking around in the bottom of the bag against each other. I let out a chesty laugh and pulled the strings shut.

"Is this?" I asked and he nodded.

"I pay attention." The smile was so faint on his face, but I could see the best parts of him fighting to come back to the surface.

"How romantic." I kissed his cheek, letting my lips linger against his skin. "I can't believe you brought this on a carry on." I laughed.

"They're not looking for teeth." He shrugged, "It's not illegal to carry them."

"What did we miss down here?" Ronan asked, changing the subject.

"There is a big fundraiser event that we will be sponsoring in El Palacio on Saturday. President Ramírez has demanded my presence. I need all three of you to come with me." I had already told Mateo so he had no input, but Santos and Ronan looked at each other with apprehension.

We'd had plenty of conversations about the politics behind the cártel, that the only way to claim my empire was to rule it from every angle. I needed to solidify my place in our world, make it so the Flores name held power once again.

"All three of us?" Ronan asked, raising an eyebrow up suspiciously.

"Is that a problem?" I crossed my arms, waiting for them to dare deny me.

"I mean you just plan to show up like, 'Hey, I'm running for office, here are my three boyfriends and expect them to elect you?"

I hated when he knew better than I did.

"I haven't figured out the logistics of it all, but I need all three of you there with me. It will make me feel more at ease," I told them.

This fundraiser was a way to reintroduce me to the world, let everyone who mattered know that the Flores Cártel was once again its rightful regime. Of course, only those who really mattered would know me for who I really was, everyone else would see Celia Flores, daughter of the prolific politician Rafael Flores. For all they knew I was coming home after studying abroad to follow in my father's footsteps, first a mayor, then a governor, and eventually a senator just like my papá.

This was my campaign announcement. This was also where the cártel would seal major agreements with the heaviest hitters in the country. They'd have our protection, our guns, our drugs, we'd have their money. Because I had my family's fortune, the ledger, and the connections, I was able to attain everything my tío was promising, for much, much less.

A bargain anyone would be stupid to pass up.

It was also a trap. The fundraiser was sticky, sweet bait set out to lure my tío into our hands. He'd think we were unprepared, careless, and ready to celebrate. He would surely come for us. But we were more than ready, more than expecting him.

"What are you so nervous about?" Mateo asked with a laugh, like he couldn't believe I was scared of anything.

20

Santos

"**S**he's worried they're gonna call her white-washed, gringa, Americana," I told them, she winced at the words I'd been hearing my entire life from the people who called me family.

Having parents who didn't teach you the language of your people, who didn't teach you about heritage or culture, that was a curse in itself. Celia was young when she lost her family. She didn't lose her language but with time she lost that piece of herself that belonged down here.

Now that she was on this side of the border again, her confidence had shattered. She was just as lost here as I was.

That wasn't true. She had and she lost, I had never had it at all. And maybe it's true what they said, about better to never have it at all and shit. Because Celia looked like she was in pain, and mentally on the verge of losing what little grip she was holding on to.

She was carrying too much on her shoulders, and she refused to let anyone else bear the brunt of it for her. To take some of her load off.

"They aren't wrong," I told her and she scowled.

We'd finally arrived at the villa, and she was so pissed at me she practically opened the door before the car had come to a full stop. I grabbed her wrist, pulling her to me and slamming her against my chest.

"Let me go," she yelled, beating her other hand against my chest while my brothers got out of the car, confusion written all over their faces.

"What's the matter? Are you mad because I'm lying or are you mad because it's the truth?" I asked her.

"Fuck you! You don't know what it's like." She was crying now, and even though it wasn't my intention to hurt her, I needed her to know she wasn't alone in feeling this way.

"Don't you think I feel it too? Lost out here, because it *should* be home, but it's never been *my* home? Don't you think they feel it as well?" I pointed to my brothers.

"Do you not want to be here?" she asked, her eyebrows furrowing heavily in the middle.

"Now when did I fucking say that, morena?"

"I think what he's trying to say is that it's okay for things to not feel right, to feel out of place here even though it was your home once. We'll make it home eventually, together. We can belong here too," Mateo said.

"He's right. I am afraid of what they'll think of me," she admitted.

"Fuck them," Ronan finally spoke. "It doesn't matter what they think of you. At the end of the day they will still come begging for what you have to offer," he reassured her. "You're enough."

She exhaled and turned on her heels, stepping towards the villa. We followed behind and suddenly she stopped and faced me, sticking her pointer finger in my face, her nostrils flaring hard.

"Call me white-washed again and I'll add your teeth to my collection, querido."

I knew I had crossed a line, but she needed to understand she wasn't alone in these feelings. I'd been in her place my entire life, pushed into a corner by my family because my only parent who spoke spanish failed to teach it to me. The other didn't give a shit if I was connected to my culture and eventually I found myself a grown man, too afraid to learn something new for myself.

"Maybe we should hire a tutor?" I asked my brothers, as we made our way inside the villa.

Mateo agreed and Ronan shrugged like he didn't give a shit either way.

"Whatever you guys think is easier for you," he said, and I frowned.

"What? You're too good to learn the language of the country you're going to be living in?" I asked, not hiding the snark in my tone.

Celia laughed from the front and stopped in her tracks again.

"You mean they don't know?" she asked him.

"Know what?" I demanded.

She laughed harder, a borderline unhinged sort of cackle, and she slapped her hands down onto her thighs in disbelief.

"He fucking speaks spanish." She could barely get it out, she was laughing so hard.

"What?" I asked, not hiding my outrage.

How the fuck I managed to know an asshole for half my goddamn life and not know he spoke an entire other language was beyond me. Ronan shrugged and walked on in front of us like he didn't want to answer any questions. Mateo looked just as stunned as me but not at all pissed off. Celia sobered up from laughing to finally speak again.

"You think he would have survived a minute inside my house if he didn't learn spanish? Take note boys, these are the 'little things' women fall head over heels for." She winked and caught up to Ronan, lacing her fingers into his.

"What the fuck man?" Mateo asked, just as much confusion in his own expression.

"Did you know he spoke spanish?" I asked him.

"Now that I think about it, I remember him saying he had to fight to not get sent down to South America for a mission when we were in the Seals. I just never thought too hard about it, but it makes sense." Mateo scratched his head. "Barely fucking fair if you ask me, he was probably a kid when he learned it."

"He's always gonna be two steps ahead of us when it comes to her," I told him.

"It's not a competition," Mateo reminded me.

"But it could be, and it would be fun to lower him down a few pegs every now and then." I smirked.

He returned it.

"I kind of like how that sounds."

My phone buzzed and I pulled it open, a photo of Celia's tits filled my screen, Ronan's dick squeezed right in between them, the head of his cock just barely grazing her lips.

"How the fuck did they have time already?" Mateo said, astounded, running towards the stairs.

"I fucking told you man, we need to form an alliance." I laughed, following behind him.

We jogged through the villa, sliding on the tile floors until we reached her bedroom door and pushed it open, to find Ronan between her legs, his head buried in her cunt while she whimpered softly.

"I thought you weren't choosing, morena," I teased and her eyes found mine.

"Who said I chose anything? He just undressed me first," she said, moaning just as he ran his tongue up and down her slit.

"Spare me, I haven't been inside her in w—" She didn't let him finish, she pushed his head back down, bucking her hips against his face as she moaned and writhed around from pleasure.

I looked over to see Kane was already undressed.

"Are you coming?" she asked and my dick woke up like it had been personally summoned by her.

Ronan thrusted three fingers in and out of her while his mouth worked her into a frenzy. Her thighs clenched shut, squeezing his head and she cried out, her climax flooding out of her and coating the sheets.

She was fucking beautiful.

She could have anything she wanted.

And she wanted us.

There was nothing that made me worthy but suddenly I didn't care anymore, I was done fighting my own mind. Maybe instead of spending my life worried about what made me good enough for her I would just start working on *becoming* good enough to be hers.

"What do you want from us?" Mateo asked her.

She smirked, her chest heaving up and down as she came down from her orgasm.

"Te quiero," she said, like it was just that easy.

"There's three of us," I reminded her.

"And I want all three of you," she repeated, getting up on her knees.

Mateo climbed onto the bed, and she extended her hand out to me, pulling me close to her while I still stood on the floor. She reached for my belt, and I helped her undo my pants, pulling them down my thighs and letting my cock spring free from the confinement of the fabric.

She bit her lip. More nerves than seduction.

"Morena, you don't have to—"

"You don't get it, I want to. I have to," she told me, her eyes a little too shiny with emotion.

"Why?" I asked.

"Because if I can't, then he won. Then it means he *did* take something from me, and I just... I just can't let that happen."

"I'm sorry," I told her, her eyebrows scrunching in the middle.

"For what?" she asked.

"For not seeing it then, for not realizing *how* you needed me. I'm sorry I let you down. I won't fail you again," I told her, gripping a handful of her hair in my fist and pulling her to my cock.

Zerkos got off the bed and went rummaging through a dresser drawer for something. Her lips parted and I slid inside, feeling her hot mouth accepting me with ease. Her lips wrapped over her teeth, and she moved her head along with the guidance of my hand. Mateo positioned himself underneath her, grabbing her hips and guiding her down to his dick.

Each pump of his cock inside her vibrated from her mouth onto me as she moaned around my shaft. Her back teeth clinked over the metal bars of my Jacob's ladder, sending a jolt of pleasure up my spine and drawing my balls up higher.

Not yet. I told myself, slowing up on her movements and loosening my grip on her hair.

"Does that feel good? Is Mateo all the way inside you?" I asked.

She nodded and mumbled a response with my cock inside her mouth.

She had tears streaming down the side of her face, but she hadn't asked me to stop, and something told me she needed this for her own healing. I squeezed my grip around the hair on the base of her skull once more and pulled her to me, shoving myself as far down her throat as I could.

"Oh fuck." I breathed out just as her tongue swirled around one of the bars in my piercing. "Your mouth is perfect."

The bed dipped from Ronan's weight as he climbed onto it, opening a bottle of lube and squeezing it out onto his cock before letting it drip down to her ass.

"Are you ready for me, Flower?"

21

Celia

I thought I was ready to answer but it wasn't his fingers inside me that I felt, preparing to open me up so that his cock could slide inside with ease. No, it was the head of his manhood, pushing against the tight barrier of my ass while Mateo made no effort to slow his methodical thrusts into me from below.

"Puta madre!" I dropped Santos from my mouth in order to cry out just as he pressed his way in, bottoming out inside me.

I was so full. It was the kind of sensation that felt so unreal it seemed wrong, feeling both their lengths sliding in and out of me, stretching me to the brim and rubbing against each other through a thin barrier of skin.

"Oh God,"I cried out again just as Santos gripped the back of my hair once again.

"God isn't the one filling up all your holes right now, morena," he reminded me, pulling my face towards him so that he could use it for his own pleasure. "Should I stop?" he asked just low enough for me to hear, making me realize I'd closed my eyes again.

I shook my head side to side and blinked up at him.

If I stayed looking at them, they kept me grounded. Kept me from glimpsing into the memories I wanted to stay locked tight in the vault inside my head. Because I knew that when I looked up it wasn't the face of a monster that I would see, it was the face of someone who loved me. The face of someone who did whatever he could to keep me safe, and I did the same for him. That's what our scars meant, they meant we loved each other, and that someone else felt threatened by that.

Guillermo didn't deserve my fear, and he didn't deserve an ounce of my memories.

I took a deep breath and shifted my eyes up to him, seeing nothing but love and admiration in the reflection of that hazel stare. He slowed down like he could sense my thoughts and he cupped my face with the palm of his hand.

"Morena?" he asked, furrowing his eyebrows.

"No, please. Don't stop." I shook my head with barely enough time to open my mouth again as he slammed his way in, hitting the back of my throat with every thrust of his hips. They were somehow in sync, each thrust hitting the deepest parts of me like a steady metronome.

So many hands were reaching out, caressing, stroking and rubbing every sensitive part of me, making my head spin from an overload of pleasure.

In and out, in and out. They filled me up, stretching me past what I thought was possible. The first orgasm came from a buildup, my core tightening as it waited in anticipation for the release while my body slow climbed that diving board reaching higher and higher towards bliss, ready to submerge into the water. I couldn't cry. I couldn't scream. Each attempt only muffled by Santos' pierced cock thrusting deeper into my mouth.

"I'm gonna come," he whispered, his eyes staying fixed on mine before he held my head in place, his entire length sheathed down my throat as he emptied his release so deep inside me I couldn't even taste his salt on my tongue. I fought back the urge to gag everytime he hit the back of my throat but the sound of me choking on his dick just made him moan louder.

He pulled out of my mouth, his cock slapping Mateo in the forehead, making him scowl. I couldn't hold back my laughter as he shoved Santos away from him, but it was cut short when Ronan yanked on my hair. He pulled me against him, forcing me upright so that my back was pressed to his chest. I dropped my hands to Mateo's sculpted abs, holding myself in place as they both moved in and out of me.

"Oh F—" Ronan cut me off, releasing my hair and wrapping his fingers around my throat.

His thumb stroked up and down the sides gently before he applied pressure. I moaned, closing my eyes to surrender just as fingers slid between my folds and forced a burst of pleasure to cascade all throughout my body. I wasn't sure who they belonged to, and sparks of color were blooming throughout my vision. Just as I was getting to that floaty place my thighs shook and weakened under me, my orgasm coursing through me like a broken power line sparking over wet asphalt.

"Oh fuck yeah, sunshine," Mateo breathed out underneath me, one set of fingers still digging into my hips tightly while the others continued to torment the bundle of nerves full of heat between my thighs. "You're squeezing my cock so good."

Just as he said it, he put all his power into one final thrust, painting my insides with his hot, sticky release. I was breathing heavily, drops of sweat running down the side of my face while Ronan thrusted in and out of my ass slowly and methodically.

"How are you not done yet?" I asked, looking back at him, his hand still positioned around my throat but in a gentle hold.

"Done? I plan on being inside you for so long that our bodies fuse together, and they'll have to medically separate us." I started to laugh but he pulled me off Mateo, the sudden odd feeling of still being full in one hole but not the other always left a confusing need.

"More," I begged just as Ronan pulled me with him, sitting back against the headboard of the bed, spreading my legs apart.

Mateo's cum dripped out of me, coating the base of Ronan's cock while he guided my hips against him slowly. That's when I noticed Santos had been standing a few feet away watching this whole time. He stroked his pierced shaft up and down, his fingers purposefully hitting each bar every time he moved his hand.

He was a brown fucking God and I wanted to lick every scar on his beautiful body. Ronan's hand traveled down, his fingers rubbing me while he taunted my puckered hole with his thick length. I moaned, another sharp bolt of pleasure striking my core while he played in mine and Mateo's cum.

"Ven a mi," I demanded, shifting my eyes back to Santos.

He obeyed silently.

I reached out, my fingers tracing over each fucked up scar from wounds that had been barbarically reopened multiple times. He let out a stuttered breath. Ronan curved his fingers entering me and moving in and out of me. I reached up, clutching Santos' forearms.

"Oh... Oh God," I moaned just as Ronan adjusted us into a more reclined position so that Santos could climb on top.

One fist firmly planted into the mattress while another hand explored my naked body humming in approval as his fingers twirled my nipples between them. Ronan's fingers moved away to make room.

I gasped, feeling him position the tip of his cock at my entrance.

His chest pressed against mine, forcing me harder against Ronan. And then he entered me, each delicious inch of his throbbing erection slid inside me with ease. Each bar of his piercing pushing me closer and closer to another orgasm from the sensation.

"Oh fuck." Ronan groaned. "I can feel your piercings."

"Shit, that's so fucking hot, talk dirty to each other," I whined needily.

Santos chuckled, like he knew the power his mecha-cock had.

"You gonna come from my cock rubbing up against yours Zerkos?" He was challenging him, which made me realize they were in a better place than when they had left.

Something happened while they were gone.

They'd somehow healed.

"Please" I moaned, feeling my overspent body climbing to try for one more orgasm like it hadn't already run a marathon's worth of them.

I reached down, finding my clit still sensitive and swollen but desperate for that friction I craved that I knew would send me right over the edge. I made slow circles, relishing in the feeling of the two of them moving against each other inside me until I could no longer contain it.

My climax burst out of me like a riptide, swallowing up everything in its way as I fought for an opportunity to breathe in between filling my lungs with sea water. Violent and potent, leaving me deaf to all sounds around me momentarily.

"Fuck." Ronan gripped me tight, emptying his release inside of me and pumping me full of his cum as if my orgasm had taken him with me as well.

He moved my hair out of the way and turned my chin to the side, exposing the side of my neck to his mouth. His tongue dragged against my flesh, licking the salty sweat from my skin before he slowly pulled out of me. I shuddered, my body still convulsing in tremors from the powerful aftershocks of the full body orgasm they wrung out of me.

Ronan rolled away and just as I moved to get out from under Santos, he gripped me tight and stood from the bed, keeping me impaled on his steel adorned length. I wrapped my thighs around his waist, feeling him deeper inside of me as he walked me over to my private bathroom.

"I'm not done with you yet, morena," he whispered into my ear, opening the door.

I held his face in my palms while he toyed with the shower controls, and once his eyes found their way back to me, I pressed my lips against his. It was tender, far sweeter than I would have thought possible for two people raised on violence and death. He walked us under the hot stream of water, guiding my hips up and down his shaft in a slow and torturous rhythm.

"I don't think I can come anymore." It felt impossible, there were literally no fucks left inside of me and he was still trying to draw them out somehow.

"Is that a challenge?" He smirked pushing me against the cold tile wall.

I turned my head just in time to see Ronan and Mateo striding into the bathroom, cocky looks on both their faces as they watched Santos thrust into me with a feverish passion.

"Put a timer on, if he takes more than five minutes to get her off I'm stepping in," Ronan threatened and Mateo barked out a laugh.

"Bet I can get her to do it without even using my cock," Mateo responded.

Santos growled into my ear like their back and forth was throwing him off, forcing him to slam into me harder to prove something. My back slid up and down the wall each time he pounded into me, and despite my pessimism I could feel the impossible happening.

My core tightened and I felt it building up inside me again. As if he'd already unlocked the cheat codes to my body, he observed and responded, moving his fingers down to my clit to rub gentle circles, forcing my thighs to clench tighter around him.

"Oh shit!" I gasped, feeling the wave wash me over into nothing but a liquid mess of bones, limp in Santos' hold as I seized from my climax, milking his cock until he had no option but to follow me into oblivion.

The other two stepped into the shower, pulling me off of him while still holding me up, washing my body with care. They followed the same gentle devotion when it came to dressing me, Mateo slipping one of his shirts over my head as if his clothes were the only uniform I was allowed for my sleep.

Waking up every morning to his smell was a comforting feeling. Like no matter how wrong the day could go, at least at night I was surrounded by his love. Ronan carried me to bed and just as he slipped me under the covers, I realized the others were leaving.

"Wait," I said sleepily. "Can we all sleep together?"

They looked to Ronan who only shrugged, crawling into bed on my side. They both followed, settling in on my other side and wrapping themselves around me.

Life was starting to go right.

My heart started beating fast at the thought, because life never went right.

I didn't understand success. I didn't know what it was like to get what I wanted, to have a dream that was coming to fruition. When all you knew was failure, it became a comfortable place to set up permanent residency. Why try to accomplish something when I was so good at just... giving up? The thought alone was terrifying.

Mateo wrapped his arm around my waist and pulled me into his chest like he'd done every night while Santos and Ronan were away.

"I can feel you crying Sunshine," he whispered into my ear. "Was it something we did?"

I shook my head, doing my best to keep my tears silent and undetected. Ronan's snoring let me know I was doing a decent job.

"Pass her here," Santos whispered.

Mateo didn't wait a second, tossing me over his body so that I was positioned between him and Santos.

"What's wrong, morena?"

I looked between the both of them, the tears streaming down my face as I struggled to verbalize what I was feeling.

"I'm just… I'm just… too happy?" I said, unsure if that was even the emotion I was experiencing because it had been so long since I'd felt anything even remotely close to this before in my life.

"Is that a problem?" Mateo asked.

"Yes. I don't deserve it."

"Yes you do, Celia." Santos' voice was cold, cutting, with a kind of reprimanding tone.

"No. I don't. We're bad people who do bad things. I haven't even begun to scratch the surface of all my sins to come. I don't deserve this. I don't deserve to feel this way." I shook, the silent tears pouring out of me like there was no turning back from this revelation.

"Tough, morena. This is the life you chose. You had plenty of opportunities to leave, now it's time to throw away any guilt, any conscience you've spent the last twelve years growing. You can be a bad person, and still be happy." He wiped the tear collecting at the corner of my eye before it fell.

"Who gets to define what's bad and good anyway?" Mateo asked.

"My body count was double my age before I turned fourteen," I admitted for the first time in my life.

I heard a heavy sigh.

"I get that you're going through some sort of, imposter syndrome bullshit right now. You're looking for any reason to throw in the towel. You're feeling like you don't deserve all the things you've spent your entire life working for, fighting for, and then running away from. But here's the thing Celia, if it's not you, then who? Because I guarantee your uncle will sleep through the night in this very bed after he kills you, and he won't cry a single tear over all the good things he'll get from your death. And *he* most certainly doesn't fucking deserve them." It was Ronan saying everything I needed to hear, letting me know he hadn't been sleeping as hard as I thought.

I inhaled a stuttered breath, filling my lungs up as I repeated his words in my head.

If not me then who?

My fucking traitorous hermana?

She wouldn't have cried over me. She wouldn't mourn me the way I mourned her. She would slit my throat and take everything that was mine. Everything I would have gladly shared with her.

When did I become such a soft fucking pendeja? I turned to my side, facing Santos and letting Mateo snuggle me into him again. Ronan's snoring started up once more and I let the sound of it calm me into a sleepier state, running my fingers over the scars on Santos' chest, reminding myself I would kill her not just for my own revenge, but for his too.

Retribution was coming, and I would find the Celia I buried deep inside me a long time ago to wield it.

That would help me sleep at night.

22

Celia

The best part about this whole fundraiser gala was that all I had to do was throw money at it. An absolute joy for someone like me who needed minimal interaction with people outside my personal circle.

At the end of the day, I just wanted to tell my people what they needed to do and expect it to get done. It was a fair request to keep myself out of social situations unless they absolutely required it.

The gala demanded it unfortunately, but at least all I needed to do was show up and look hot.

Which I was failing to do.

The Prada box was opened, and the dress was already laid out on the bed for me. Ronan's choice, because I'd still yet to develop a sense of personal style. I really was more of a sweatpants and someone else's T-shirt kinda gal. But this was the event of the year, and it was a big fucking deal.

I painted my lips a dark plum color, opening my lips into an O shape to let the matte shade dry. I was never quite fucking sure if you were supposed to do that or press your lips together to spread the color around.

I was really inept at all this feminine stuff, but it's not like I had someone to teach me. I spent most of my childhood as my father's shadow and when we *were* forced to be apart my mother wasn't discreet in her desire to keep me at a distance.

Her own fucked up way of protecting herself.

I guess I wouldn't want to get close to my kid either if I knew the chances were high that they were going to grow up to kill my husband. I loved my papá, but I was glad he died because, in reality, the odds would have been against us. Historically, time proved cártel seats weren't passed down in peace, they were taken with blood and glory.

The birth control implant in my arm itched from the thought of breeding. The idea alone was laughable. I was thirty years old and probably hadn't even processed a third of my childhood trauma yet. Was I gonna pop some kid out and chain him to that dungeon like my father did to me for the sake of making them a 'better person'? Was I going to force my child into something they likely wouldn't have chosen on their own if they could understand?

No.

I wouldn't be bringing a child into this fucked up world.

I stuck on the sticky strapless bra to my left boob, hooking it onto the right to create the insane illusion of cleavage that I'd never achieve on my own. I wasn't even fully dressed for the night yet and I was already looking forward to taking all this mierda off and crawling into a pair of Ronan's boxers and one of Mateo's shirts.

The three of them walked into the room just as I stepped into the dress, pulling it up to my shoulders and giving them my back so one of them could do the clasps. I gasped looking into the mirror just as Santos finished.

"I-I can't wear this," I said, completely horrified at what I was looking at.

The dress was stunning. Black, strapless with a sweetheart neckline and a tight bodice that hugged all the way down to my hips before the fabric dropped loosely to my ankles. It was essentially backless, stopping right above my ass and leaving my back completely exposed.

That was a problem.

Part of my vault of traumas—I needed to keep locked up tight.

"Yes you can," Ronan said, turning my back away from the mirror and forcing me to look at my own face.

"I can't. Find me a jacket if I *have* to stay in this dress," I told Mateo, knowing he wouldn't argue.

"No." I watched Santos step behind me in the reflection of the mirror, my eyes following him as one of his hands ran up the front of my body, while the other trailed softly along the scar on my back.

It looked worse than I thought possible. It didn't heal right. It had re-opened so many times in that basement just from the way they had me chained up, hanging by my wrists that it didn't allow for it to scar and fade. No, it was raised up, purple in some places and red in others.

It was a reminder of the women still in that Bratva den, locked in cages and waiting to be sold. I would find a way to go back for them.

"No?" I asked, turning away from him as if he'd never seen the scar before.

He wrapped his hands around my shoulders and turned my back towards the mirror again, this time turning my chin to force me to look in the reflection.

"Fucking look at yourself." He sounded angry, his fingers gripping my chin a little too hard, but it was a welcome kind of pain.

The kind that was supposed to wake you up from a bad dream.

"Don't cover it up. Show them exactly why you're the most feared woman on the planet. Show them why they should be grateful for the opportunity to bow at your feet." He licked his finger and wiped the makeup that covered the scar on my cheek. "There, that's better."

He gave me a soft, sideways smile. It was always sideways now. With the way the scar on his own face pulled at his skin it didn't let it be anything but perfectly crooked. He was right, I couldn't ask him to accept the way he was now if I couldn't give myself the same amount of kindness.

"Fine," I relented before turning back to face him, wrapping my arms around his neck. "You know, she wasn't wrong…" I admitted.

"Who?" he asked, furrowing his eyebrows in confusion.

"My sister…" I said with hesitation, unsure if she was even that to me anymore. "You do look more handsome with that scar." I brushed his curls out of his eyes so I could see it better.

I reached up onto the tips of my toes and pressed a kiss to his eye.

"Te quiero," I whispered.

Mateo cleared his throat, reminding us we weren't alone, and I shrugged, walking back to the bathroom to do one final cloud of hair spray over the curls I knew weren't going to hold all night. No curl could survive the genetics of heavy, pin-straight, Indigenous hair. I was practically Cinderella now, fighting the clock until they'd dissolve back to normal.

El Palacio would be full of civilians at this time, but as the guest of honor it was expected that I would be late. Dominico said it was important to make them wait for me, to make an entrance.

Seemed pompous as hell, but if I recalled correctly that about summed up Rafa.

I'd almost forgotten there was almost no distinction between politician and drug lord in these parts. It wasn't until I was greeted by the military police that I remembered I had paid them to be here.

Funny how that worked.

They kept their faces covered, too afraid of ending up in my ledger.

It was alright, I didn't want men on my side who had too much to lose. I wanted the ones who had already lost it all. There was a distinct difference in the kind of work ethic the two groups put in. The door to the limousine opened up from the outside, a valet waiting with his hand stretched out for me to take. Ronan slapped it out of the way, getting out first and helping me out himself.

"Play nice now, or I'll swap you for the other white boy," I teased.

Mateo and Santos followed behind, a sizable difference to not draw any suspicions but still close enough that anyone who saw knew they were with me. People likely thought they were my own private bodyguards.

Not a wrong assumption either.

"Excuse me? You think they won't be able to tell if your date suddenly goes from blond to black haired?" he asked.

"Not the time for an 'all gringos look the same' joke?" I winked, biting back my laugh.

"You'll pay for that one later, flower. Mark my words," he whispered into my ear as he led me up the steps to El Palacio.

One of the grander buildings in the city.

Photographers' cameras went off nonstop, the constant flash lighting up the dark night sky for us as we walked down the red carpet to the government building. It was beautifully decorated inside. They'd gone all out with my money to make it so. Beautiful black roses covered every banister, and decorative ribbons hung all around made from silk and paper tissue. Bar tables filled the space covered with black silk tablecloths with decorative white lace layered above them, a centerpiece of large candles on each one.

"Señorita Flores." A man tapped my shoulder. "I was instructed to show which way you will make your entrance from." He spoke in spanish, pointing down a tiny side corridor with a set of narrow stairs. "The steps will take you to that balcony there," he showed me exactly where I would be appearing in front of the public for the first time.

I really was Celia Flores again.

I couldn't dig up Cecilia if I tried. That bitch died in Sokolov's trafficking ring.

That was the thing about my enemies, they kept trying to fuck with the dead, but they didn't realize I was the queen of can't fucking kill me. They were going to have to hit me harder than that if they were going to keep me down. Only Santa Muerte knew the day of my death.

I took a deep breath, knowing only one of them would be able to come up there with me.

"Take Santos," Ronan said, as if knowing I wouldn't be able to decide between the three of them.

I nodded, looking over at the balcony again, lined with gold and draped in black and white that wrapped around a spiral banister that led towards the grand staircase. It poured out into the gallery where everyone else waited for me to appear.

It was a bit of a whimsical moment, something I would have been prepared for if our lives had never gone awry. I would have grown up here. I would have likely had my quinceañera here. My papá would have introduced me to the world and made some sort of announcement about me someday following in his footsteps. Letting enemies and allies know.

But that was all ripped away from me.

I would be introducing myself to these people.

These strangers.

Santos gave me his arm and I laced my hand around his bicep, squeezing tight for an extra boost of emotional support. He led the way up the stairs, and I followed behind, the stairs too narrow to allow us to walk side by side. It was a service entrance, something likely built for servers and other employees of El Palacio.

There he was, waiting for me at the top. Presidente Ramírez. I'd been doing my homework for the last few weeks. He was forty years old and in the second year of his term. One of the youngest presidents in my country's history, and his mission was to cut down on street violence and child deaths due to drugs and gangs.

I was more than willing to make nice.

"Señorita Flores, it's so nice to finally put a face to the name I've been hearing so much of." He picked up my hand and pressed his lips to my knuckles.

I could hear Santos' teeth grinding behind me.

"Behave," I whispered, "Likewise Ramírez. I hear you are doing great things for our country."

"Please, call me José Luis."

"Well, José Luis, I was pleasantly surprised by your willingness to work with me and my people. I don't want to jump the gun, but I am hopeful I can make you see the positives in supporting my campaign."

"I am not an ignorant man. I know everything that happens in my country—"

"Your country?" I cut him off.

"Like I said, I am not an ignorant man. I know this country's history. I know you are the prodigal daughter returning. Lazarus coming back from the dead."

My interest piqued.

"And what do you have to say about that?

"Ignacio Flores is a crass man. He has no taste for politics or social decorum. The only game he can play he doesn't play well. His henchmen are unmanned, loose in the streets, feeding drugs to the children and the whores. Anyone who crosses him faces a temper tantrum and risks a bullet to the back of the head." His face twitched like there was a deeper story in there.

"So. The enemy of your enemy is your friend?" I asked him.

"With conditions of course."

"As long as you hold my leash?" I clarified.

He smirked. "You're far more intelligent about the inner workings of our world than I expected from an expatriate, Celia. May I call you Celia?" he asked.

"You may not. I am not an expatriate, and I take offense to that. I was forced out of my home country as a child by a stupid man with dangerous delusions and too many idiots willing to do his bidding." I did my best to reign in my anger, but these days I had no tolerance for ignorant men.

He raised his hands up in defense and chuckled again like I was a kitten with sharp claws he thought too cute to scratch him. I liked them better when they underestimated me. I'd allow him to think he was the one in control, because at the end of the day I was smart enough to know having him on my side was how I'd grow.

I'd force my way into politics with one hand and with the other I'd rule the criminal underworld. His time would run out, mine would not.

I paid attention to all my lessons.

"My apologies, Señorita Flores. It was not my intention to offend. There is much gossip and very little truth when it comes to why the Flores family left México." He put on his charm once again, not seeming to actually be worried about offending me.

"Let's move on, José Luis. I think you'll find me to be a reasonable woman to work with." I cut the drama short, letting him know I wasn't interested in gossip.

He nodded to me and then whistled over a nearby usher.

"We are ready," he told him, motioning for both of us to stand in front of a dark curtain.

The usher disappeared, but minutes later the curtain pulled back, revealing the edge of the balcony and the crowd of people below, waiting on our descent. They clapped politely, the quiet encouragement of upper-class socialites was the same, no matter which side of the border you were on.

There was always someone who thought they were better than everyone else.

Santos remained a few feet behind, giving the illusion of a bodyguard instead of a lover. My papá's lessons always in the back of my mind, directing my every move. A strong woman in politics was one who didn't have a man at her side, but behind her. Once I had established myself, I wouldn't hesitate to introduce my men to the world as mine.

But I had to play the long game, and to do that I had to make sure I was allowed on the board first. A mayor elect with three lovers? That was far too much for Guadalajara. President Ramírez rested his hand on my low back as he walked to my side. I recoiled from the touch as his fingers grazed over my scar.

I could feel Santos' glare burning like a hot laser over my skin, scorching José Luis' hand off my body without even looking back at him. We descended down the staircase, one step at a time, politely smiling and waving to the upper-class drones below us.

The minute I stepped down into the gallery, I became self-conscious. Hundreds of eyes staring at me from all angles. My weaknesses, my flaws, my scars all out on display for them to judge.

Santos' arm was heavy on my shoulder, telling me I could do this.

I *could* do this.

Fuck my scars.

Fuck what they thought. At the end of the day I was the best thing that could happen to them because I was the only one who could put things back to the way they were when my papá was around. And I would do it better than he did.

I was a violent woman, who survived a violent past and had a violent history. Scars were minimal compared to the damage I'd actually done in this world. I wasn't here to make friends. I was here to gain respect, to tell them I was someone to be feared.

I was fucking home and no one else was going to take that away from me ever again.

We spent the next hour walking from table to table, Presidente Ramírez introducing me to his colleagues and supporters, letting them know that if they supported him that they now supported me too.

All he wanted was to keep the kids out of it and reduce deaths in the street. That was such an easy thing to abide by that it felt like I was cheating him out of a good deal. Ignacio had set the bar so low that I was going to be a shining beacon of hope for these fuckers.

I'd have to send him a thank you letter before I deprived him of his guts.

"Señor Presidente." Dominico appeared, nodding to the president before turning to me.

"Dominico, how good to see you. I had heard whispers of your return to politics. It's true what they say then, those who support the Flores family do it for life," he joked, knowing damn well what he was actually saying.

The only way out was death.

Since neither Dominico or I were dead, then he belonged to me.

"Likewise, Ramírez. I'm actually here to show Senorita Flores to the conference room. The rest of her campaign party awaits," he said politely.

Ramírez barked out a laugh. "Like father, like daughter. I remember Rafael was always working, even during parties and social events. I hope you don't inherit all his bad habits. Live a little, eh?" He raised the drink in his hand before taking a sip.

"Claro. Maybe after I win the election I can finally relax." I gave him a smile that was all business before letting Dominico lead the way through the gallery, Santos on my heels barely allowing space between us as he followed. I scanned the room, searching for Mateo and Ronan but by the time I had found them they had already taken note of us and began to walk in our direction.

"Give me a minute in the ladies room, go along without me," I instructed Dominico and veered off towards the sign pointing to the restrooms.

I didn't have to turn my head to see if they were following me. I knew they were.

I opened the door to the bathroom and walked straight to the sink, standing in front of it and taming the stray hairs back down while I took a moment to just…breathe.

23

Ronan

Álvarez drew the short straw and stayed outside the door, guarding the bathroom from any unwanted visitors. She was distracted, fixing her hair in the mirror and touching up her dark lipstick. I looked over to Mateo and gestured to the stalls. Without speaking he moved ahead, opening each door to make sure it was empty inside.

Prowling quietly her way, doing my best to remain unnoticed while she was still in her own world, all her self destructive thoughts clearly weighing down the more reasonable part of her brain. She didn't need to be doubting herself before she walked in there. She needed to show them she knew exactly who she was and who they were in comparison to that.

I moved towards her from behind, slowly wrapping my grip around her throat and urging her head up. She let out a soft exhale, those black eyes devouring me into her abyss with little effort as she gazed up at me, slowly parting her lips in invitation. My free hand roamed upwards, following the curve of her waist until her breast was in my hand and she moaned responsively into my mouth.

"I-I can't." She broke our kiss. "I'm already late as it is."

"Make them wait," I demanded, undoing my belt. "They bow to you, not the other way around, reina." Her skin pebbled up at the use of the nickname.

"In this dress? How am—"

"Stop making excuses, sunshine. Bend her over Berserk. I want to see your cum drip down her thighs."

I reached down, grabbing the hem of her dress and gathering it in my hands until I'd lifted it up past her hips.

"What if someone walks—"

"Shut up, flower." I let go of her breast and placed my hand between her shoulder blades, with a forceful push I shoved her down, fully bending her over the counter.

She moaned again, this time it echoed through the chambers of the bathroom, bouncing off the tile walls and back to my ears like a siren song straight to my cock. I pressed the hard steel of my length against her, and she turned her head to look back, eyes wide open like she didn't expect me to be ready for her.

I'd been hard all night, a mixture of anger and jealousy every time the fucking president of Mexico ran his hands up and down her back. I'd spent the whole time blowing up Santos' phone asking why he hadn't cut the bastard's fingers off yet, but I already knew my answer.

We had to play fucking nice. I wasn't going to be the man standing in her way. Not after everything we'd been through.

My hands roamed her thighs, giving her ass a big squeeze before I decided to slip my way between them, finding her panties soaked with arousal. I wedged my fingers inside the fabric, pulling it to the side and sliding two fingers between her folds, coating them in her slickness. She whimpered, the side of her face pressed into the marble of the bathroom counter top while she nibbled on her bottom lip.

"Ronan." She called out my name while I continued to toy with her clit, closing her eyes and reaching back to touch me. "We really don't have time," she protested again but only with words.

"It's not up for debate. You may be in charge of that empire out there, flower, but we both know you belong on your knees for us." I gripped her chin and turned her face forward, forcing her to look in the mirror.

I dropped my hand from her face, keeping my gaze locked on her expression in the mirror just as I pressed the head of my cock at the entrance of her pussy. She turned her head to look back again, this time I wrapped her long silky hair around my wrist and with a hard tug I corrected her gaze once more.

Her eyes narrowed with a look full of fire that reminded me of how she stared at me in that high-rise. But it wasn't hatred I saw, and maybe it never had been all along.

"Are you provoking me on purpose?" I tugged harder, forcing her chin to lift higher and a groan made its way out of her chest just as I made my way inside her fully.

"It's so much better when you're angry." She licked her lips, her eyes finding mine in the mirror.

I pulled out slowly, almost all the way before slamming back in at once. Her mouth gaped open, and her eyes shut as she reveled in pleasure.

"Eyes open," I growled in her ear, picking up my pace and thrusting into her feverishly.

Her eyelids flew open at my command. She stared into the mirror, first watching herself with curiosity as she bounced forward with every jolt of my cock, then moving back to me. With one hand on her hip, guiding me in and out of her and the other still wrapped tightly around her hair, she whimpered as she got closer and closer to her release.

"You don't get to come yet," I whispered in her ear, releasing her hair.

Still fully sheathed inside her, I brought her arms behind her, pressing her wrists together at the small of her back.

"You let him touch you as if we weren't watching." Mateo spoke from a few feet away.

Her eyes widened, a smirk playing around the corner of her lips.

"What did I tell you would happen?" I asked her.

She screamed out with my next thrust, this time her gaze moving to Mateo's dark stare.

He hadn't moved at all, leaning against the wall with one foot supporting him and his arms crossed over his chest. Their eyes locked, an intimate moment between them while I continued to pound into her over and over again.

"What did he tell you would happen?" Kane asked her, his voice laced with darkness.

She moaned and writhed against my cock every time I slowed up my movements to torture her further. Her cunt dripped down onto my pants, the wet sounds of us joining together filled the air along with her screams.

"Answer him," I hissed in her ear bringing my hand down to her ass with a hard clap.

A sound erupted from deep inside her chest, confirming just how much she still liked that.

"He said," she cried out with my next thrust, a hand slipping from my grasp that reached between her legs to get herself closer to relief, "he was going to punish me."

"And that means you don't get to come yet." I slapped her hand out from within her dress and she whined, backing into me to feel the full length of my cock deeper inside her.

Mateo let out an unhinged laugh, finally kicking off the wall and walking towards us. He leaned his head to the side, that manic twinkle in his eye I recognized so well.

"Maybe we should stuff her full of our cum, have Santos come in here and do the same before we send her off to her meeting. Then she can think about what she's done while we drip down her legs," Mateo threatened, her eyes jerking to the side to glance at him and she groaned again at the feeling of me pulling her by her wrists to lift her chest higher into the air.

"Fuck," she cried out, getting closer to the edge.

It was a nice threat, but not one we could deliver on. Not when she was already squeezing my cock with a vice grip kind of hold. She'd be coming undone soon enough regardless of whatever I said to try to keep her from it.

"I think she likes the sound of that." I lifted her from the counter so I could see the lust-drunk look on her face in the mirror.

"I thought you were supposed to be in my corner," she reminded him through labored pants just as he reached for his zipper.

He smirked.

"You let him put his hands on you, Sunshine." His voice was low and husky, a dangerous promise hiding behind it.

I moved faster now—in and out—finding myself getting closer to my climax with each pump, my balls drawing up higher as I fought for my release.

"He's the president," she said. "I have to be civil."

Her eyes found mine again in the mirror's reflection. Her erotic sounds echoing repeatedly became the urgent catalyst to my orgasm, forcing my cum to spill out inside her with one final thrust of my hips.

I pulled out slowly, ignoring her desperate pleas as she attempted to push herself back onto my cock.

"He's the president, but you're the queen. I told you this was punishment," I whispered in her ear before pulling her away from the counter and turning her to face me.

"I'm not gonna lie, you're making it damn hard to not want to do that again if this is my punishment."

Mateo yanked her by the hair, pulling her to him with a swift move that had her gasping once her ass slammed against his cock, hard and ready for her.

"Then we'll just have to keep teaching this lesson to you, won't we sunshine?" he asked her.

"Yes!" She cried out, as he entered her.

I had the perfect show watching the mirror, watching him plow into her while he held onto her wrists. It was hotter than I ever thought possible, watching someone else have their way with her. And for some reason all I could think about was why it took me so long to be okay with it.

"Clean me up," I said, turning to face her, her head level with my cock as he kept her folded halfway.

She wet her lips before parting them and swirling her tongue around the purple head of my cock. She lowered her head, taking me further into her mouth and sucking with a vacuum-like force. I removed myself from her mouth, putting my dick back into my pants and ignoring the wet spot before I turned back towards the door to tag my best friend in.

The scowl on his face when I pushed open the bathroom door let me know he understood exactly what was happening inside and was feeling pissed about being left out. I tapped him on the shoulder and gave him a nod to let him know it was his turn, his eyebrows softened, and he pushed his way inside, leaving me to guard the way.

I leaned against the wall, arms crossed at my chest while I listened to my two best friends fuck the only woman I ever loved.

Death really made you see things more clearly.

I understood why Celia had always been so goddamn obsessed with it. Leaving tequila and weed offerings on her altar when we were just kids and telling me to not pay any mind. Almost dying gave you a new perspective on things, nearly losing everyone you cared about in the blink of an eye even more so.

Having Celia at the cost of either of my brothers' lives would have been like drinking a little bit of poison every single day. Not enough to kill you, but just enough to keep you sick and miserable until the end of your time.

A well-to-do looking socialite walked towards the bathroom. I stuck my arm out in front of her and shook my head. Before she could open her mouth to protest, Celia's screams of pleasure leaked out through the cracks in the door. She widened her eyes, giving me a condemning look as if I were the one that was in there right now.

Well, I had been.

She turned her back to me, marching away with an appalled look on her face. Mateo pushed through the door with a satisfied expression that he didn't bother to hide. Santos followed after, and just a minute or two later Celia walked out, lipstick pristine and chin held high. Her dress hugging her curves once again.

"You're not worried about what they may think of you coming out of the bathroom with two men?" I asked her and she laughed.

"Baby, I don't know if you remember, but my papá died in the middle of a senate campaign. No one is batting an eye that I'm not taking a piss by myself." She walked in front of me, and I stayed a few steps behind, happy to play the part of a bodyguard.

It wasn't like I was pretending. I would have easily cut through anyone who tried to get to her. She walked through the gallery and down a wide hallway until large double doors appeared. She took a deep breath, standing straight with her shoulders pulled back.

She was putting up her mental armor and readying for battle.

All I could do was hold her flag.

No, all she *needed* me to do was hold her flag.

And I would hold it till my arms gave out and the colors ran red with the blood of her enemies. I knew she was capable of spilling it all on her own.

24

Celia

They sat there, waiting for me, filling up each seat at the table in the conference room and leaving the head of the table for me. Men I remembered from my papá's regime, all of them highly opinionated, some clearly bitter over the nepotism in our way of life. None brave enough to actually attempt to try the same though.

Sure, originally I may have earned my title in a less than favorable way, just being born to the right family. But now, none of them could deny that I'd bled my right to call myself queen.

I had already sat down and spoken with most of the men here one on one, for the majority of them, like Luciano Amaro, I already knew we saw eye to eye. Some others hadn't formed an opinion of me yet and we had only been acquainted. A few had already proved to be rooting for my failure, probably thinking that I would be their chance for power.

Men like Fernando Garcia who were just hoping to catch me with my pants down so he could fuck me in the ass and blame it on my not being Mexican enough for his liking. But of course, he couldn't deal with Ignacio himself, so he'd only scrutinize and shame me until it came time for me to do the hard work of ridding the world of my tío.

Then he'd miraculously find the courage to challenge me in hopes of taking everything I'd worked hard to build.

Idiot didn't know I was a servant of death.

You couldn't kill those who worshiped La Muerte. Only she decided when we went.

My time was far from up.

They all stood but Fernando stood once I entered the room. I made sure to let my gaze linger on him as I walked past every other man seated before arriving at my own chair, giving him a dose of my bad side. My father had been gone too long, I would bet good money Fernando here had crossed the line and settled for my tío. Maybe I was just cynical and untrusting.

Great qualities in a leader.

The more I thought about it the less I tolerated him sitting at this very table.

"Good evening Señores—" I switched to spanish.

He interrupted, raising his hand in the air, waving it as if he alone had the authority to stop me from speaking.

"I'm going to cut short the pleasantries, Celia. It's been a long night waiting for you to show your face, why don't we speed things up here so we can all go home?" The fucking audacity of this man made me fight every carnal instinct that screamed at me to throw a knife into his face.

I noticed César in the corner, twirling the sharp point of one on the tip of his finger. He didn't look up; he didn't need to. Both our thoughts were in the same place so when the corner of his lip twitched, I knew our minds were back in the past. The moment he threw that blade in my cousin Carlitos' cheek was the very same moment my tío decided he'd had enough of not being the biggest man in the room.

Too bad for him, even with all the giants now gone, I was still bigger.

"I assure you that just because I'm wearing a dress, it doesn't mean my cock is smaller than yours Fernando. On the contrary, I'm wearing this dress because it is actually so fat it can't be contained by a pair of pants." A few men chuckled quietly to themselves.

He scowled, taking a beat to think up something clever to retaliate, but I was faster.

"Your hostility towards me only proves that I've already succeeded in what I came here to do. Own this country.

You're angry that a woman has done in two months what you have failed to do in fifteen years." I stopped and addressed the rest of the room, "What you all failed to do."

There was an awkward beat of silence but it only tasted like the failure of mediocre men. Regardless of how far their loyalty went, there was no denying every man in this room at one point entertained the idea of having the cártel for themselves. None had been brave enough to try to claim it.

"Now, if you are done trying to prove whether or not your dick can hit a g-spot, let's move on to what really matters here. Ignacio needs to die. This week preferably." I gave the deadline wondering which one of my men would prove themselves worthy of being my right hand.

I wasn't hopeful about any yet.

"You're barely Mexican. Why should we have to listen to anything you have to say when you're saying it with a gringa accent?" He said the words with a bitter expression on his face.

I extended my hand out and before I had even blinked there was a pistol in my palm. I didn't bother to check to see who'd placed it there. Only a few voices gasped out loud as I flipped the safety off, nostrils flared at the man who dared insult me.

"Maybe if I hadn't been so busy trying to survive after you all tucked your tails between your legs and went into hiding when Rafa died, I could have dedicated more time to perfecting my spanish."

"So, you're better than Ignacio because Rafael had a hand in you?" He scoffed.

"No, I'm better because I learned who I can be *in spite* of the pitiful men who stood in my way. Get the fuck out of my sight if you want to stay alive." I pointed to the door and Miguel stood up to forcefully escort him out.

"Rafa would have put a bullet in his head," Dominico said from the far end of the table.

"You think I made the wrong call letting him walk out of here?" I asked the men I knew I had no choice but to trust as my council.

"I think it was a kind decision," Luciano answered. "Some men deserve kindness, some do not."

"And Fernando Garcia?" I asked.

"We shall see what he deserves," he said, and I nodded back at him, taking his words as a request to leave and see what Fernando was up to unsupervised.

He stood up and followed him out, back into the gala.

"I have a primo who is acquainted with one of Ignacio's soldiers. I can send him inside with your word, jefa," Miguel answered, sticking to business and moving past the unnecessary drama that had just taken place.

"It's a good idea, better we know where he is than to wait for him to come at us. Even if we are prepared." I nodded my approval. "Get on that. The faster we kill the hijo de la chingada the faster we can focus on the things that matter, the things that make us rich." They all nodded their heads, agreeing that money was the reason for it all.

"Thank you, Miguel," I acknowledged him once again. "Everyone go." I waved the rest of the room off. "We'll continue this once Ignacio is dead." The room cleared out faster than I expected. I sat there in silence, staring at the Rufino Tamayo painting Rafael let me pick out when I was thirteen for this very room in this government building. I didn't realize the momentousness of the occasion then. A child of a crime lord, decorating the walls of a federal building with a painting made by an Indigenous artist. Almost like the statement alone was the art itself. It was too low on the wall, because he thought I should be the one to get to hang it. I was seven years old the first time I spun around in these chairs, and I was fourteen when I first sat through a meeting.

Dominico was the last one out the door, but he turned back to face us before exiting.

"She needs to learn," the old man said, shaking his head.

"She doesn't need to learn shit," Mateo spit out in my defense.

"What do I need to learn?"

"You came here wanting to do something different, but this is a wheel that never stops turning Celia. You wanted to do better than your father, but you can't. If you show these animals a moment of weakness, they will eat you alive. So you better fucking eat them instead. That's the secret to all of this."

"If you knew that, then why did you still come along when I said I'd do it differently?" I asked.

"Because you came in with this brand new attitude, bright eyed and filled with hope. Those intentions mean something, they make you someone worth following. If you leave, someone else *will* take your place, they circle like vultures just waiting for a crack in the foundations."

"Don't I know it." I looked over to Ronan and exhaled heavily, remembering his losses.

"If you ask me, you're the right person for it, Celia. And that's not because of all the work I watched him put into you, but because of something that I think grew inside of you after him," the old man said.

"What if I'm not good at it?" I asked, my voice wavering.

"You could kill all your enemies, baby, and the only person still standing in your way would be you," Ronan said.

It was the kind of realization that sunk itself so deeply into your psyche that you felt it shake you to your core.

"Leave," Santos told Dominico.

I didn't bother waiting to see if he'd completely left the room before I tore my mask off and let my walls down. I hated that anger always manifested itself in tears now, like my body just couldn't process the overload of emotions and the only way to let it out was to cry. I thought I'd built that shell around my heart, that it kept me protected. But it turned out all I did was emotionally constipate myself for years and now it was flooding out like trauma diarrhea.

"Why are you afraid of getting everything you've been fighting for?" Mateo stepped up to me and lifted my chin up, wiping a tear before it dropped.

"I don't know how to accept success."

I clenched my fists around the arms of my chair tightly, biting my lips until I could taste the liquid metal in my mouth. I could feel them, their shadows hovering over me and the heat of their protective shield. Ronan's hand was first on my shoulder, then Mateo's on the other side. Santos kneeled down in front of me, wrapping my hand inside both of his.

"Morena," he whispered.

"What if this was a huge mistake?" I whispered the words I feared the most.

"How could it be? This is your destiny," he said, like he hadn't wanted to escape this kind of life since I first knew him.

"Maybe it wasn't. Maybe it's Caro's. Maybe I'm stealing that chance from her. What if I'm just a fucking fraud?" I covered my face, too ashamed to fall apart in front of the guys I loved so much.

"Is this because of what that idiot said?" Ronan asked, and I nodded my head.

"I just feel like a sham. Like I fooled everyone. Maybe a long time ago this was my destiny, but what if I'm not meant to be here anymore?" I asked, looking up at him, hoping for some answers.

"Then fake it till you make it sunshine." Mateo squeezed my shoulder as he whispered in my ear from the other side.

"What?" I choked out, surprised at his response and he shrugged his shoulders.

"No one knows what they are doing. And if they tell you they do they're fucking lying," Ronan finished Mateo's thought.

"I'm drowning in doubt," I confessed, the tears welling at my eyelids.

"Come back up for air, we can't save you from yourself," Ronan lamented, a sad tone in his voice. "I wish you could see what we see. You're a fucking force to be reckoned with. You've survived hell and you'll survive this too."

"I wish I believed that. I just have this feeling like—"

"Don't even fucking say it." He read my mind, knowing exactly what kind of turmoil was crashing through my mind.

Death.

The end.

I was always thinking about it.

She was my gravity.

The center of my universe.

Everything moved because death allowed it so.

This could only end in death.

This could only end in death.

It was the only way out.

My heart began to race, and I shut my eyes, taking a deep breath in to try to calm myself before the panic set in again.

Not here. Not here.

"What would make you feel better right now?" Mateo's husky voice honeyed its way out in that way only he could sound, letting me know he was ready to cater to any and all of my needs to anchor me back down to reality.

I looked up at him through my eyelashes.

"Do you want to kill him, sunshine?" he asked, no judgment in his tone at all, just a desire to fulfill my need, whatever it be.

I looked between the three of them, mouth slightly agape at the fact they all had the same expression.

"I think so," I said quietly nodding my head.

"Find him. Bring him back here." I heard Santos already on the phone behind me.

Then I heard the deafening boom in the distance and the ground trembled beneath us. We didn't have to guess or speculate what had happened.

We all already knew.

"Find César, there's Diablos on standby. Make sure no one is hurt, and get all the civilians out," I told Mateo. "Find the president, make sure he's safe," I told Ronan.

"Come with me." The last instruction went to Santos, I squeezed my hand around the Glock and the four of us made our way out of the conference room.

Pandemonium had broken out at the gala. Smoke was filling the air fast and people were running through the building, shouting and screaming for each other in a wave of chaos.

He may have been inadequate for all intent and purpose, but my tío had a knack for dramatic murders—I'd give him that.

It would end today though.

Obviously, Fernando had been a distraction, a way to get my tío and his men in the building to fuck this party all to hell and cast a shadow over my name. He didn't understand that I was the shadow, the very thing that loomed over the memory of my family's name. I was annoyed at myself for not seeing that farce for what it was.

Santos walked in front of me, shielding me from anything that might come towards me in the thick wall of smoke.

"I think we need to get out, Morena, there's too much smoke," he yelled over the screams of the crowd rushing towards the doorways to the outside.

Another tremor shook the building, and the rearmost walls began to collapse, bricks cascading into a pile on the ground as Diablos and cártel soldiers worked alongside military police to empty El Palacio and get everyone out safely.

"No. This is our chance. We have to find him," I told him, my eyes tearing up from the insidious fumes overwhelming me.

He didn't argue, pushing through the crowd desperate to get out as we forced ourselves in the opposite direction, deeper into the building.

Two girls in their early twenties were huddled together on the floor, coughing and yelling for help. I pointed them out to Santos and we both rushed over to help.

"You need to get out of here. There's too much smoke, the building is coming down," I shouted in spanish.

"She's pinned under the boulder!" One of the girls responded.

Santos and I both reached for the boulder, finding it too impossibly heavy to move.

"Together," he said, and I nodded. "One, two, three!" We barely lifted it three inches off the ground, but it was just enough for the uninjured girl to pull her friend out from under the rock that had her trapped.

She began wailing, either from the feeling of her foot being free, the pain, or the shock of the entire situation.

Probably all of the above.

"Head towards the exit, find the men in leather," I told them, pointing towards the crowd.

"You think he's still inside?" he asked me, one girl over his shoulder and the other clutched to my arm as we helped them towards the exit.

25

Celia

"No. He's not here," I told him, stepping into my tío's mindset and realizing what this truly was.

"What?" He looked at me with confusion, putting the injured girl on the ground so she could find her people. "But the bombs—"

"His men, yes. He's not here, he's not this ignorant."

"Then where is he?" Santos asked.

"The Villa." My skin pebbled though I was the one speaking the words. This would end where it started, the very place my tío began his disruption to my life would be the very place it would end.

Cathartic.

That's how it would feel too as I skinned him alive and plucked the teeth from his mouth like feathers from poultry. My papá once said his revenge was so close, he could taste it, smell it in the air.

He died that very week.

All I could taste was blood. All I could smell was blood.

That was enough to tell me that death was on her way.

Santos and I rushed out of the building battling through the chaos of bodies gathered at the front of the collapsing building as it slowly crashed its way to the ground from the weakened foundation.

"Text César, tell him to bring Mateo and Ronan home with him. Tell him to keep ALL of the men outside the villa," I instructed Santos, charging through the crowd while looking for the vehicle we'd arrived in.

"Where are you going? You can't go off alone, Celia." He wasn't wrong, my tío's men along with whatever stray Los Muertos soldiers he'd collected were likely all lurking around here, waiting for us to flood out of the building like mice scurrying from the fire.

"Then keep up with me," I told him, finding an orange Mastretta parked away from the crowd and unblocked by other cars. "Are you driving or am I?" I smirked at him, memories of our youth flashing through my mind.

"Get in," he said, taking his jacket off and wrapping it around his elbow before breaking through the driver's side window.

The alarm went off, but it was already far too loud between the sound of the flames engulfing the historic Palacio, the sirens of the ambulances and firetrucks in the distance arriving, and the screams of innocent people attempting to piece together what had happened. He brushed the broken glass from his seat before unlocking the passenger door for me. Santos reached into the electronics of the car, yanking out a wire that shut off the blaring of the security system before hotwiring the engine to start.

"It's been a long time since we've done this." He smirked, his hand casually dropping to my thigh and slipping through the slit in the side of my dress.

"We never did it like *this*," I reminded him.

"*You* never did it like this. If you think for one second it wasn't all I thought about during those drives, those runs we made, you're fucking crazy, morena." His hand rubbed up and down my skin, calming me as I fought to slow down the current of excitement running through my veins.

Cálmate. There was a bigger end game here.

Me and Ignacio.

One of us would die tonight.

I almost didn't care which one.

Closure was kind of like that, like it didn't matter how things ended as long as they did. People seemed to be satisfied as long as they knew the ending. I didn't get the need, why did the book always end just when you got to the part where the main character finally found happiness?

You spent all that time watching them suffer, you cheered them on hoping they could have their happily ever after. When they finally did it was a five-page epilogue with some stereotypical idea of what happiness looked like. A pregnant belly, a picket fence, no threat of death.

Maybe it ended there because they couldn't possibly describe something they didn't understand. Maybe none of them actually knew what it truly meant to be happy. You couldn't write happiness if you didn't experience it for yourself, your readers would surely know it. They'd see past the pretty lies in the words you spelled out and see the sad person beneath it all.

Maybe authors were just truly unhappy people, forcing imaginary creations to undergo the cruel darkness that lived inside their own minds as if the characters weren't simply mirrored shards of themselves.

Certainly cheaper than therapy.

Not that I understood anything of the sort. I was allergic to healing. The thought of being examined under a lens gave me hives.

Or maybe I had just become bitter. Cynical over time, and maybe that was the problem. I'd never been delusional enough to think that I could ever earn myself a happy ending. When I turned thirty, I realized I was really only ten years away from outliving my papá. A rare feat for a Flores. That was what brought me to the Black Crow

Brotherhood's door in the first place. I was alive because I was lucky, and I knew that luck would eventually run out.

I might have not been ready to die yet, but we weren't the ones who got to choose that day.

Santos pulled into the villa with a screech as he yanked on the emergency break. He opened his door, but I wrapped my hands around his wrists and pulled him back down to me.

"I want him alive."

He grabbed the back of my neck, closing his mouth around mine and sliding his tongue between my lips. Kissing Santos was like inhaling summer in the middle of the snowy winter, like drinking clear tequila with no chaser.

It was liquid fire.

But it didn't last nearly long enough. He broke free, and the right corner of his lip curled up.

"Then you shouldn't have brought me." He got up, walking around the car and opening my door for me.

"Who said chivalry was dead?" I joked.

He pulled his phone out, scrolling through the texts before shoving it back in his pocket.

"Zerkos and Kane are headed here now, we should wait for them," he said with a wince, like he expected some sort of angry outburst at his logical suggestion.

"We should. But I'm also well aware my uncle will use anything I give a damn about to get to me, and to get what he wants." Both could be one in the same, depending on how you looked at it. "Which is why I need you to stay out here. I don't need distractions and I don't need him to use you against me."

A deep V formed between his eyebrows.

"Fuck no morena, I won't be at the mercy of the unknown again. I won't be helpless," he said with a rising panic as if it was something he had to prove to me.

"You're not at the mercy of the unknown, you're at *my* mercy Santito," I whispered, tapping his cheek with my hand gently. "I need to do this alone, if I'm not out in thirty you can come look for me."

"Screw that. You can't seriously think I'm just gonna let you go in there on your own, to possibly fucking die. You don't know how many men he might have in there, and you don't know what's waiting for you," he screamed.

"I had to watch Guillermo hurt you, over and over again. Every single day I watched him carve you up, I watched him maim you and kill your spirit. I will not risk hurting you again Santos. Whose sins are you paying for at this point?" I asked.

"I'm fucking coming, stop being so goddamn stubborn." He grabbed my wrist, yanking me towards his hard chest with a slam. "We're done making stupid decisions Celia." His nostrils flared out passionately. "We do this together."

I stared at him for a long moment. So many words and emotions silently passing between us. "Let's go," I sighed, releasing the safety on my Glock as we walked towards the side of the villa.

I didn't know how many men he had inside, but we only had so much time before the cavalry arrived. It wasn't that I wanted to do this alone, it was that I *needed* to do it alone. I needed to kill him for the sake of my family, for the things he broke within us… within me. The minute the others arrived it would become a shootout.

I knew exactly where he was, and I knew exactly how to get there without being noticed.

"Are we not going inside?" he whispered.

"Not through the door." I led him through the side of the villa, ducking under the windows and staying closer to the shadows as we snuck around the building.

Once I found the right window, the one just below the veranda door of my papá's second story office, I peeked inside the glass to see if I could see anyone. It was empty.

"Give me a boost to the balcony," I whispered.

He clasped his hands together to hold my foot and lift me up. It was just barely enough to get my arms up onto it. I muscled my way, struggling to get my lower body up on that balcony. Fuck, how much did my legs weigh?

"How am I supposed to get up there?" Santos whispered, too loudly, and I shushed him with a reprimanding stare.

"I'm sorry Santito. I told you I have to do this alone." I gave him one final look before I turned my back to him, ignoring his hissing of my name from below.

"Celia! What the fuck!"

I pulled a bobby pin from my fancy but now disheveled hair and forced it into the lock, jiggling it until I felt the resistance I needed and turning until I heard it click. I opened the door slowly, finding the room still dark and empty. A cloud of disappointment loomed over me. I really thought I'd find him here, waiting for me.

I thought at this point we'd been doing this dance long enough that we moved in sync, a macabre choreography of carnage that only ended with shallow graves. We'd been playing cat and mouse for years and I hadn't noticed I'd become the predator, checking behind the curtains to see if I could strike him first.

Was it all in my head? Was he even here?

My stomach dropped at the thought of him still being at El Palacio, wreaking havoc and promising death to all the men sworn to me. My fears were short-lived. Just then, I heard heavy footsteps and a deep voice barking orders in spanish from outside the door. I ran to my papá's giant oak desk, scurrying underneath just in time to hear the door creak open and see the light shining into the room from out in the hallway.

I smiled to myself, my confidence skyrocketing.

Ignacio never let me down before, why would he start now?

I heard his man anxiously telling him that a car pulled up to the property, but they couldn't find us. I hoped Santos was smart enough to stay undetected, reassuring myself that I'd brought the right man along for the job. Ronan would have broken through the front door with open fire, cutting down my tío's men by the handful until one of them shot him dead.

This was too personal to go down that way.

There was only one person who needed to die. Two who truly deserved it.

But today wasn't *my* day, so one would do.

He kept the light off, slow footsteps tapped on the floor one at a time as he made his way closer to the desk. My heart thundered so hard in my chest I thought surely it would give me away. His feet appeared right in front of me, with a screeching sound he dragged the chair from the desk and plopped down.

Oh, he was making it too easy.

I didn't believe in karma, but it seemed like the bitch was really on my side lately.

A knife to the foot, then a bullet to the head.

No, that would be too quick.

And too loud.

I had to kill him quietly unless I planned to deal with however many men he had trapped in this house with us. I was a ballsy pendeja, but the thing about being a bad bitch, was also knowing your limits.

I heard the flickering of the lighter letting me know the pompous dickhead actually thought he was going to smoke a cigar while he waited for me to walk into his trap. Like I was that easy to kill. I was feeling sort of fucking offended about the whole thing.

My heart sped up even more and I gripped my knife tighter, the sweat in my palm coating the handle of the blade as I tried to figure out which foot I was going to be stabbing. Then his hand reached into the desk, his fingers wrapping around my throat as he pulled me out and slammed my back against the desk. I couldn't cry out from the pain, he squeezed too tight, his sausage-like fingers crushing my windpipe and putting painful pressure on my eyes.

I sent my arm flying, hoping to stab at him, but my body was too focused on self-preservation. My free hand struggled with his grip around my neck while the other fought to keep the blade in my clutches. He pulled me by the neck, lifting my head off the table just enough to slam it back down with force. I bit back a yell, hoping the noise wouldn't call his men in for reinforcement.

"Maldita puta," he cursed me. "All this trouble just for a few million dollars," he spat out and I wheezed, slapping and scratching at him while I felt the crushing power of his grip squeezing my arm painfully.

He truly knew nothing if he thought this was over a few million dollars.

It was over *billions*.

It was over everything that was meant to be mine.

I spit, landing right in the middle of his face and painting a disgusted look onto his expression as he fought to decide whether or not he was going to risk giving me a chance to free myself if he cleaned it off.

He pulled me by the throat once more and sent my head flying down twice as hard as before. I cried out in pain, and he squeezed my throat tighter.

"This is over Celia. You will pass the credentials of the dungeons to me, or you will die right here, right now."

I cackled in his hold, the deranged look on my face only provoking him further into a rage-fueled spiral.

"If you kill me, you stay just as fucked, just as poor, and just the same sorry excuse for a jefe that you've been this whole time. So fucking kill me payaso. You don't scare me anymore."

He slapped me across the face, the steel force of his palm cutting into my skin. A pool of liquid metal slid over my taste buds while I mentally accepted my death.

The pressure near my eyes was unbearable as he squeezed even harder, completely disabling me from taking even the smallest sip of air back into my lungs. My vision went fuzzy, specs of colors floated around in my vision.

Maldición.

Was I really going to fucking die like this?

After everything?

"My men will be up here soon, then I'll make them teach you why your father should have never put the stupid idea of a reina del cártel into your naive little mind. I'll let them each take a turn with you, one by one, till you're begging me to kill you sobrina."

"Better not, tío," I rasped, not even sure if he could make out the words as I forced them out of my mouth. He loosened his grip slightly like a dumb, curious bastard, eager for the rest of my sentence. "Maybe I'll fuck them so good they'll drop to their knees for *me* instead."

"Zorra," he spat out venomously, letting go of my throat just to strike my face once again.

I coughed, swallowing a lungful of air.

"Is it not as fun when I weaponize the very thing you all tried to convince yourselves was a weakness?"

He didn't get to answer.

A deafening boom came from somewhere in the house making us both turn our necks as if we'd see what was happening through the closed office door. Santos was creating a distraction, and fuck if it wasn't hot as hell that he could offer me his help without treating me like I was powerless.

"Looks like your men are busy," I taunted, sending my foot up between his legs with as much force as I could muster.

He wheezed from the pain, relaxing his grip around my neck to clutch his manhood defensively as he cursed me in spanish. It was all the time I needed to scamper away, just far enough to give me time to retrieve my gun from the floor under the desk and pull it on him.

"Now tío querido, did you *really* think it was going to be this easy to kill me, or did you come here just to offend me?"

He moved to reach his hand behind him, but I lodged a bullet into the very same shoulder to stop him from pulling out his own gun. He cried out in pain, but the shaking of the villa's foundation let me know his men were far too preoccupied to come to his rescue.

"And here I thought I was going to have to kill you fast and miss out on all the fun. Looks like Carlitos won't be welcoming you to hell just yet." I smirked watching his eyes go wide.

"What did you do to my son?" he seethed, which only furthered new confusion.

"What do you mean what did I do? I killed that pendejo months ago." I laughed plugging another bullet into his other shoulder when he attempted to reach back once again with his uninjured arm. "Vamos tío, I was really hoping to draw this out."

"Sadistic, just like the rest of your family. Your temperament is more suited to *lower* positions, you can't handle what it takes to be jefe," he insulted me through pained grunts.

"President Ramírez seems to think I can, which begs the question... where does that leave you if I'm running the cártel they all recognize as the tried and true version?" I gave him a sinister smirk, stepping closer to him now that he'd dropped to a seat on the ground, arms limp at his side.

"Must be so easy... to fuck your way to the top," he labored out.

I clenched my back teeth together, counting backwards in my head while I silently told myself that future me would regret not killing him slowly. He was antagonizing me on purpose. Pushing me because he knew it was over for him now and all he could do about it was hope I'd deliver it quickly.

I had no such plans to do so.

"I gave him a quick death, because he was a stupid bastard who didn't know any better. But you tío, I'm gonna take my time with you. I'm going to kill you a little every single day until I tire of playing with you. And when you're dead, I'll use your bones to pick at my teeth after meals, to comb my hair, and to clean under my fingernails. I'll burn everything else you've ever touched. Including Carolina," I promised him.

There was a look on his face that could only be described as utter confusion. Which only let me know one thing, and it was the only thing I needed to know.

My tío was no longer in charge. Someone else was just letting him pretend to play the part.

"How long has she been running the show?" I asked.

He hocked a bloody wad of spit onto the ground by my feet.

"It's going to get really smoky up here soon by the smell of things tío. I'd love to move us somewhere more comfortable but I'm real inclined to leave you here if it might get me answers." I raised the Glock up once more, hoping I wouldn't have to shoot him once again.

There was only so many bullets you could put into a man while still expecting him to stay alive for long-term torture.

"Both of you are just like your mother. Bloodthirsty. Constantly thinking with violence first, assuming the Ortíz name still means anything around these parts and that you can use it to your advantage. You think just because you have both families' blood in your veins it means you deserve this any more than I do?"

"You knew?" I asked him.

"Of course I fucking knew, we all fucking knew. The only person who didn't was you and the sorry excuse for a man that was the Ortíz boy." I barely gave him a chance to finish before putting the next bullet in his knee cap.

It was one thing to spew his mierda about me, but César was blameless in all of this.

"What do you know? Who killed Diego Ortíz?" I asked, hoping I'd get any crumbs that could help me unlock all the bullshit secrets our parents buried with them.

"Everyone knows Ortíz killed his own son." He coughed, blood splatter flying everywhere.

"Why would he do that when he needed a successor?"

"He didn't, at least not anymore. He was marrying your mother to be head of the Flores family. Diego was done, he wanted out. No one gets out alive, you know that better than anyone don't you sobrina?"

"Thanks for the reminder, tío." I stepped one foot at a time closer to him until I was standing over him.

I placed the heel of my stiletto over his bleeding kneecap and put my weight into it, ignoring his screaming pleas as well as his cursing and name calling.

There was no bird who could outsing a serenade by a man on the verge of death.

26

Mateo

There was nothing quite as chaotic as evacuating a building full of people whose language you didn't speak. No wait, there was something that topped that. It was getting a text from Santos saying that Celia was headed to the villa to kill her uncle and that she somehow found a way to ditch him in the process.

He sent a photo of him next to a blown up Mastretta with text underneath saying, 'SOS, probably will get killed by cártel soon' and I practically bulldozed through every civilian in the crowd gathered outside El Palacio in order to find Ronan and rush the fuck out of there to our girl's aid.

It wasn't that I didn't think she was capable of doing it herself. It wasn't that I didn't think she couldn't handle the fight.

It was about how the fuck I was supposed to go on if she somehow needed me and I wasn't there?

Again.

I peeled onto the main road, the tires screeching against the asphalt as the car drifted sideways before entering the grounds of the villa.

A burning sports car was now crashed into the front of the house, blocking the doorway. A portion of the upper level collapsed over it while the flames engulfed Celia's childhood home. Ignacio's men struggled and fought each other to climb out of the building as fast as they could, but each time one of them found their way out Santos would shoot them down.

I hadn't fully parked the car before Ronan jumped out, in full Berserk mode he pulled two pistols out, firing them off simultaneously towards the incoming lackeys to give Santos a break.

"Where is she?" I roared out over the sound of bullets flying in the fire taking over the mansion.

He pointed to a balcony up in the distance.

"She went up through there," he yelled.

"You let her go by herself?"

"I'm gonna fucking tell her you said that," he thundered at me. "She'll have your balls for saying anyone *lets* her do anything."

"I will actually pay you to keep your fucking mouth shut about that. Help me get up there." I nudged him, both of us leaving Zerkos looking more than capable of handling the mess of men scrambling to get out of the villa just to be shot. The pile of bodies was making it harder for them to crawl out of the blazing embers.

"She was in there." He pointed at the glass door that led to the veranda.

"Give me a boost up," I told him. He didn't hesitate, clasping his fingers together and sending me up with a grunt.

"Hey, what the fuck man? Help me up," he called out from below while I ran into the house.

The smoke was filling every inch of the villa, spreading its thick cloud all around me until I could barely see my hands in front of my face.

"Sunshine," I bellowed out, trying to fan some clarity into my vision but I couldn't avoid the involuntary tears that came from the smoke wafting all around me.

I couldn't see her, but I could hear her labored grunts and the sound of something banging.

"Sunshine!" I screamed again, this time not hiding the panic in my voice when the thought occurred to me that it might be her struggling for her life I was listening to.

I followed the sound into the corner of the room until I was close enough that I could see the scene in front of me. A brutal sight to behold. Celia Flores sitting on her uncle's chest as she bashed the butt of her gun into his face over and over again. Blood splattered over her and poured down his neck.

His face looked fucked, and he wasn't moving, which led me to believe he was dead as hell considering all the blood on the ground, but she didn't let up.

"Sunshine, we gotta get you out of here, there's too much smoke." I grabbed her arm, but she fought me off, yelling a feral screech before sending the gun down against Ignacio's face once more. "Baby, please. Let me get you out of here." I reached for her face and pulled her chin towards me, getting as close as possible as I could so she could see straight into my eyes.

She took a deep stuttered breath, breaking the feral trance she had found herself locked into.

"Get *him* out of here," she said coldly, tilting her head back towards her half-dead uncle before standing up and walking back towards the veranda, where the smoke rolled out easily into the fresh air. I could barely see her anymore, but her voice was still crystal clear when she spoke, despite the roaring of the flames outside the door. "I'm not done playing with him yet."

I didn't bother to check his pulse or give him the dignity of being carried. I dragged the sorry fucker by the leg until I'd made my way out to the balcony once more and then, without any care, I shoved him off of it the same way Guillermo had done to me when Los Muertos attacked the Black Crow high rise.

Maybe Celia had the right idea.

An eye for an eye felt really fucking right.

The Diablos Locos and Celia's men were all pulling into the property just in time to watch the flames engulf the building completely. She was already in Ronan's arms by the time I made it to them, slowed down by dragging Ignacio's corpse along the way.

"What do you want to do with him?" he asked her.

"Have Dominico lock him up in the dungeons, can you ask Emory to keep him alive for now?" He nodded to her before taking Ignacio's leg from me and dragging him over to the group of cártel lackeys who were clearing out the pile of dead bodies out front.

Before I could even ask her how she was doing, Ramírez was already stepping up to her, and in three long strides he was practically touching her again.

"If that is Ignacio Flores you have there, I'm afraid I must ask you to surrender him to the police Señorita Flores. The list of crimes he must pay for is longer than I care to read."

"Then that is *not* Ignacio Flores, and I would appreciate you allowing me to mourn this violent attack I've suffered tonight in my childhood home, José Luis," she scolded him as if he she didn't care what his title was.

"Celi—" he began but I cut him off.

"It's Señorita Flores to you, Señor Presidente. And weren't you just telling me, moments ago, outside El Palacio how you were deeply indebted to Miss Flores for saving your daughter's life?" I reminded him, making

Celia's expression soften into a smile while the president's jaw ticked in annoyance.

"I have to turn him in to the authorities. How else am I supposed to convince my followers—your supporters—that he won't be a problem anymore?" he asked her in a hushed voice as if I had no clue what fucking shenanigans they were up to.

"That's your problem to deal with José Luis. Figure it out. I'll double my previous offer towards your budget." His eyes widened at my suggestion. "But Ignacio Flores is mine, this is personal. Es familia," she reminded him.

He gave her a nod and turned back towards the police cars flashing on the far side of the villa's property.

"His daughter?" she whispered at me with a look of disbelief on her face.

"Yeah, look at you. You're practically a superhero," I told her, nudging her ribs with my elbow.

She gave me a smile, and though it was meant to be genuine, the attempted murder on her face really changed the whole vibe. Her smile faded, like she caught my train of thought and didn't like where it was headed.

"Is this... too much for you? Too dark for you?" she asked. "I know with the Crows you were all at least *trying* to do some good where you could. Here... I don't know if there is any good here." She bit her lip, letting me know she was going into that place in her head where she let all her insecurities take over.

"Sunshine, the difference between me and you, is that you hate the darkness and I'm in love with it. It pulls me in, it consumes me. The thing is, Celia, you *are* the darkness, and whether you love yourself or not is irrelevant because I love you enough for the both of us. If I have, for one moment, given you the impression that by your side wasn't the place for me, then forgive me." I brushed my thumb over the dried specks of blood stuck to her skin. "There is nowhere else I want to be."

"Promise?" she asked.

I answered without words, pulling her into my chest and pressing my lips into hers for just a second before remembering there were so many people gathered outside. Zerkos eventually made his way back to her side and Santos joined us as well. One by one her council members left the property after checking in with her and eventually all that was left were the Diablos Locos who had been waiting for instructions.

We stood there, watching the villa burn down until César finally made his way over to say his goodbyes. He'd fulfilled his end of the bargain and earned his freedom, without death.

"Te amo, Princesita," he told her, punching her shoulder softly.

"If I can ever repay the favor, just say the word." She didn't hug him, and he didn't reach for her like I would have expected them to.

Maybe because it would be harder to face the emotions than either of them were prepared for.

"Actually…" César said. "You could tell that stubborn doctor to come back over the border with me."

"What?" She looked at him like she didn't understand.

"That Irish skin, she's gonna burn up down here Princesa. My Médico ended up signing up for a Doctors Without Borders program, so I'm... desperate for a good club doc," he told her, scratching the back of his head nervously.

"Desperate for a good doctor, or desperate for *that* doctor?" I instigated, hoping to force the words out of the man myself.

He gave me a cutting look, but Celia paid no mind.

"If you think I can make Emory O'Connor do anything—" Celia started.

"No, she's just as hard headed as you are. But she's indebted to Zerkos, and she'll go— or stay—where he tells her to."

"I'll see what I can do, Lobito." She reached up on the tips of her toes and placed a kiss to his cheek before he turned around and walked into the mass of leather vests congregated in a circle.

I'd kind of miss the bastard.

And I'd never fucking tell him that.

From the outside looking in, it reminded me of when loving parents dropped their kid off at college and stuck around that first day just to make sure they were settling in okay. Now César would be packing up and heading thousands of miles back to Grimm's Reach, because she had proved she could make it on her own.

"What do you need?" I turned her towards me, wiping a rogue tear that fell from the corner of her eye.

"I need to change out of these clothes, I need a torta like nobody's business, and I need to squeeze the truth out of that ugly pendejo," she said, looking up at me. "In that order."

"And the villa?" Zerkos asked.

"Let it burn, there's another home further south, away from the city. It's smaller, but since The Diablos are gone it'll be just big enough for us all," she explained. "There's another villa adjacent to the property and the Crows can house there."

"Send me the address," Ronan said, casually tossing the keys to Santos.

"Where are you going?" he asked him.

"To get the lady her torta. I'll meet you there." He smirked, and she leaned into him and pressed a kiss to the corner of his lip before turning to Santos and changing her expression into a frown.

"You had to blow up the fucking Mastretta?" she chastised him, flicking her hand in the air to wave him off.

"You ran off like you have no regard for your own safety." He scowled, raising his voice back at her.

Oh. This was going to be an actual argument.

"Because I knew if you went in there, I'd have to worry about whether or not you were going to come out alive too," she yelled back, stepping up to him and getting as much in his face as she could, considering her height.

"So that's how this works? You get to decide whether you live or die while you put us on a shelf to look at us, and keep us safe?"

I spaced myself from them, unsure if this was a "we" thing or a "they" thing. I saw both sides of the argument, and for that reason alone I knew I needed to get the fuck out of here before either of them tried to drag me into their corner.

"At least then I don't have to go through the pain of thinking I'm going to lose any of you all over again. If you're waiting for an apology, it's not going to come from me Santito." She emphasized the nickname like she wasn't happy to be saying it at all.

"Kane, are you not going to say anything?" Santos called out to me, ruining my plans to try to stay Switzerland for this entire thing.

"Uh, well... I mean..." I scratched my head anxiously, "She was handling herself pretty well all on her own. She didn't need me." He didn't like that, scowling deeper at my response. "What? She doesn't need any of us dude."

She laughed, forcing the expression on his face to harden and the scowl on his forehead to deepen.

"Let me remind you of the week she spent in that Bratva cage. Let me remind you she was drugged, starved, and sold *twice*. And maybe you forgot but I had to spend an entire week watching her get mouth raped by my own fucking cousin. When it comes to the four of us, the three of us die before she ever gets hurt, *that* shouldn't be a hard rule to follow." Santos was rarely the type to yell, hardly the kind to verbalize so clearly why he was upset.

He never talked about what happened in that basement. Chalked it all up to it being *her* experience even though he was the one bearing most of the visible scars. She'd been marred by it too, but they were both processing it on such opposite ends of the spectrum that it was easy to forget they went through it together.

Like everything that came her way *made* her who she was, no matter how awful or painful it might have been. While for him it was ripping him apart. He stormed away, heading towards the several options of cars that had been left behind. Her expression had deflated to one full of pain and remorse.

I sighed heavily, dropping my shoulders before pulling her in again to place a kiss on the top of her head.

"Where the fuck are you going?" she asked as I turned away from her.

"I'm gonna see if Zerkos is still around for me to catch a ride with him. You should go with Santos," I told her, knowing damn well I was risking sliding onto her bad side.

Her nostrils flared and she stared up at me through furrowed eyebrows.

"I'm not good at saying the right things. I don't even know how to fix this," she confessed, making me chuckle.

"Sunshine, you're hot as hell and twice as stubborn, but you're right, your communication skills are shit. Get in the car with Santos if you want a ride to your new home," I told her, dropping my tone into that serious one I rarely took with her.

"That's not fair."

"Tough, you wanted three guys, you gotta take care of the fragile little egos that come with them too." I pushed her in the direction he'd walked off to before I ran off to find Ronan, hoping he hadn't left me behind yet.

27

Santos

"I'm sorry," she said after five minutes of driving in silence.

"No you're not," I answered.

"You're right, I'm not."

"And you'd probably do it again too, if given the chance," I added, turning my head just in time to get a glimpse of her biting her lip like I really knew her too well for her own good.

"I guess after watching my family go through so much pain, so much violence, I thought I was doing the right thing by prioritizing your safety above everything. The three of you are my family." She shrugged, looking out the window while fidgeting with her nails.

"What do you think would happen to the three of us if he had hurt you? If he had killed you?" I asked.

"What would happen to me if it was the other way around?" She raised her voice.

I sighed.

"Stop trying to leave me all alone in this world," she chastised.

"That's not what I'm trying to do," I gritted out.

"And what would you have done had I taken you up there with me?" she asked.

"I would have k—"

"Killed that motherfucker," she interrupted, nodding like I was just so damn obvious. "You see the problem with that yet?"

"I do," I admitted begrudgingly. "But my wanting to protect you isn't because I don't think you can't protect yourself. It's because you've been doing it for so long. Don't you think it's time to let someone else take a turn?"

"Take a turn?" she asked.

"You've been looking over your shoulder for fifteen years, morena. Let us watch your back now. Can you do that?" I asked, her shoulders sagging like she was relieved.

"I can do that." She nodded, wrapping her hand over mine and squeezing.

"You can't keep running into the mouth of danger by yourself every time. It drives me fucking insane. Maybe you've forgotten that we do things together, but it's the reason why the three of us are still alive. Okay?"

"Okay." She nodded, her eyes burning straight into mine.

"Thank you." I dropped my hand to her thigh where her fancy dress had been ripped to shreds, exposing her bare leg. There was nothing like feeling her hot skin under my touch. "Did he hurt you?"

"He banged my head up pretty good." She rubbed the back of her head. "But I'll survive."

"Let me see." I told her, but she shook her head.

"You're driving."

"Let me see!" I stepped on the break, forcing the car into a screeching halt.

The smell of burnt rubber filled the car and she rushed to slide her window up, but it was too late.

"You're insane! What are you doing?" She laughed as I pulled her off her seat and folded her over the middle console so that her head was on my lap.

She tried to push off of me, but I grabbed the back of her neck and pinned her down.

"Stay still, I want to make sure you're okay." I ran my fingers through her scalp gently, feeling for anything possibly concerning.

She relaxed her head onto my lap, despite her face being directly on my dick aside from the thin layer of fabric separating us from each other. There were some pretty good bumps and a small scratch that had bled and already dried up around her hair, but considering she wasn't even complaining from the pain, it didn't seem serious.

"See, all fine," she said sarcastically with her mouth plastered onto the crotch of my pants.

"Not all fine," I grumbled, taking my foot off the break and driving on once again.

"Then let me make it better," she said with a honeyed tone to her voice, cupping my dick through my pants and giving it a squeeze.

I could feel her hot breath practically on my cock through the fabric of the designer suit she had me in. She unzipped me, way too fucking slowly, and the anticipation alone engorged my erection further.

"Oh fuck, morena," I said just as her hand reached inside my pants, the soft skin of her dainty palms squeezing around my shaft and pulling it free.

"Pay attention to the road," she reminded me, each word sending goosebumps down my spine as her exhale tickled the overly sensitive skin.

"Then hurry up and put your mouth on me." I forced her head back down, drawing a yelp from her.

Her lips wrapped around the head of my cock, barely any pressure as she swirled her tongue around, making me nearly forget about the road when she swallowed me down. The heat of her mouth was almost enough to make me come, but the way she moved her tongue around each bar of my piercings was even more intense.

I groaned, a bolt of pleasure running up my spine every time she relaxed and took me all the way down the back of her throat. She picked up speed, her saliva dripping all over my cock while her head bobbed up and down my lap.

How many men would ever get to say they got road head by the baddest cártel queen to ever live?

Her fingers wrapped around the base of my dick. She squeezed and tugged using her own spit as lube while she gagged down my cock with more than audible moans. I released my grip on her hair and trailed my fingers down her back, cupping her ass.

It was sticking up in the air, perfectly taunting me in the reflection of the passenger window. I lifted my hand up and dropped it down with a hard smack. She moaned a deep guttural sound that vibrated from her chest down to my balls.

"Fuck. That mouth." I closed my eyes for a split second, forgetting the road.

She was slobbering more now, one hand gripping my thigh for support with the kind of pressure that would leave a mark. The other hand rolled my balls in her palm, she kneaded them softly, playing with them in her hand while she continued to slide up and down my shaft. I lifted my hand up and struck down once more eliciting a grunt of pleasure from her.

I slid my hand through the rips in the fabric of her dress, letting my fingers roam under the elastic of her underwear. Her back arched further, her ass sticking up higher somehow as she reached for more of my touch. I gave her juicy ass one final squeeze before traveling further down, feeling the slickness pooling between her legs. She was so goddamn wet and it was just from sucking me off.

"Do you want me inside you?" I whispered.

She nodded, mumbling some incoherent bullshit with my cock still in her mouth.

"Fuck," I moaned, closing my eyes again before remembering it was up to me to keep us alive.

I pushed my fingers inside her, a welcome whimper from within her chest greeted me just as I made my way into her tight, drenched cunt. She groaned, the vibrations making my toes curl until I couldn't fight the inevitable any longer.

"I'm gonna come," I warned her, but she didn't let up, using my words as fuel and moving faster, sucking even harder than before like she was going to pull my soul out through my cock.

I'd never fought harder in my life to keep my eyes open, the dark of the night and the weak headlights of the car we'd stolen were proving to be enough of a challenge. Receiving the hottest blowjob known to man definitely turned the game up to hard mode.

I pulled my fingers out from inside her, drawing a disappointed grunt from her before forcing a squeal once I gripped the back of her neck and shoved her as far down my cock as possible. I moved her up and down my length, feeling my core tighten and my balls drawing tighter the closer I got to my release. I took the right turn into the address she'd plugged into the navigation system, peeling hard through the gravel driveway before pulling the emergency break just as I emptied myself down her throat.

She lifted her head up slowly, wiping her lips with the back of her hands before giving me a devilishly sinful look. She then looked past me to my window, and she settled into a proud smirk that spread to her eyes with a dangerous glow.

I turned my head to see Ronan standing next to my window and surely there Kane was on the other side of hers. He opened her door, completely devouring her with his eyes before he opened his mouth to speak.

"Damn sunshine, there's a puddle on the seat," he commented, pulling her by the waist and tossing her over his shoulder.

"I see you've made up," Ronan said with a smirk, extending his hand to me to help me out of the car.

"She said sorry." I grinned back.

"Why do I not believe that?" He laughed.

"She said it in her own way." I followed Mateo into what would now be our new home.

She said it was smaller, and in comparison to the villa it *was,* but for some reason I had been expecting a house.

It wasn't.

It was just a smaller mansion.

She was yelling something at Mateo and pounding her fists on his back.

"What's the problem?" Zerkos asked, catching up to them.

"She's mad because I told her I'd lock her up if she wouldn't take the night off." Kane smirked.

"I need to talk to Ignacio," she shouted.

"He'll be there in the morning, sunshine," he said calmly, taking her further into the house as if their head start had already given him all the time he needed to get accustomed to what would be our new home.

"He's not wrong, beautiful. Give Emory some time to patch him up, get his adrenaline back down so that you can cause him more damage tomorrow," Ronan told her.

Mateo dropped her to her feet in the kitchen, her disappointment was more than evident.

"I've waited so long for this," she told them both, clenching her fists tightly.

"So what's a few more hours?" Zerkos asked her. "Get some rest, go in there with a clear head so you don't make any rash decisions just because you're thirsty for revenge."

"It's not in me to be patient." She crossed her arms over her chest, jaw clenched tight.

"Maybe we can distract you then."

"Unlikely, I'm wound up and there's nothing I want more than to make him pay," she snipped at us, teeth bared like she wasn't taking no for an answer.

"Nothing?" Ronan looked at her questioningly, stepping towards her way too slowly.

She shook her head to confirm. His hand reached up to cup the side of her face, his thumb brushing down her lip before he pulled her to him and locked his lips around hers.

"Then I'll go kill him for you so you can get some adequate rest." He smirked, pulling away from her.

She shoved him playfully. "You're a pain in my ass Ronan."

"And I'll continue to be that till the day one of us dies, flower." He reached over the counter pulling a large paper bag and began distributing the tortas wrapped in aluminum foil to each of us as we gathered around the kitchen for our first meal in our new home.

28

Celia

I brushed my hand over the black Armani two-piece suit I paired with red bottomed overpriced heels. I couldn't deny how much better expensive clothes felt than my normal jeans and T-shirt attire. "Finally... you show your face," Ignacio groaned from his restraints.

He didn't look nearly as bad as he seemed to be last night, which made me wonder if I should have just killed him instead.

"It was a big night. Had to move into a new house and everything. Who knew the villa could burn down twice?" I mused casually.

"You won't get anything out of me," he spat out.

"Who says I want anything from you? Maybe I'm just going to make you my plaything until your body gives out from the pain. You're a bit expired viejo, I don't think you can take much these days." I walked by the metal table, running my fingers over all the surgical steel tools and torture devices.

"You should have come to me Celia, we could have done this together."

"Together? You mean after you killed my mamá, I should have come to you for help?" I laughed. "That's rich."

"I didn't kill Jamila." He pulled against his restraints angrily.

"That's not even a worthwhile lie. Jamila hated me. If you expected her death to devastate me, you were hurting the wrong sister."

"I didn't kill Jamila!" he screamed again. "Your hermana lost her shit and went out there after I left her with Guillermo. I would have never hurt Jamila on purpose," he gritted out.

I lifted an eyebrow.

Curious.

Maybe I did want something from him.

"Tío. Do you have more secrets for me now?" I tilted my head, pulling up a chair and sitting down casually as I waited.

There was no gossip better than family dirt, it was a Latin American right of passage, after all. If you came from Indigenous ancestors, we were well accustomed to passing stories down as history.

There was always time for the chisme.

"I should have been the one to marry her. She was *mine*. We had been together for years when Augustin Ortíz killed his own son and then forced her to marry my brother in an attempt to keep his hand in the business."

"And my mamá just went eagerly? The obedient little pawn she was?" I asked, unsure if I should even bother believing the words coming from his mouth.

"Your mother was as ruthless as you are. You think you're a killer because you're a Flores? Nah Celia, that's the Ortíz blood running through your veins. She orchestrated the whole thing, killed your abuelo execution style in front of your papá's men and told them they followed Rafa now. Made a big show of that ledger full of bought secrets too before she made it disappear from the face of the planet."

"Seems like she wasn't right for a cobarde hijo de la chingada like you then. You make it sound like she was perfect for my papá."

"She *was*. Then he put her fire out, kept her in the background, away from any decisions until she settled for the realization that she'd lost the very thing she'd dirtied her hands for. I would have stoked her flames. We would have controlled this country together." His upper lip twitched angrily.

"But instead, you let my psychotic revenge fueled sister kill her instead. For what? To send a message to me?"

"I told you; I didn't have a hand in it. Your sister is a loose fucking cannon. She makes bad calls up and down, she aligns herself with our enemies because she thinks she'll gain the upper hand. She's robbed me blind and used that money to pay my men to do Bratva bitch work." He spat onto the floor.

"So she *is* getting in with Sokolov?" I asked and his eyes hardened, as if he remembered this wasn't family social time and needed to stick to his promise not tell me anything.

I sighed, grabbing pliers and a rubber block about an inch in size off the table Mateo had left prepped for me. I stepped one foot directly in front of the other until I found myself across from him.

"Abre la boca or I'll pry it open with a hot knife," I promised. He didn't dare to disobey, opening without hesitation just wide enough so that I could stick the rubber block inside his mouth.

I pinched the plyers shut around his back molar, putting one high heeled Louboutin on the wall for leverage. It wasn't as easy to pry a man's tooth out without the adrenaline of survival running through your veins. But he didn't deserve easy, and I relished every pained grunt out of his chest until the tooth finally came loose.

His screams echoed through the dungeon walls.

"I asked if she was getting in with Sokolov." I pulled the rubber block out of his mouth.

"Getting in? She's nice and cozy in their family tree now. She's made arrangements to marry his eldest son." He spat out a wad of blood onto the ground.

"Since when?" I asked, trying to figure out how long my sister may have been responsible for my misfortunes.

"A year now?"

"But she was with Guillermo Álvarez," I said, knowing that what I'd seen between them in that basement was much more than something casual.

"Clever zorra that one. Smart enough to understand just exactly how to use her pussy to get far in this world. She kept Guillermo in line for me, made sure he didn't get too big for his own britches. I guess your papá didn't teach you every lesson you needed."

"Except now it looks like she's the big fish in your pond and she's about to swallow you up tío." I clucked my tongue, "all this blood and war just to hand México over to the Russians?"

He growled with disapproval but we both knew I was right.

Carolina was a garbage truck full of hot trash waiting to unload.

But she was my fucking sister.

Even if she was a pendeja.

"We can stop her together," he labored out.

"I can stop her myself," I told him, shoving the block back inside his mouth, pulling another molar out with a bit more ease this time.

I didn't give him time to mourn his tooth before jamming the pliers back and finding the next addition to my collection. One by one I pulled out his remaining teeth, all aside from the few bits and pieces that were barely hanging on in the front from my previous assault. I was sweating, my hands aching and sore by the time I finished. His head hung from his neck, blood dripping from his open mouth as he moaned and shivered from the pain.

"I gave your papá the gift of an easy death." he mumbled with difficulty.

"I am not my papá. I am the woman both of you helped to create, and you *will* feel the full force of my wrath. I will give you the death you deserve. Nothing more, nothing less."

"Where are you going?" he shouted at me as I turned to leave.

"To beat some sense into my sister."

He laughed like it was an outrageous thought.

"That's not how this ends, sobrina. It ends in blood. It always does."

"I'm better than you. I decide how this ends," I said, turning on my heels.

"You can't leave me here like this Celia," he moaned, and I laughed darkly.

"Tío, that's exactly what I'll be doing. And I'll keep you alive, and I'll come down here and inflict pain on you whenever you cross my mind, until the day I die. Unless you bore me, then maybe I could be persuaded to forget to feed you and put an end to your misery."

He groaned, yanking at his chains and making a loud racket.

I ignored him, placing the pliers back on the table and leaving the torture chamber, striding past each cell until I entered the control center of the dungeons. I gave a smirk and a nod to Taylor Constance and she returned me a beaming smile.

"How are you settling in?" I asked her.

"Well, you pay better than Ronan and considering, regardless of location, I end up between four walls with a computer for a window, I'm finding myself right at home." She laughed.

"Something about having you watching over us makes me feel warm and safe inside," I told her.

"Well, good thing I'm always watching then," she said, raising her eyebrows up suggestively, making me laugh.

"Let me know if you need anything, seriously. I'm grateful you're here. I'm grateful for all that you've done," I told her, implying that I had been made aware that if it weren't for her, Ronan would be dead right now.

"Even death can't separate me from those fuckers, Celia. I'm afraid you're stuck with me." She smiled, assuring me I had no debt to her because her loyalty was to my men.

Which was more than fine with me because their loyalty belonged to me.

"I consider it a privilege, so let me know if I can help you make yourself comfortable here."

"Just point me to a sexy woman who likes cars and I think I'll be just fine around these parts."

"I'll keep my eyes out," I told her, taking that as my cue to stop bothering her and let her continue her work.

She was already tracking down Sokolov for me, but now she was trying to find Carolina too. She really was the best at what she did, and I was thankful every day to have her on my side. My heels clicked over the smooth concrete floor, and I sent a text to Mateo to let him know I'd be heading home from the dungeons.

"You're lighting a candle before we leave?" he asked as I held the match over the wick on the seven-day candle encased in glass.

"Yes, mi vida," I told him, pouring a fresh shot for La Madrina and dropping an unlit cigarette on her altar.

"What if it burns the house down?" The look on Mateo's face was so innocent and cute it made me smile.

"I promise you it won't." I grabbed my packed bag off the bed, but he ripped it from my hand to carry it himself.

"It could happen," he mumbled.

"She wouldn't do that to me." I assured him, knowing Santa Muerte took care of her children.

"Zerkos said the jet is loaded." His tone switched into business mode like it did anytime we talked about cártel related things.

It worked. All of us, doing this together. It somehow made sense, we were moving like a well-oiled machine, and I depended on my guys with my life. On top of that, I'd found myself a solid council who I trusted to call out my bullshit, *respectfully* of course. I was only so tolerable. I was counting all my blessings and I knew they would only keep coming if I let Death loose so she could play.

When you were exposed to darkness so young, it just became something you had to embrace inside yourself. I knew now the only way to not hate myself was to love even the worst parts of myself.

After all, they were the parts that had kept me alive all this time.

29

Celia

Between Susana's knowledge of her father's day to day life and Taylor's incredible tech-stalker skills it was a piece of cake pinpointing where we were likely to find Sokolov.

Because I'm a spiritual kind of pendeja, I thought it was quite symbolic to pick Friday at midnight, when he was sure to be at the very strip club he'd kept me prisoner in for nearly a week. The very place where he drugged me and sold me like cheap meat at the market. If I was lucky, I'd get to free some girls from that very same fate tonight.

Mateo's hand found mine in the backseat of the car, squeezing it tight and ignoring the nervous sweat as if it didn't bother him at all.

"Hey," he whispered nervously in my ear.

"Hmm?" I answered quietly so that the conversation stayed between the two of us.

"I can't promise to hold back when we go in there." He furrowed his eyebrows in the middle, creating a hard crease.

"His death belongs to me." I growled.

"No Sunshine, his death belongs to all of us. I watched helplessly while you almost died because of the drugs he pumped into your system. He killed my men." He didn't stand down.

"Mateo," I gritted out, hating having to get stern with him.

"How about this," he grinned dangerously, "first one to him gets the kill?" He raised his eyebrows with his proposal, and I tilted my head at an angle while I thought about it.

"No guns?" I asked.

"If that's what the lady wants, that's what the lady gets." He gave me a shameless smirk.

"Fletch and his team will be waiting at the other exits to cause distractions and take down some of their men. We should have plenty of time," Ronan said from the front, making eye contact in the rearview mirror.

"I need you to go down into that basement and free the girls that will be in there," I told him before turning to Santos in the passenger seat. "I need you to check the dressing rooms behind the stage for any girls getting ready to be sold."

"Aye aye, jefa." Santos gave me a two-finger salute.

We parked across the street and just as Ronan was opening his door to get out, I called him back to me.

"Ronan, there was a lion in that basement last time," I warned him.

"What?" he said with a laugh of disbelief.

I was high as hell, but I remembered very vividly what I'd seen. The hot breath on my back and the sharp claws scratching against the smooth concrete floor with an obnoxious sound.

I remembered the bird's warning.

"Just be careful, okay?" I told him.

He turned back fully, reaching for me and pulling me into him despite the middle console standing as a barrier between us. His lips parted against mine, his tongue raking softly against my own for just a brief moment before he withdrew from me, leaving me high and needy for more.

"Focus, morena." Santos growled like he didn't approve of Ronan's distraction.

We got out of the car, the men strapped on their Kevlar vests and double checked all of their weapons. Ronan handed me a vest and I raised an eyebrow at him.

"I don't need that," I reassured him.

"Oh, have you become bulletproof in the last twelve years?" he said with a sarcastic tone.

"I'm not afraid to die," I explained.

His jaw ticked with anger, the scowl forming deep into his forehead.

"Put the fucking vest on, Celia." He pushed it into my chest. "I'm getting real sick of this shit." He dropped it from his hold, forcing me to clutch it fast to keep it from falling on the ground.

I turned to Mateo and gave him a questioning look, hoping he could help me with the angry blonde giant.

"I don't think you realize it, Sunshine, but every time you disregard your life, it feels like you're saying we aren't enough for you to want to do your best to stay," he said with deflated energy, scratching his head and walking ahead of me.

I sighed, turning to see Santos still standing next to me.

"What, you're not going to say something too?" I raised my voice, preparing to snap.

"No. I get it," he said, not bothering to explain himself.

He was gonna make me work for it.

"You get it?" I asked.

"Yeah. You think as long as we're safe it doesn't matter what happens to you. I get it because that's how I feel about you, how I feel about them. I'd give my life a hundred times over to make sure you three have the happy ending you deserve." He started walking away. "But if you take that vest off, I'll be taking mine off too. If you die, I die too," he said without looking back.

Pendejada.

I slipped on the vest and ran after them, buttoning my coat over the obnoxiously thick Kevlar.

"Espérense pendejos," I shouted. The insult had Ronan stopping in his tracks abruptly forcing me to slam into the concrete wall that was his body.

He turned to face me, a scowl on his face that loosened once he eyed me up and down and appreciated that I'd listened to his demands.

"Thank you," he whispered into my mouth, gripping my jaw with one hand and forcing me on the tips of my toes in order to collect the kiss from him.

"One more thing," I said, forcing a single eyebrow to raise up from him.

He didn't ask, he just waited.

"There was a bird in that basement." His expression became even more confused. "If he's still there. I want him," I told him, not leaving room for discussion.

"Do you want the lion too?" Mateo laughed.

I clucked my tongue in annoyance as I shoved him to the side. The four of us broke up and headed for separate entrances.

"How do you plan to get to Sokolov without drawing attention to yourself?" Mateo asked.

I gave him a knowing tilt of my head without explaining anything.

"Sunshine, I promise you if he sees an inch of your body tonight, he dies by my hands." His expression was serious, fully devoid of humor.

"I guess we shall see." I winked, picking up the pace and walking ahead of him.

I slipped on my coat and nervously patted at it after fastening the buttons, hoping the vest was well hidden underneath. Mateo slipped on his suit jacket and did the same. It was bulky as hell, but these idiots weren't paying enough attention. They didn't know we were coming.

That alone would be their ending.

We paid our cover fee and walked in through the front door, the bouncer unchaining the velvet lined rope after checking our fake IDs matched the names on the list that Taylor had hacked into and gotten us on. I set off the metal detector just as I had expected, but I stuck my boots out, letting the metal buckles clink loudly to justify the alarm. The guard ran the hand paddle over my body, seemingly satisfied when it only sounded after he brought it down to my boot buckles once again and let us go.

The purple velvet covering every inch of the place smelled of stale smoke and none of the hanging neon lights matched. I was overly made up, playing the part of arm candy while Mateo had the ID of some well-to-do billionaire Taylor had conjured up for him and put on the club's VIP list.

The same list all the vile men who came here to purchase women were on. We walked through dark halls together while some less than cheery bikini-clad server led us to the area where the show would be.

Calling it a show made my stomach churn.

Flashes of memories cut through my mind like shards of glass, broken and fragmented from the drugs they'd pumped into my body after days of starving me. I slowed down, palms sweating as I realized what killing Allisher Sokolov would mean to me.

A freedom in a way.

The death of Cecilia.

The death of everything I had pretended to be while running away from who I truly was. The death of an entire world inside of me really, according to Yevtushenko.

We had been sitting at our booth for less than two minutes before a cocktail waitress came by to get our orders. Mateo asked for a soda with lime, she eyed him suspiciously but jotted it down anyway.

"Fortaleza?" I asked, and she nodded her head.

I held up two fingers indicating I wanted a double and she turned away to fetch our drinks. The stage lights flashed on just as she set our glasses in front of us. I reached for the glass, ready to put the straw in my mouth but Mateo covered the top of the glass with his hand, shaking his head at me.

"Not here."

I didn't have to ask why. There were a million reasons, and though I wanted a drink to calm my nerves I also knew I needed to do this with a clear head. Clean, fast, and viciously.

And there was no way I was gonna beat Mateo to him if I was drunk.

"I'm going to the bathroom, text me if things start to seem off," I whispered in his ear, sliding past him on the booth and feeling his hands cup my ass while I slid by.

I ignored his low growl, walking past all the other tables and not taking notice of the disgusting filth who assumed the shape of men, waiting to buy a girl. The cocktail waitress pointed the women's bathroom out to me and thankfully I seemed to be the only one in the building who wasn't already working here.

It was totally empty.

I took off my coat, removing the bullet proof vest and dropping it to the ground.

Sorry boys.

Change of plans.

I unzipped my dress from the side and stepped out of it, folding it neatly and shoving it into a corner with the vest knowing damn well that if *anything* went right tonight, the chances of me making it back here to collect my belongings were slim.

Charged it to the game.

A worthwhile offering in exchange for Sokolov's blood.

I took one last look in the mirror, fluffing up my heavy hair and wiping stray lipstick from the corner of my mouth. I was in that same matching black lingerie that all the girls in this building were wearing, well at least something close enough that no man would be able to tell the difference.

I patted the outside of my boot, feeling for the knife I'd hidden inside. I didn't need a gun for this. I would have to do it from up close. I always knew that I would have to, and in a way, I needed that. Now I just needed to get to the boss man.

I slipped my hand into my bra, feeling for the tiny zip lock bag that contained my secret weapon for tonight. I took a deep breath and sent a silent prayer to Santisima. I walked out of the bathroom, turning back into the hallway and headed towards the stage when a cocktail waitress passed by me with a single drink on her tray.

"Is that for the boss?" I stuck my arm out in front of her and she looked at me with an anxious and hesitant expression.

"He said you were taking too long, asked me to come get it for him myself. Probably better you don't bother him right now unless—"

"No, take it!" She pushed the circular tray towards me, and I nodded, giving a sympathetic smile while she headed back towards the main area with the stage.

I rushed down the hallway, unsure which one of the doors would be Sokolov's but knowing I had a limited amount of time to find him. I pulled the baggy from my tit-pocket and opened it up, pouring the powder into the drink and stirring it with my finger until it dissolved into the vodka clear liquid once again.

Alright. Deep breath, he's just a man. All men can be killed, that's the one thing they all have in common. I picked the door all the way at the end of the hall, knowing it would be easier to go back the way I came if someone caught me.

But fate was good to me now.

After all, the bitch knew she owed me for a lifetime of pain.

He sat in his leather chair behind a desk, as if he were doing the most important work in this ever elite establishment. He was busy on his phone, not bothering to look up as I set the heavy glass in front of him.

"Your drink," I said, turning around and reaching for the door handle.

"You're new," he said, making me question whether it was a statement or if he was waiting for me to confirm.

Was he so well involved in his business that he would know every bar girl walking around here in his cheap underwear he bought by the masses? Would he recognize my face when I turned around? Would he remember me?

"Y-yes," I answered nervously, turning around and smiling through pressed lips.

"All the new girls have to give me a dance. You haven't given me one yet." He licked his lips, staring me up and down as he put his phone on the desk.

Just drink the fucking vodka pendejo.

"W-well, I'm working," I blurted out hoping it would be enough to thwart any suspicion.

"You work for *me*," he reminded me. "What's your name?" he asked.

"Susan." I smiled, remembering his younger daughter's name was similar and watching to see if there was any change in his expression.

Nothing.

"Dance, Susan. Remind me why I keep you well fed and paid." He sat back into the chair, forcing it to recline a bit.

He turned up the volume of the small speaker that sat on the corner of his desk, the same early 2000s soft metal playing out on the main area crackled from it. I swayed my hips from side to side, walking towards him one foot at a time between sensual movements that went along with the beat. I ran my hands through my hair before dropping them down to my chest.

If he were any other man, I'd be riddled with insecurities and shaking from self-consciousness. But he wasn't going to survive to tell the tale of the Latina who couldn't dance well, and the closer I got the more I realized that wasn't what he was thinking at all. He licked his lips in a suggestive way and spun his chair to the side, away from his desk to give me room to climb over him.

I turned around and folded in half, touching my ankles and shaking my ass directly in his face while he made low hums of approval. The song switched to *Aerosmith's* 'Walk This Way' just as he pressed his face to my crack and took a real-time grown man sniff.

I paused, mortified before continuing to move my hips like I wasn't eighteen kinds of uncomfortable. I flinched at the feel of his hands as they gripped my cheeks and squeezed hard just as I came back up.

"You better get used to men touching you sweetheart," he said in his sharp accent. "Otherwise you'll be back on the streets soon," he threatened, letting me know that even the employees in this hellscape were hardly there by choice.

I turned to face him, knowing I was risking him recognizing me by giving him the time to stare, but not once did his eyes move up from my chest even when I climbed onto his lap to straddle him. I took the opportunity to grab his glass from the table, grinding onto his erection to keep him focused on me until I poured it into his mouth.

He moaned, swallowing the drink as I licked up droplets from the corner of his lips hoping it wouldn't be enough to fuck me up on the drug. His hands ran up my sides and he cupped my breasts over my bra, squeezing too hard without care. I fought a wince, biding my time until the heroin kicked into his system.

I had no idea how long it would take, but I trusted Dominico when he said he gave me enough to tame a lion. Sokolov wasn't a lion but I knew his obsession with using the drug meant he not only peddled it himself, he favored it. I knew the drug world well, and I wasn't above it. I knew as the leader of the cártel I would suffer serious losses if I refused to distribute them.

The thing was… drugs weren't the problem.

It was society's response to it. It was the way addiction was handled with either a prison sentence or death. People like Sokolov depended on addicts falling prey to these drugs so that he could keep them in his vicious cycle of imprisonment. I saw the look in the cocktail waitress' eyes when I told her the boss was angry.

Sure there was fear, but the hazy look in her stare told me she wasn't fully here either. I remembered the feeling well. The song switched again to something with a hard beat that I didn't recognize, and the Russian crime lord pulled me closer against him, pushing my hips down into his unimpressively semi-soft erection. My legs dropped from the sides of the chair, so I arched my back, pressing my tits into his face to distract him from my hands reaching into my boot for my knife.

His eyes drooped and he leaned his head back into the chair, but in the same motion it fell down like it was too heavy for him to control. I smirked. *Gracias Dominico.* Maybe it was daddy issues, but in a way, I seemed to find a paternal-type bond through him. One that didn't require lessons in a torture chamber.

I wasn't angry at my papá. He did what he thought was right, and in a way, all his *teachings* helped me to survive, molded me to become who I am today. But I also knew it was my duty to make sure a child was never robbed of their innocence in the way that I was. President Ramírez's request wasn't outrageous, and it was something I intended to do myself once I had been fully established as the *sole* head of the cártel.

I gripped his short blond hair tightly in between my fingers and yanked his head up, his eyes struggling to blink open as I brought my face as close to his as possible.

"Te acuerdas de mi?" I purred into his ear while looking into his eyes and waiting for the acknowledgement to flash through them.

His eyes narrowed as he tried to piece together who I was but either he was too high from the possibly lethal dose of heroin I'd drugged him with, or I'd really just been a blip in his life. I still had nightmares from his cage and the pendejo couldn't even be bothered to remember my face.

"Where is Carolina Flores?" I gritted out, yanking his head hard with one hand while the other fished inside my boot for the knife.

Finally that spark of recognition lit up in his pupils, and just then gunshots rang out outside the door.

30

Mateo

She'd been gone way too long, and rather than believing she somehow might be in trouble, I had a feeling that she'd gone out of her way to find trouble herself. She just couldn't wait, she wanted to see his death and she wanted it by her hands.

As much as I wanted to see the bastard bleed under me I knew it was her right just the same, if not more. I wasn't angry that she wanted it that badly, I was angry that she kept risking her life so carelessly. We all were.

I flipped up my phone and texted Santos;

ME: Celia just went rogue. May need backup.
Santos: Rgr.

I casually walked through the main area into a narrow hallway with a lit up bathroom sign. I pushed through the women's bathroom to see if I could find her, ducking low to search for feet but all I could see was a pile of clothes in one corner. I pushed the stall open and sure as shit it was her clothes and her bulletproof vest.

Goddamnit.

Just as I exited the bathroom some big guy walked past me and made his way to the end of the hall, standing post in front of a door. Well, well well, thanks for making it easy for me pal. As I walked closer his face turned with curiosity, like he wasn't sure if I actually had the audacity to square up to a man his size.

I remembered his face. I remembered him in that room when Celia was tied up and drugged after being sold to us.

So I wouldn't feel so bad about killing him to get to her.

"Oh, hey big guy," I cooed out with my hands raised up in the air to the scarred-up, ten-foot tall motherfucker guarding what was surely Sokolov's door. "Remember me?"

He tilted his head and his hand twitched like he was thinking of reaching for his gun. But I was faster, ducking under and swiping my feet below him. He fell to the ground with a hard thud, practically shaking the foundation of the old building. I slammed my heel into his wrist, immobilizing his hand and reaching for his weapon first before tossing it away.

The lady said no guns.

"I'll kill you," he spat out before I felt the weight of his foot against my chest that sent me flying against the wall.

I pushed myself up, watching his eyes slowly shift to the gun several feet away.

No sir.

I barrel rammed into his stomach, punching over and over, each time releasing pained cries from the Bratva lackey. In one quick move he threw me to the ground, the taste of blood filling my mouth and pain shooting through my body from the force of the impact. He stood, a pissed off look on his face that said he considered me annoying at best.

He was too big for us to do this standing.

I knew my odds off the ground with a man this size.

This time I beckoned him, flipping my palms up and making a 'come here' gesture to taunt him. He scowled, and like an angry bull, he charged. But before he could crash into me, I dropped to the floor and swiped my feet over his ankles again, knocking him off balance.

I didn't delay, crawling on top of him and practically tea-bagging the son of a bitch as I laid my fists into his face repeatedly. His fists pummeled into my side, each one a heavy boulder against my body forcing me to spit blood with every hit. I ignored them, gripping his head tightly in my hand and despite his yelling and his savage strikes,

I slowly fought against his muscles as I turned his head to the side.

He lifted his top half off the ground, grasping at my arms to stop me but giving me just the space I needed to turn his head by force. It wasn't easy, a man that large had muscles in his neck that were bigger than my wrists. I dug my fingers into his face, fighting against him as he screamed and fought me until I heard the final crack, severing his spinal cord and making him go limp. I let go of his head, struggling to stand up from overexertion and pain. I stumbled towards the wall, resting on it as I caught my breath.

It was the sound of the guns firing behind me that catapulted me back into action, grabbing the gun from the ground and pushing open the door Sokolov's man was guarding. My jaw clenched tight at the scene I'd walked into. Celia's face jerked to the side with shock and eyes went wide at the sight of me. A smile stretched over her face from ear to scar as the man's blood pooled around her hand. It dripped down her arms, her chest, and over her legs.

She was straddled over an older man with silver hair and a tracksuit while wearing nothing but lingerie, one hand gripping his hair tightly while the other held a dagger plunged deep into his mouth from the bottom of his chin.

Allisher Sokolov.

Or it *was* him once.

"You're impossible." I shook my head, closing the door behind me.

"Are you mad at me?" she asked, her expression turning sweet and innocent.

"You're impossible, sunshine," I repeated, pulling her off of him and covering her with my suit jacket. "Seems like the whole gang's inside now, we need to get the fuck out of here," I told her, pulling the knife out from his chin and shoving it into his temple with ease as the blood poured out of his neck.

"Did you make contact with Ronan and Santos?" she asked,

"Who do you think is out there making all that noise?" I pulled the clip out of the dead Russian's gun to check how many bullets were left.

Eight.

I'd have to make do.

"Check him for a weapon," I told her. She nodded, patting Sokolov down and fishing inside the inner breast pocket of his jacket before pulling out a 9mm Luger.

"Stay behind me," I said, putting my arm out in front of her when she tried getting past me to open up the door.

She gave me a look full of sharp knives.

"If you're feeling suicidal, let me know sunshine. I'll take you out myself and do it quick so it's painless. Now get behind me before I knock your ass out and carry you over my shoulder." She looked at me with her mouth gaped open like she couldn't believe I was taking this tone with her, but I was finally starting to understand why Zerkos handled her the way he did.

She was a fucking brat, begging to push every boundary she came across and I wasn't sure if it was because she was aching for a punishment or because she simply didn't know how to live without conflict.

She smirked, gesturing her hand at the door to let me know she'd be a good girl from here on out. A voice message came in from Santos. It was hard to make out with all the noise, but I could hear broken up shouts as he panicked about finding Celia.

"I got her. Regroup outside," I sent back to him.

"I'm cornered. I need help." Santos' voice came in clearer on the next voice message.

"Where are you?" I sent back to him.

"Stuck inside the fucking DJ booth," Santos yelled into his speaker.

I gnawed on my cheek, looking back at Celia.

"Mateo," she warned, knowing exactly where my mind was going. "I swear on all that is—" I interrupted her, pulling her into my body and pressing my lips into hers roughly.

She responded, parting her lips for me and letting my tongue invade its way into her mouth. Her free hand ran up my chest, caressing the side of my cheek and raking through my hair as we deepened our kiss.

"Reina," I whispered into her ear, doing my best to pronounce it the same way I'd heard the others. "Please," I begged, pulling back and looking into her black eyes.

"I can't stay here, not knowing what's happening out there," she yelled, not holding back her emotions. "You can't keep me here, in the dark, with all those guns going off, just waiting for someone to rescue me." Her eyes welled up with tears but not a single one fell.

I knew what she meant when she said in the dark, she didn't mean the quality of the light in Sokolov's office. She was talking about history repeating itself, her traumas. She couldn't handle the idea of being helpless and blind to what was happening out there, while we, her family, might be in danger.

Fuck.

"Fletch, I need cover." I sent the audio message and waited for a response.

"Where you at boss?" he yelled over the background noise.

"Trying to make our way to the DJ booth."

I pulled her close behind me and opened the door to find Russians, cártel grunts, and stray Crows alike dead on the ground. Men hiding behind bodies and open doors shooting towards this end of the hallway. We couldn't go back the way we came.

"Run to that door on my count." I pointed to the door across the hall from us, it was only five or six feet away, but a bullet didn't care about that kind of distance.

It was still far enough to die getting there.

"One... Two... THREE!" I pushed her towards the door, barreling myself in front of her and hitting an incoming Bratva soldier dead smack in the chest with a bullet just as she pushed open the door to reveal the backstage area.

It was a complete clusterfuck out there—bodies lying on toppled tables, blood and booze dripping from every surface of the place. Any civilians were likely nice and dead at this point, not that there was much to feel guilty about.

Every fucker inside this place was here to buy a woman.

We gave our men one rule only.

Don't shoot the girls.

I pushed Celia against a corner, sheltering her from any Bratva asshole in the audience. That's when I noticed the three dancers huddled in the opposite end, using the blind spots in the stage to their advantage for cover. I put my index finger over my lips to signal them to stay quiet, and they nodded fearfully, crouching down further.

I could only hope that they had no reason to fear for their lives. Sokolov's men would have had no need to injure or kill any of the women who were working here, and our men weren't set out for that kind of mission. As long as they avoided a stray bullet, they could make it out of this.

Right now, I needed to focus on getting my best friend and keeping the woman we loved alive.

31

Ronan

They were supposed to be waiting outside, waiting for a signal or some word from us that it was time to go inside and wreak havoc on Sokolov's little slice of hell when I got the text from Kane that Celia had snuck off and was now missing.

"Let me find this stupid fucking bird, or she'll never let me live it down," I whispered into the phone, unsure if I was heading in the right direction in this pitch-black basement.

There was a dripping of a faucet somewhere in the distance, loud and constant enough that in the two minutes I'd been down here it was already driving me to the edge of madness. If anything was alive down here, it was certainly insane from it.

"I'm not waiting anymore Zerkos, I'm going in." Santos clicked off the line and I sent a voice message to Fletcher and Ethan to let them know it was time.

I pulled my glock out, just in case, and delved further into the dark abyss of the basement, kicking the bodies of the Bratva grunts who'd seen me breaking in through the window.

"Dirty slut," a kid's voice called out, couldn't have been more than ten years old.

My fury ripped through me, and I pounded my heels through the space, no longer afraid of who I'd find down here because I knew I'd rip through them in order to free the child that had found themselves stuck in Sokolov's grasp.

I pulled my phone out to shine the flashlight, trying to find the source of the voice and only seeing empty kennels stacked one on top of the other. If they weren't down here, then they likely were already up there, being sold off.

"Lion!" the kid yelled from behind me, but just as I spun to find the voice my light shined a mere foot away from the gigantic jungle cat asleep in the corner.

There was a heavy chain joined to the wall and it connected to a metal collar on its neck. In a matter of seconds my emotions ranged from pure unadulterated fear for my life like I'd never felt before, to feeling like the luckiest bastards alive.

That leash was all the friend I needed in this world right now.

I took a few steps back, my shoulders hitting against something and causing a loud rattling and wings flapping behind me. I sent my arm back just as I turned to see what I'd stumbled into, knocking what seemed to be a small bird cage off a table. My reflexes were faster than my own brain, catching it before it had a chance to fall and injure the parrot inside but not quick enough to stop it from having a full-on, aviary-style freak out.

There was no greater piss-your-pants type of moment like feeling the hot breath of a giant feline on your back. To hear the low growl of an animal you know you'd likely never be able to defend yourself against just seconds away from you. I jerked forward, diving onto the ground with the bird cage glued to my chest as the Lion rose to his hind feet, paws stretched up into the air while its leash kept it from coming any further.

Fucking Christ.

I was getting too lucky. Which meant it was going to run out soon. I rolled out from underneath him before he had a chance to drop his paws onto me and scrambled backwards. I shouldn't have been shocked, she warned me about the goddamn lion, but for some reason it seemed too outrageous to believe. Guns went off upstairs and I knew my time was being cut short. I could only hope Santos had been able to successfully free the girls that had been kept in these now empty cages before bullets began to fly up there.

"Slut!" The bird parroted out, relaxing me at the realization that the voice didn't belong to a child.

Was I more angry that I'd been sent on a mission to rescue a foul mouthed bird, or that said bird was now impeding me from heading straight into the fire myself? I backed up as much as possible from the roaring cat, getting away from the lead of his chain so I could finally turn my back to him and run. I took the basement stairs three at a time, pushing the door open with my shoulders to total chaos.

Our men had completely overrun the place from every entrance and exit, bullets flying through open air as Sokolov's grunts shot at us from every angle. I slipped back through the basement door, dropping the bird's cage on the ground.

"Alright little dude, I'll have to come back for you."

"Cocksucker!" the little shit cawed out like it understood me.

I pulled a second pistol from its holster and readied myself, opening the door and shooting first at the Bratvas standing just a few feet away from me. Soon as they dropped to the ground Ethan came charging towards me with a grin on his face like I'd just saved his life.

"There's a fucking bird on the other side of this door. Get it out of here," I told him.

"Are you fucking serious right now?" His eyebrows creased in the middle of his forehead.

"Deadly. That bird is fucking family to her." I gave him a flat stare before I turned and headed past the hallway, following the sounds of yelling and bullets flying.

Sokolov's men used the corpses of their patrons as shields while their fingers stayed glued to the triggers on their automatic rifles. I slid behind the bar, both guns ready to fire, but there was only one small waitress, covered in blood hidden among the bodies.

"Stay hidden okay?" I told her and she nodded her head. "It'll be over soon."

I peeked my head up above the bar to scan the room. There were five Bratva's shooting into the booth, too many of them for me to see who may be trapped in that corner. A bullet whizzed past my head just a hair away from my ear and I sank to the ground once more. Then I heard her scream.

Guns readied at the top of the bar before I raised my head up to see out again. I cleared a path for them, Mateo at her front and Fletcher on her six as they ran towards the DJ booth. I shot at the men surrounding it, taking two down so that Mateo could slip inside for protection.

I needed to make my way there. I hopped over the bar one bullet flying straight into a Bratva grunt's head, as I dropped my head just in time to avoid one to the brain myself. Celia shot three times, one bullet missing but the last two hitting the remainder of the men surrounding the DJ booth.

From another door, four more men ran out, their semi-automatics burning through the room at rapid speed. Fletcher was giving her cover and shooting at Sokolov's men hiding behind toppled cocktail tables as they ran towards the DJ booth to Mateo. The bullet hit Fletcher dead center in the forehead, his body falling limp in front of her. She didn't scream but her eyes went blank, wide and full of a terror I hadn't seen in her before.

She'd killed plenty of people before.

She'd been a child killing other children. She murdered innocents. She took the life of her own family. But she'd yet to see a good man die. One that had pledged to protect her, one that had fought for her and now alongside her.

I charged, dropping my body over hers as fast as I could, shielding her from the incoming rain of bullets as I laid on the ground on top of her.

"Are you hit?" I asked, crawling behind the DJ booth and pulling her into me.

She had that vacant look still on her face like she wasn't fully registering the chaos all around us.

"Baby, I need you present for this." I gave her cheek a hard tap and she blinked at me in shock.

"Fletcher—"

"Is dead," I confirmed. "We can mourn him later, we have to get the fuck out of here," I said it to her but it was meant for me.

I'd lost plenty of brothers in the middle of action. The battlefield wasn't the place for grieving unless you were prepared to drop into the grave as well.

"Okay," she whispered, shaking her head.

"If you're in the building, get the fuck out." Santos said into his phone, advising our men to head out.

"Sokolov?" I asked.

"He's dead," Mateo confirmed.

"Pluto?" she asked me with worry.

"Ethan got him out," I assured her, watching her shoulders relax.

"Any captives?" She asked.

"Four were tied up backstage. They're already loaded into the van," Santos answered.

"Let's roll the fuck out of here then." I reloaded my clips, tossing a gun to Mateo.

"Wait," she yelled, her eyes wide with a look I didn't recognize from her.

Worry.

"I love you. All of you pendejos."

I raked my fingers through her hair, a soft smile pulling at just one side of my face. She looked between the three of us, no response needed on our part. She knew how we felt. She knew how hard the three of us loved and fought to keep her.

She was saying she loved us in case she died.

We wouldn't return the sentiment because we knew she *wouldn't*.

I remembered the candle she'd lit, and I pulled her chin towards my face.

"You're protected, remember?"

She smiled and nodded, some of the weight seeming to lift off her shoulders.

"Ok, take cover," I warned them, Mateo and Santos dropping their bodies over her despite her clueless protests.

My brothers and I were so in sync I didn't have to let them in on the full scope of the plan, they knew me well enough to read the signs and react accordingly. I pulled the grenade from my belt, pulling the pin and tossing it over the booth towards Sokolov's men surrounding us.

They yelled but the blast soon overpowered any other sounds in the room. The high pitch sizzling in my ear muffled any chance of communication between us. I grabbed a smoke bomb next and pulled it, tossing it over and letting the smoke fill the room to give us the cover we'd need to get the fuck out.

Cries of pain amplified throughout the room and bullets flew aimlessly through the smoke. Santos and Mateo surrounded Celia, the four of us moving together in a tight huddle towards the exit. A sharp pain hit me in the chest, sending me stumbling backwards and dropping to my ass.

"Ronan!" Celia cried, but I waved her off.

"Get her out of here, it was my vest," I wheezed, taking a second to catch my breath on the ground.

"Mudak!" I heard in the distance.

They dragged her out screaming, reaching for me. But I would only be moments behind. Bullets were still whizzing by, and the smoke was burning my eyes.

The bullet cut the air behind me, nearly hitting me from behind. I checked my six and ran for it, stepping over the dead bodies to get to the neon EXIT sign. Footsteps charged towards me, but I couldn't bother to turn around to see who was coming, my eyes watered heavily from the smoke, I wouldn't see them until it was too late.

It wasn't easy for a man my size to be tackled to the ground. So when it happened, it took me a few moments to register what was happening. Those were all the seconds he needed to throw his fist into my face not once, but three times.

I pressed the barrel of my glock into his gut and pulled the trigger repeatedly, plugging six shots straight into his stomach. Blood pooled out of his mouth, and I rolled him off of me to let him die in peace. I sprinted to the exit, pushing the door open, hurting but relieved to have gotten out in one piece.

The fresh air invaded my lungs with no warning, a sharp gasp filled my chest as I took a moment to get my bearings back before looking around. Emergency vehicles surrounded the building, cop cars, and flashing lights of every sort gathered outside. Celia sat on the edge of an ambulance with a blanket wrapped around her while a paramedic looked her over, Mateo and Santos on each of her sides.

Her eyes lit up when she saw me but the scowls on my brothers' faces told me we had much bigger problems. I scanned around, seeing a few other women being looked over by other EMTs and some giving statements to federal agents.

Then I saw Ethan, walking towards me while wearing a vest that read FBI on it.

I saw red.

"You fucking rat," I charged towards him, fist high in the air but my brothers got to me first, holding me back from dishing out what he deserved.

"In our fucking house!?" Santos yelled from behind me, his fury just as strong.

He raised his hands up defensively, looking back and waving off the concerned agents who were watching. I fought against Mateo and Santos' hold on me, knowing damn well they were keeping me from a prison sentence by containing my rage.

"Ronan stop," Celia yelled, jumping off the ambulance and standing between both of us with her hands on each of our chests.

"Looks like I lost *two* brothers in there." I gritted out, nostrils flaring widely.

"Zerkos you're still my brother. Fletcher was still my brother," he said angrily like he had any right.

"You don't get to say his fucking name." Mateo added.

I pointed at the building like he would magically appear in its stead. "Fletcher would have ripped you apart if he knew you were a fucking pig."

"The whole time?" Mateo asked innocently.

Ethan didn't answer, he just gave him a look like he'd regret hearing the words themselves.

"We'd been trying to nail down Sokolov for five years before the word spread about the Black Crow Brotherhood. It was a long game to play undercover but I knew you could get me him. I would have preferred alive, but

I'm not angry about one less asshole in the world," he said like we'd done him a favor.

He was all business now, showing his true fucking colors. Reminding me why the only good cop was a dead one.

"You fucking—" I lifted my fist up again but Santos held me back, Celia still keeping herself between us.

"You came to México," she said, a frown in her expression that told me she didn't trust him just the same as me.

"I knew it was just a matter of time before we ended up in Sokolov's steps, thanks for not making me wait too long." He smirked. He fucking had the nerve to smirk.

"And now?" she asked him.

"Now I think it's time you find your way back down to the other side of the border, Miss *Gomez*." He emphasized her old alias before looking back at the rest of us. "All of you. My boss isn't looking to arrest any Crows for this, but if the investigation gets messy, he won't be there to back you up. Which means I won't be able to either, brothers," he said like it upset him.

He'd completely crushed my reality in a matter of seconds.

"You're not my fucking brother." I shoved past him, crossing my fingers no other boy in blue would be harassing me while I tried to make my way to the car.

"I know right now you don't want to hear this," Mateo said behind me just as I reached to open the back door, knowing damn well I was too angry to get behind the wheel right now. "But if he hadn't… betrayed us," he considered his words carefully, "we would probably be looking at federal prison right now."

"You're right. I don't want to hear this," I confirmed, scowling at the site of the white parrot in my seat.

"Cocksucker!" he chirped, tugging at the final fiber of my patience as I shut myself into the car like an angry child.

I was always the person being lied to.

Every goddamn fucking time.

At what point would I learn and stop trusting the people around me?

32

Celia

Wounded wasn't even close to the right word.

Ronan was hurting badly from the sudden loss of two friends he considered family. Despite my men's justifiable anger, I lingered back in an attempt to get more information from Ethan, but didn't find out too much that wasn't already obvious.

He was a nepotism baby, both his parents were in the bureau which meant by the time he was a senior in high school, he knew he'd already been accepted into training and was making his way through the ranks. He'd been obsessed with human trafficking issues since he was young and decided to make it his life's mission to save those who couldn't save themselves.

Despite my feelings towards bootlickers and those who wore the boots themselves, he wasn't a bad guy. But that didn't mean he deserved Ronan or any of the guys forgiveness, even if he had given us a legal pass. It didn't seem like he was seeking it either, that badge was the blade that cut the threads of their bond, and now there was no room left to heal the damage.

He'd go his way and we would go ours.

I sat next to Ronan in the back, opening up the cage and letting my foul-mouthed little friend climb up my arm and perch onto my shoulder. He buried himself into the nook of my neck, using my hair for warmth and comfort.

"Whore!" he shouted ten minutes into the drive, breaking the uncomfortable silence in the car and forcing a laugh from Mateo.

We all laughed, unable to hold back and pretend like the bird wasn't able to lighten the mood.

"I'm so sorry," I told them all, shaking my head, unsure which thing exactly I was most sorry for.

Maybe if I'd kept that vest on, Fletcher would still be alive, maybe if I hadn't gone looking for Sokolov by myself none of this would have happened.

"Everything that was supposed to happen did. Fletcher didn't deserve to die, but I can promise you he would have rather it been him than any other innocent person in that room. You included," Mateo spoke.

"I'm not innocent," I reminded him, but he just cleared his throat like he didn't want to get into it.

I didn't either.

They'd just suffered a monumental loss, the last thing I needed to be doing was throwing a pity party for myself over guilt.

There were very few things in this life I allowed to permeate my conscience.

Leaving Ronan was one of those things.

The deaths under my name could not be.

That was a lesson I learned long ago to ensure my own survival.

We stayed a few extra days in Cove City. It was all the time we needed to bury Fletcher and allow his family and the Crows to mourn him before we all headed back south. My sister was nowhere to be found and after a few days of paranoia and constant checking behind my shoulders, I finally concluded that she went into hiding for self-preservation.

We were doomed to repeat my papà's fate.

Chasing each other until one of us had finally drawn our last breath.

An exhausting concept I had already long tired of.

Once we'd returned back to México my phone blew up with missed messages from Ramírez, dozens of texts and phone calls telling me it was not wise to leave the country this close to election season.

He needed to be reminded that he was working for me, not the other way around. But I was too exhausted, too burned out on death and violence to be anything but apathetic to the entire situation.

Our hacienda was waiting for us, not many lights turned on despite the fact Chiyo and a few other family-related Crows were living there as well. My heart dropped at the thought of having to explain to her what happened. Why Fletcher wasn't with us and why he wouldn't be coming home.

We didn't even share a language.

Like my thoughts alone were powerful enough to summon her, she came running through the doors at the sound of our car pulling into the property. She waited at the entrance with hands clasped and one by one we stepped out of the vehicle.

She ran to us, as if she'd been expecting him to come out of the car as well, slowing down to a stop with a confused look on her face once she saw there were only the four of us. She looked past as if maybe there would be another car following us, as there often was. My men had gone home to tend to their wounds, the Black Crows that remained would be arriving from Cove City within the next few days.

Ronan looked away, Santos looked down, Mateo stuck his hands in his pocket. She turned to me as if she was waiting for me to confirm what she feared.

I shook my head, unsure of what else I could do or say.

Chiyo dropped to her knees, a heavy sob blowing out into the wind.

It wasn't fair, their love hadn't gotten a real chance before it had been crushed to nothing but dust.

But maybe we weren't all supposed to get a chance.

I looked at my guys, realizing I had not only gotten a second, but a third and fourth chance as well.

It definitely wasn't fucking fair.

The men walked towards the house, brushing past her with awkward glances and no words of comfort.

They had none for themselves, how would they conjure them for her?

I stopped in front of her, standing silently while she continued to cry, her tears falling down her cheeks and wetting the soil beneath her.

"Where am I supposed to go?" she asked.

It was the first time I'd heard her voice.

"You don't have to go anywhere. But if you decide to leave, wherever you go, I'll help find a place for you there." I assured her.

"I'm starting to think, there's no place for me in this world." She lamented in perfect English, letting me know my original belief about her being the smartest person in the room wasn't wrong.

She played them all.

But regardless of wits, ferocity, or strength, there was one human flaw that forced every human to crumble in pain, to split into shards of themselves.

Grief.

Loss.

La muerte.

I'd long forgotten that pain. When I laid in the hospital bed with a bullet in my shoulder at the age of fifteen and mourned my entire family, I had begged Santa Muerte to cast her protection over me like a comforting blanket, not to prevent me from dying but to prevent me from feeling what death inevitably did to all of us.

It took.

It robbed us, not only of the people we loved but of the parts inside us they helped to create.

I saw how badly she was hurting, even if it no longer resonated within me.

"I'm sorry. He was a good man, and I would have preferred if it would have been me instead." It was all the comfort I had to give her.

It was the truth.

Handling my own pain was enough of a chore, I couldn't find that place inside myself to sit down with her and cry for the life that was lost. Trying to find words of comfort was nearing an impossible task, and I wasn't sure if it was because I'd been molded to be this way or if it was the human condition itself.

"Take as much time as you need, my home is yours Chiyo," I told her, walking towards the entrance and leaving her to mourn privately, unsure if that was even what she really needed.

"Señorita, you have a guest in the piano room," my maid let me know as soon as I stepped through the door.

I sighed, thanking her and mentally preparing myself for whatever bullshit Ramírez would throw my way. I wasn't in the mood to deal with him, but it looked like he was going to make that my problem anyway. I understood the importance of keeping a powerful man in my pocket, my papá had taught me that lesson well. But it was clear José Luis thought I was his tool, not the other way around.

I wanted to say it was a credit to my work ethic, my influence, my power.

But I knew the reality.

The pussy between my legs made him think I was someone he could use and manipulate to his desire. He was about to learn that my pussy was still the biggest cock in the room, despite what he thought he knew.

I sent a text through our group chat, letting the men know I'd be in a meeting and not to interfere before I left my phone on the bookshelf by the door. I glanced over at Santisima's altar, the protection candle had burned all the way down to the bottom of the wick, all the wax gone and the glass stained a dark black color. I pushed my way into the room, but it wasn't Presidente Ramírez waiting for me.

"I thought I'd make this easy on you. Bring the fight to you, woman to woman and all," she said as I walked into the room.

"You think you'll be able to kill me and my men will just let you walk out of here scot-free? You think once you've murdered the mayor elect of Guadalajara, you'll just be able to take my place in everything I had a hand in?" I raised an eyebrow and she cackled loudly.

"Carajo, no. But it *is* impressive how fast you've taken over down here. He really did teach you everything, hmm?" she asked, the envy turning her eyes a bright green color. "Regardless, I have no intention of doing any of that anymore."

"Then why are you here?" I asked, growing tired of her incomplete thoughts.

"Think of this as your final test hermana. We all know you can't be reina if there is someone left to challenge the throne."

"So what? You came here to die?" I laughed out, crossing my arms over my chest.

"Bueno, no. You're going to kill *yourself*," she said matter of factly.

"And why would I do that, Carolina?"

"Because my big sister would never kill me, she'd kill herself first before she ever hurt me. And she'd make sure that whatever happened, that I'd be okay in the end, since she failed me so deeply before." There was so much hatred and delusion in her eyes that for a moment I almost considered her words.

"While all of that is true, you're not my sister anymore. How long have you been watching me suffer from a distance? How long have you been putting obstacles in my path? How long have you been sharpening the knife our tío wanted to use to kill me?" I raised my voice, stepping towards her slowly.

She smiled something sinister, like my reaction was everything she'd been hoping for.

"You give him too much credit. He was weak like papá, he wanted to leave you in peace to die in America, old and disconnected from cultura. The credit goes to me. Who the fuck do you think put you in that Bratva cage to begin with? The moment I saw you outside that bar in Cove City I sent your photo to Guillermo to set the pieces in motion. He signed your death warrant and put the timer on his own primo. Between that and my future sister in law giving Dezy Junior all the intel to feed back to Sokolov, I knew we just had to wait for the right opportunity before they left you all alone and defenseless.

"You've been after me all this time?" I asked. "Why?"

"You think Ignacio gave a fuck? He wanted you alive so that he could force you to open up the dungeons and he'd let you go free. He underestimated you the entire time, he underestimated me too. That's why it was so easy to take it all from him. He should have known better. A Flores won't ever stop fighting for what's theirs."

"That's where you're wrong." I shook my head. "I would have gladly let you have it all. I would have walked away for you before you tried your best to take everything I care about from me."

"The pinche gringos and little Álvarez? Please Celia, I was doing you a favor. It's easier to choose one when you don't have to."

"I'm not choosing, they're all *mine*," I declared, grinding my teeth together.

"Regardless, you wouldn't have walked away. It's not in our nature."

I thought about it.

I wanted to argue, to tell her that I was better than them. Better than her.

But I wasn't.

I wanted this. It was mine.

If I let her live, we were doomed to play out the same scene until one of us finally killed the other, repeating our family's curse.

I would break it now, save us both the pain of a miserable lifetime.

Correct my papá's mistake.

I would kill my sister.

Because for the first time in my life, I had something to live for.

33

Celia

"So then, how did you expect this would all go down? You were always the one with the flair for dramatics hermanita." I gave her a side-eyed look. "You can't really think my men won't come looking for me in anything short of a few minutes."

"It's actually *them* we're waiting on." She smiled from ear to ear.

"What did you do?" My heart dropped. "How did you get in here?"

"There's always a hole in the security, Celia. You should always expect that if you have enemies alive, there is someone close to you, working with them." She wasn't fucking wrong, and I wasn't sure if I was angry that she was giving *me* lessons, or if it was because I'd been so naive to not suspect otherwise.

And I already knew which pathetic pendejo it was that had betrayed me.

Fernando Garcia.

He'd involved himself in our business just long enough to get what he needed to feed it back to my sister.

"How many of my men did you kill?" I asked, wondering how many lives I'd have to push down and bury beneath the reach of my conscience.

"Just your security here. Kept your little maid alive if she promised to bring you inside without suspicion and lead your boys up to their rooms without a fuss. Looks like she gets to live after all." She walked towards the wet bar and unscrewed the cap to the tequila and poured two shots.

"Why are you here? Did your fiancé not tell you that his daddy is dead yet?" I hardened my eyes, waiting for the change in her expression.

She schooled it well, but she didn't hide the way she momentarily froze. As if all her thoughts had bombarded her at once with all the possibilities. If Allisher Sokolov was dead, then his son would be the new Bratva king.

"Good. Then he'll be twice as pleased when I come home wearing your crown." She narrowed her gaze my way, downing her shot and wiping the stray drops spilled from the corner of her lips.

"Or maybe he won't need a wanna-be cártel bitch if he's got his own." I suggested, throwing her off.

I thought this would be hard. That her death would be another scar in my psyche that would never heal. That I'd carry the pain of this my entire life. But when I looked at her, I saw nothing but the sum of my pain over the last fifteen years. How differently this would have ended had she stayed at my side instead of coming at me from behind

I truly believed Death always had a plan. Maybe I'd been made to mourn Caro all those years so that when the time came for her to die by my own hands, My heart would already be calloused over. The wound; already healed before the knife could cut me down.

"Why did you kill Mamá?" I finally bothered to ask.

"Because in the end, she favored you most," she said bitterly.

"Ha! Jamila had no love for me, you're delusional. You were her favorite."

"Then why did she refuse to tell me where our fortune was? Why did she hide that key from me when I went begging her for it? Why did she choose to die over letting me be reina?"

She wasn't my little sister anymore.

She wasn't anything to me anymore.

"To keep you safe you fucking idiota."

We were taught that family was everything. That no one from the outside would love you and be there for you like your blood. But here I had created a family with three men who I'd give my life for over and over again. And there stood my sister, asking me to bleed myself open for her.

She poured herself another shot and finally picked the other glass up in offering to me.

Fuck it.

I grabbed the glass and downed it knowing my sister wasn't smart enough to use poison against me or drug me like the men who held her leash.

And if she was, then I guess I deserved to die for being stupid enough to trust her.

"Ronan," she chirped, her eyes lighting up, making me turn around to see him with a purpling eye and his wrists bound tightly.

The gun pressed to the back of his head was held by a bald man. I could only assume he was working for the Russians. There was one more Bratva on his other side, because clearly it would take two men to outmatch Ronan Zerkos. His green eyes were raging with anger, and just as he opened his mouth to speak the Bratva grunt bashed the butt of his gun to the back of Ronan's head. He dropped down to the ground unconscious with a hard thud.

I screamed, but before I could run to him Carolina had a gun cocked and the sound of the safety coming off forced a chill up my spine.

"Tie her up, Adrik." She nudged her chin at me and the same grunt who'd knocked Ronan out pulled my arms in front of me with little to no effort despite my best attempt to fight against him.

He pulled a zip tie from his pocket, closing it around my wrists too tight before walking over to Ronan and doing the same to him.

"You're going to sit right here hermanita. We're going to play a little game," she said, using her gun to gesture to the Victorian style red, velvet couch with two matching chairs across from it.

"What the fuck are you talking about?" I sat down, doing my best to hide the creeping panic that came with the thought of how many men might be hiding in my home right at this moment.

"You said you didn't have to choose between them. Let's up the stakes shall we?"

Mateo and Santos came in next, both looking worse for wear than Ronan had, not a shocker considering their size compared to his. Three grunts surrounded them, all with guns pointed at their backs as they pushed them further into the room. That's when I realized one thing was not like the others.

Among her 'soldiers' was Fernando Garcia.

Traitor to the Flores Cártel.

Mateo's eyes registered Ronan before looking my way, the worry etched deeply into his expression.

"Celia." Santos rushed to me, but a shot rang out, the bullet hitting a framed piece of art causing the glass to shatter and spray onto the floor.

I screamed, trying to get up once more but Carolina pressed the gun harder against my temple.

"Everyone sit," Carolina commanded, eyeing Santos with a hateful stare. "Away from *her*," she clarified.

They both took a seat on opposite chairs from me, Ronan was still on the ground knocked out next to us.

"Wake him up." She gestured to her Bratva lackeys.

Which begged the question, where were her cártel men?

Loyalty must have been hard to buy these days. I didn't need to blackmail for it, I had earned it.

"Where are your men?" I asked with a smirk.

"These *are* my men," she gritted out.

I laughed, forcing her upper lip to curl up.

"Fine, then where are Ignacio's men?" I clarified.

"Dead."

I didn't press any further.

I didn't need to.

They were dead because she killed them. Because they refused to bow to her and her deranged plans of washing away everything the cártel was by merging it with Bratva bullshit. We didn't deal in the sale of flesh, and we never would. There were many fucked up things I was willing to be blind to for the sake of money and power.

Human trafficking was not one of those things.

They slapped Ronan's face a few times until he finally woke up, roaring, and readying himself for a fight before the gun in front of his face reminded him of our situation. We were outmatched, and worse yet we were outgunned.

"Glad you could join us, Ronan," Carolina said in a cheery voice. "You were always like a brother to me, you know?" She sighed. "Way more than that pendejo César."

Ronan's jaw hardened, the muscle bulging as his brain slowly pieced together what was going on.

"What's your plan?" he asked.

"Well," she drew out the word. "My big sister is going to pick one of you to die, before I kill her."

"Why?" I asked.

"Because you don't get to have everything you want if I didn't. And let's face it, neither of these cabrones fucking deserve it either." She pointed her gun at all three of my men.

"And if she doesn't?" Ronan squinted like the pain of the hit to the head was catching up to him.

"Then I'll make her watch me kill *all* of you, before I kill her." She placed her index finger over her lip like she was thinking. "In fact," her eyes widened, "I *will* kill you all." She laughed loudly, clapping her hands together. "Why leave witnesses? We just upped the stakes again hermanita. Now we're choosing who you get to watch die, while the others die after watching me kill you."

I turned my head to the side, my eyes burning straight into Fernando Garcia's hateful stare. He thought he was clever, that he'd fall to his knees for my sister and somehow steal it all out from underneath her.

Lackeys with too much ambition always thought they could rule. They didn't understand the game, they didn't know the logistics, and they certainly weren't blood thirsty enough for it. At least Carolina had the taste for it, even if she was shit at the admin portions of the job.

"Hurry up, or I'll choose for you." She demanded.

"Choose me, flower," Ronan said softly, "There isn't a world for me if you aren't in it and I can't watch any of you die."

I shook my head, tears pooling at my eyelids as I refused to make the decision.

"It's me, morena. Say it," Santos demanded but I hung my head down, looking away from all of them. "Don't make me go through this again."

"I can't," I refused, crying as my entire world crashed around me and I realized there was no one left to save us, there was no one who would care.

Fletcher was dead and gone, César had gone back to his motorcycle club, and we... we had been bested, just a foolish and rookie move was enough to be the blade in our guillotine.

"How romantic," she said sarcastically. "You have two minutes." Her voice dropped to an icy tone as she stepped back and sat on the piano bench, noisily clanking the keys without an ounce of skill in her bones.

When the worst thing that could ever happen to you finally happened, the whole world slowed down. You played every action, every thought or movement you had leading up to it, wondering if at any point there was any chance of it going any other way. If you could blame something other than yourself for leading down this path of no return.

"Caro! Stop! Let them go," I cried, raising my head shamefully.

If there had ever been any doubt in my mind that I needed to kill her, if there had been any shred of love left inside of me for her, it had rotted and festered right before me. But that didn't matter, because she was going to be the one getting the last laugh.

I'd already gone through the pain of losing Ronan... twice.

A third time would kill me.

But for once I didn't have it in me to be a selfish bitch. He'd suffered my loss too many times as it was, and he didn't deserve to watch me die. If that was the only gift I could give him in this life, it would have to suffice.

"Have you made your choice hermanita? Or shall I choose for you?" She spun her pistol towards Mateo, his big brown eyes full of fear.

I nodded slowly.

Every second up to this moment was still replaying in my head.

What could I have done differently?

What could I have changed?

Even if I had gone inside with them together, none of us had weapons on us after our flight.

Hindsight was more than twenty-twenty here.

I had cost us our lives.

"Wait," I shouted just as I heard the click of the safety.

"It's okay sunshine," Mateo attempted to calm me while Ronan shouted, telling her to point the gun to him instead. "I love you fuckers."

Santos' hazel eyes had a blank fog rolling over them, something I recognized from our time in his primo's basement. He'd given up. He didn't care if he was the first or the last to go because he knew this was how our story would end. I think somehow, we all did. Our protection had run out, and in the end people who dealt in death were almost always next to die.

"Ronan!" I screamed. "I choose Ronan," I sobbed, closing my eyes so I wouldn't have to meet his.

"I love you, flower."

"I'm sorry, baby, I can't let you watch me die. I love you," I explained hoping that he'd be able to somehow forgive me in his last seconds of life as if it would matter at all.

We would all meet again in hell.

I was sure of it.

Me and the demons who found themselves at the end of my leash willingly.

Just as we had figured it all out, it would be over.

I guess only good people got happy endings.

What had I ever done to deserve something more than exactly this?

"Wow, I was not expecting that one, I'm not gonna lie. Really thought she loved you more than that Ronan." Carolina chuckled, the blast of the gun ringing out was almost as loud as the scream that barreled out of my lungs.

But it wasn't his body that dropped down to the ground, it was the bald Russian. The shock and surprise of Taylor Constance charging into the room with her pistol burning hot had us all freezing in the moment out of disbelief.

Her distraction was enough to throw my sister off and give me the chance I needed to overtake her.

I elbowed her in the side, using my bound wrists to knock the gun from her hand.

"Por que consigues todo?" she spat out, yanking my hair and ripping it from the scalp.

I screamed from the pain, sending my bound fists down to her face simultaneously.

Gunshots rang out all around us, but I couldn't focus on anything but Carolina, knowing if I took my eyes off for even a split second she would use that as a chance to kill me. Taylor said she was always watching, and though there was a part of me that wanted to question the breach in my privacy, I couldn't help feeling anything but grateful for this window of opportunity she had given us.

"Porque soy mejor," I hissed out, bashing my forehead into her nose as I pressed both my hands down into her throat, earning a forced choking sound from her. "Soy mas grande," I panted, cutting off her breath. "Y quiero eso mas."

She scratched at my arms but the weight of my body sitting on her chest was too much for her to push me off. My fists moved on their own, repeatedly coming down her face with all the force my arms could muster. Her screams of pain muted in my ears and my vision lost focus as my muscles repeated the action my brain no longer connected to.

Her bones crunched under my hands and eventually the burning sharp pain radiating through my extremities dulled. The bullets died, or maybe they just ran out. The room went quiet. Nothing but the sounds of my fists still hammering into her face. I felt hands on my arms, pulling me back and lifting me off of her.

I screeched a feral sound, panting heavily through my rage.

"Your hands, morena," was the only thing Santos could manage to say.

I looked down at them, bloody, cut up with shards of bones from my sister's face sticking out of them. Wrists still bound, my middle fingers broken and bent into awkward shapes. I didn't bother to look at her face to see the damage, I knew she was long past dead. I opened my mouth and the involuntary wail of a broken woman echoed out of my lungs.

Santos was there to catch me as I fell into him, his hands no longer zip tied and able to hold me to his chest as I mourned my little sister for the second time.

"Call an ambulance," Mateo said with worry in his voice.

Ronan was already on his phone and the way he paced back and forth let me know everything was not okay.

Then I saw Taylor, on the ground, eyes wide and blood pooling at her mouth. Mateo hovering over her with his shirt pressed into a wad against her stomach.

"Taylor!" I rushed to her side, unable to touch her without feeling a burning pain against every part of my hands.

Santos cut my restraints before lifting her head up under his lap.

"I told you, that I'd do anything for these fuckers." She choked on her own blood with a smile, her eyes fluttering closed.

"Taylor, keep your eyes open," I commanded her.

We'd lost too many innocent people already.

They'd lost too many of their friends.

I was not worth these deaths.

Santa Muerte please.

Why them and not me?

"You can't shroud me from pain if you keep taking everyone from me!" I screamed, my tears falling over her face and my yells not registering any reaction from her.

As if La Madrina heard my plea, the sounds of the ambulance drew closer and closer to our home.

"We have to get her into the main area," Ronan instructed, reminding us of the dead putos in the room that were going to be drawing more attention to the situation than we needed.

"Call Dominico, have him reach out to Ramírez to clear this mess." My voice sounded hoarse though I couldn't remember screaming. Santos nodded as Mateo and Ronan lifted Taylor off the ground and carried her out of the piano room.

The paramedics rushed in, loading her into the gurney while trying to explain to Mateo in a language he didn't speak that he'd have to meet them at the hospital separately. He didn't take their no for an answer, climbing in anyway and disappearing with the sounds of the sirens.

I stayed sitting there on the floor, paralyzed and numb as I thought about the last half of the year. Was this who I had been meant to become all along? Had there been another path set out for me that kept begging me to stay the course, but I just refused to follow it? Or was my destiny always meant to be one filled with carnage and death?

I was built for it.

I knew I was.

I shook off the imposter syndrome crawling up my spine once again and reminded myself that I'd made every promise against my enemies come true.

"Raa Cocksucker!" Pluto's voice jarred me out of my thoughts, making me involuntarily laugh as I looked up to find Ronan holding his cage.

"Hola Amigo." The tears rolled down my face and he turned his little head to the side as if he was trying to recognize my pain as something he understood.

"Hola Puto!" he cawed, forcing my tears to stream down faster with my laughs.

"I didn't know you spoke spanish."

Ronan sat, placing the cage on the ground and bringing me into his lap. The bird alluded to conversation every now and then, mostly letting us down each time it turned into repetitive insults. He plucked the sharp bones sticking out of my hands one by one, the burning sting a welcome pain. We sat there together for an hour before his phone rang. He lifted me up to reach for his cell in his pocket.

"Where are you?" he asked as soon as he answered.

"Okay, go without us. We'll meet there soon, ask Kane if he needs any clothes."

I waited anxiously for him to disconnect the call and give me all the information.

"Santos made contact with Ramírez, he'll make sure there are no questions from the paramedics. Dominico is sending a crew to clean the bodies up while we're gone." He lifted me up to my feet, my legs barely able to hold me. Instead of letting me get my bearings he lifted me up into his arms, carrying me out of the room and taking me up the stairs.

"Where are we going?" I asked.

"Taylor's in surgery," He told me, some of the weight of the universe lifting off my shoulders.

"She's not dead?" The tears began again, I no longer fought to wipe them or prevent them from falling.

I think I had finally learned that crying didn't make me weak.

It made me someone who felt pain.

"Looks like she's gonna make it." He carried me through my bedroom and sat me on top of the closed toilet lid once we reached the bathroom. "We can go to the hospital after I get you cleaned up. Get your hands checked out. The mayor elect can't show up to the hospital covered in blood."

He walked to the shower, turning it on and adjusting the faucets to a warm temperature before helping me to stand. He pulled each item of clothing off of me with complete and total care, being careful to not hurt my hands any more than they'd already been damaged.

"I love you," I whispered into the air, unsure if it was even loud enough for him to hear.

He looked up at me from a kneeled position as he undid the buckles on my shoes and helped me out of them. I had a million ideas of what might have been coursing through his head right at this moment.

Nothing said I love you quite like being the first one picked to die.

"You're my entire world. It was the right choice," he reassured me, the sobs pouring out of my soul with a ferocity I'd never experienced before, making me unsure if I'd ever be able to stop myself from crying again.

He helped me into the warm stream of water, washing me gently and avoiding doing anything but letting the water carefully roll off my skin to avoid any more pain. My hands throbbed, but it was the kind of ache you could ignore. The kind that reminded you that you finished that very thing you sought out to do.

I'd won.

Todo es mio.

Even if it had cost me just as much.

34

Celia

"And you're sure she can be trusted with... my secrets?" I asked my dearest friend through the phone awkwardly pinned between my cheek and my shoulder.

"Dr. Hernandez is very well recommended for her professionalism and her discretion in your circles. I've sent all her information to Dominico *and* Taylor, if they didn't find any reason to be suspicious, then neither should you, Celia," Emory said in a condescending tone..

"I've just never really done this before. Not like this, not with the intent of bearing it all," I explained anxiously.

"And that's why it's never worked for you before. Real communication requires work, consistency, honesty. Things we all know you don't excel in. If you can't give her the bare minimum, then don't bother wasting her time," she snapped at me as if she knew I was starting to chicken out.

"Ouch amiga," I said with a laugh.

"It's a waste of *your* time too, if you can't respect her time, at least respect your own. You will never heal if you don't sort through your damage. It's not up to them to fix it for you."

She meant my guys.

She wasn't wrong, I couldn't lay the burden of all my problems, my fears, my traumas on them. Sure, they could be there for me, but it wasn't up to them to always have to clean up my messes.

It had been a week since Carolina had died and I hadn't slept more than three hours total. It wasn't that I couldn't sleep, it was that I was afraid to. Afraid to close my eyes and deal with the aftermath of every horrible thing I'd done to claim the throne I could finally sit on.

"How's Grimm's Reach?" I asked, the sarcasm in my tone too clear.

"I don't want to talk about it, don't change the subject," Emory snipped at me.

"Fine," I said. "Besos." I hung up without another word, knowing she would be mad for about thirteen seconds before she got over it and found something else to irritate her instead.

With some struggle, I used my wrists and the few uninjured fingers to put my phone in my purse, standing at the door as if I hadn't just had an entire conversation in front of this person's house, trying to decide whether or not I would be going in at all. I knocked with my elbow, my hands still badly injured, wrapped in gauze and splinted.

"Cecilia Gomez?" The elderly brunette opened the door to her modest home.

I nodded, appreciating that Emory was thoughtful enough to not give the name that was associated with my political career. Dr. Hernandez wasn't a stupid woman, she would have had to have been living in an alternate dimension to have missed my face plastered around the news with the upcoming election.

The fact she was opting to stick with the alias let me know Emory might have been right about whether or not the doctor was trustworthy. She led me through her home until we reached double wooden doors that opened into a beautiful office. A rich mahogany desk sat in front of a backdrop of bookshelves, nothing but psychology textbooks displayed on the shelves.

She gestured to the sofa and took a seat on the opposing chair. I followed suit, sitting down as well.

"Thank you for clearing your schedule for me on such short notice," I told her.

"I understand you've had a family tragedy recently. Is that where you'd like to start?" she asked, getting down to business without asking a single word about me.

I fidgeted with my hands nervously on my lap.

"Actually, I'm not sure. I've never really done this before, I'm not sure where to start…" I told her truthfully.

"Here's the thing Cecilia, in order for me to help you out of the grave you've dug for yourself, I need to understand just how deep you've dug it. That's the only way therapy can work." she said, as if she somehow knew everything that was going through my head without knowing anything at all. "Start with what hurts the most."

I nodded my head, letting out a deep exhale before opening my mouth.

"I spend a lot of time wondering what would have happened if my father had a son…"

Epilogue

Two months later

"Congratulations to the newest mayor of our beautiful city," Ramirez announced in the town square in front of El Palacio. "Celia Flóres has my vote of confidence not just because of the legacy her father left behind. His footprint will always be stamped into the sand of our city's history, but because of her passion to do the right thing for our people, for my home town. I can't wait to see what she does in the upcoming years." He raised a glass of champagne into the air as he talked me down from the podium.

I had just delivered my acceptance speech, thanking all those who campaigned for me and the citizens who supported my infiltration into politics. They didn't know Celia Flóres wasn't just their mayor, but the jefa of the biggest crime organization in central America.

Not knowing would keep them safe.

Coming to terms with the fact that there were no good guys or villains was something I had to do as a child in order to sleep at night. There were just people, some who did worse things than others. Some of us enjoyed doing bad things, and some of us did it under a justifiable premise that it was for a better cause.

I wasn't ready to define where I fit into that mold and there was likely a good chance I'd never need to.

Dominico and Luciano waited for me on either side of the steps as I descended from the stage, joining the crowd to listen to the rest of President Ramirez's speech. He had big plans, which required big money, and that's where his vote of confidence started and ended with me.

But I'd already proven to him that I was a woman of my word, spreading the message loudly that any child found being used under my name would result in lethal consequences to the perpetrators. With the dungeons reopened there was no need for deaths in the streets anymore, we handled our business quietly and in private.

I'd made fast changes and lucky for me, I hardly had to lift a finger to do it.

"They are waiting for you inside for photos, let's make this quick eh, reina? We have that amnesty meeting with the new Bratva leader later today," Dominico reminded me.

It was just a video call, but it was necessary to be punctual, to be civil. Allisher Sokolov's eldest son, Viktor had taken over after his father's untimely death. There was no hiding the cártel's involvement, especially when I sent my sister's head and his men's desecrated corpses back to his door as a message.

He was fresh on the throne, just as I was. We both understood the nature of the game and his father's death benefited more than it hurt him. The sting of my sister's loss and knowledge that the cártel couldn't become something under his control and manipulation likely didn't feel great either, but now he was free to marry whatever unfortunate soul would capture his attention.

If anything I'd done him a favor.

But still, we had to make nice. Forgive, not forget, but let lo pasado ser el pasado.

Set up rules and establish boundaries.

The border would be one, to start. Some shithead racist had been elected and it looked like we had gotten the hell out of the United States just in time to watch the fireworks from the good seats.

The military police nodded towards my men, an amusing show of respect, considering they still covered their faces in fear for what my soldiers would do if their identities were discovered. Ramirez and I had an understanding, as long as they stayed out of my way, I had no reason to get in theirs.

Politics were boring, I knew well why my papá dreaded his civil duties. I was much more inclined to the blood and gore side of the business. Reporters and photographers took my photo, all of them calling to me at once and not giving me the opportunity to focus on a single camera at a time.

Flashes filling my eyes and a sense of victory and accomplishment washed over me at the realization that I'd done everything that I'd set out to.

Not bad for una muerta.

Hell, I'd even been resurrected from the dead.

Luciano and Dominico stayed by my side, reminding me of every single photo of my papá that existed documented in history. His men were always at his side too, ready to take a bullet for him.

And it wasn't just the two of them, they all believed in what I stood for, in doing things differently. In ruling with respect.

I'd long burned the ledger as a show of good faith, erasing every trace of blackmail and debt each name had acquired and given them the option to stay rich and by my side or go retire with my blessing.

I didn't lose a single soldier that day.

But I had one left to let go of.

Santos was tired of war, tired of gang life, tired of violence. Which was good, because he couldn't afford another scar on his body anyway. We'd moved out to a secluded hacienda so that he could spend his days relaxing in the sun like the goddamn perfect househusband he'd become. I knew he was done with all the death the minute his knife sliced through Guillermo's throat.

I promised myself I'd never let him take another life in my name again.

I had to let go of all my chefs because he'd decided cooking was solely his responsibility. He settled into a life of comfort easily and nothing made me happier than to see it. He deserved this freedom.

Ronan was the head of my security team now, because God forbid he let my safety be under someone else's control. I preferred it that way, it kept him close to me in my everyday life and I was glad to always have him within range.

Mateo easily fit into the dungeons, preferring to keep a place in my cártel and getting his hands dirty where it counted. He was a fast learner, and Dominico was teaching him everything he'd need to learn so that the old man could retire rich and in peace.

I pulled my phone out to check on Ignácio through the surveillance feed, wondering if the day would ever come where he'd give up and die so that I could stop dragging this on. In some ways I kept him alive for me. To punish him anytime grief took over for the things that I was forced to do because of the path he put me on. Some days I kept him alive because I was a monster who enjoyed hurting him.

Some days I kept him alive because I was tired of killing my own blood.

"Are you ever gonna put that poor old man out of his misery, Flower?" Ronan asked, not hiding the amusement from his face as I pocketed my cell phone once again.

"Kill him? He's family Ronan." I laughed, walking past him.

"Your idea of family has a really wide range Sunshine," Mateo added. "Exhibit A, the fucking bird."

"Don't bring Pluto into this." I shook my head, waiting for him to open the door to the Escalade for me. "He's my goodest boy," I chirped.

"You know, it wouldn't hurt to talk me up half as much as you do that parrot," Mateo complained, getting into the car behind me and shutting the door.

Ronan chuckled from the front, Santos was already waiting for us all in the passenger seat. I straddled Mateo and ran my hands through his hair.

"Mi vida, I didn't know you wanted to be my goodest boy." I smiled, pressing my lips gently to his as Ronan pulled away.

"Sunshine, I want to be your everything, whatever you'll let me be I'll be it for you. Quiero ser tu todo." He blinked slowly with a smile forming over his face.

"Now, now, you know what I said about using Spanish against me," I whispered into his ears as his fingers traveled up my side.

"How can I resist when I know how wet it gets you?" He peeled my suit jacket off, sliding his hands underneath the thin satin material of my tank top, his touch just light enough to send a chill up my spine.

"Mmm," Escaped my throat.

"No fucking way, you start that shit now, while I'm driving, and I *will* pull over," Ronan said from the driver's seat.

"Then you're going to have to pull over because I'm not stopping," Mateo taunted from beneath me, his hand cupping my breast and his tongue raking against my neck.

I gasped as he lifted my top up and placed his mouth over my nipple, his tongue swirling wildly across the hardened bead. I cried out, my sounds forcing a growl from Ronan's throat from his frustration.

He veered off the road going into the desert.

"What are you doing?" I shouted.

"Taking a shortcut," Ronan gritted out like he was angry we were starting without him.

It wasn't my fault somebody needed to drive.

I gasped at the feel of Mateo ripping my suit skirt at the side, making room for me to properly spread my legs and sit into a deep straddle over his engorged erection.

"More," I moaned as he kissed up my neck, his fingers gripping my back and pulling me somehow even closer to me.

His hands traveled lower, giving my ass a hard squeeze before his fingers slipped through my thighs, coating themselves in the slick arousal forming between my legs.

"Fuck." I tipped my head back while he toyed with my clit.

His hands gripped at the fabric of my torn skirt and with one more tug he ripped it completely up the side, pulling it off of me and freeing me from the little barrier it provided.

"Let's see if I can make you come before we get home." He smirked, pulling his monster cock out of his pants and slapping my pussy with his thick length.

He lifted me, hovering me a few inches above his lap as he positioned himself in the center of the backseat before spinning me and facing me forward.

"I want them to have a good show," He whispered in my ear just as I made eye contact with Santos through the mirror in his visor.

His smirk was *almost* unnoticeable.

"Take her shirt off," Ronan instructed.

"Watch the road," Santos chastised.

"I can do both," he countered.

Mateo didn't fight it, lifting the silk top up and pulling it off my shoulders before tossing it down to the floorboard. I was completely naked now, exposed and legs spread wide over his lap, his thick throbbing cock waiting to find its way inside of me. His hands caressed me, moving all over me as he reveled in bringing me to the point of begging.

I wasn't past it when it came to them.

I would only ever beg again for them.

"Please," I whined desperately as his fingers rubbed up and down against my clit.

He lifted me up again, this time positioning the thick head of his cock right at my entrance, no warning or declaration before penetrating me with the full length of his steel.

"Oh fuck!" I gasped.

"Do you think he can make you come before we get home, Flower?" Ronan teased, pressing the button on the smartscreen display of the car to show the GPS estimated time of arrival at less than six minutes.

I shook my head, knowing it would only increase the challenge and fuel Mateo to prove me wrong even though I knew damn well it would likely not take him more than four. He pulled out of me, emptying me, and leaving me with an aching need.

"Drop your knees to the floorboard," he commanded, bending me over the middle console so that I was smack dab between Santo and Ronan.

He pulled my arms out from behind me, placing my ankles in each hand before I felt his palm press against my low back, urging me to tilt my tailbone up towards him.

His hand moved to the back of my head, pushing me down further into the middle console so that my breasts were smashed up against it. I moved my cheek to the side. I was turned to see Santo, eyes full of lust and desire like he was wishing he'd picked the back seat himself instead.

His nostrils flared and he adjusted himself with the next thrust of Mateos cock slamming deep inside of me.

I cried out, biting my lip as each thrust of his hips hit deep inside, bringing me closer and closer to unraveling.

Santos moved my hair out of my face, tucking it behind my ear while his eyes stayed glued to my face, like my expression was the best thing he'd seen yet.

"How good does his cock feel, Morena?"

"So good. So good," I mumbled, the discomfort of my position somehow making it easier to lose myself to the pleasure.

Ronan chuckled, the engine roaring louder letting me know he'd stepped heavily onto the accelerator.

"Half a mile," Santos announced, his taunting forcing Mateo to pull all the way out before sending his full length deep inside of me all at once. His fingers found the bundle of nerves between my legs, giving me just enough of the friction I craved to let go.

Three more full thrusts and the build up inside me finally crashed, my orgasm pulling me under, forcing me to let go of my ankles and cry my release in Santos' direction while Mateo kept my head pressed down and thrusted into me repeatedly.

He didn't come, but he tucked himself into his pants regardless.

Ronan peeled into the driveway, the car drifting slightly from the use of the emergency break at such a high speed before we came to a full stop. Ronan jumped out of the driver's seat and dashed in front of us, barking Spanish orders at anyone who might have been hanging around out in the open as he yelled at them to go into their rooms.

I screamed as Mateo tossed me over his shoulder, naked, ass bare and facing the sun. I lifted my head off his back to see Santos following close behind, his eyes narrowed as he focused on me with a predatory gaze.

I moaned hard with the feeling of a hard hand against my backside as we crossed the threshold, not having to be told that it came from Ronan before seeing the satisfactory smile plastered across his face.

Mateo carried me past the living area and out into the courtyard, dropping me onto a long leather bench. The three of them loomed over me without moving. They were lethal. They were mine. We were always together now, always the four of us. Santos was the first to drop his pants to the floor, his pierced cock standing tall and threatening me with pleasure.

"You know, we *can* take turns right?" I laughed, but their expressions remained hard.

"But you scream so much louder when it's the three of us ruining that greedy cunt of yours." Ronan's words were so filthy they alone had the power to start the fire inside me up again.

"Make room." Santos closed in on me, sitting behind me and practically pulling me onto his lap with my ass over his cock while his hands traveled down my thighs.

He spread my knees apart, running his fingers up and down my slit. I dropped my head back to his shoulder, a moan falling through my lips as his touch sparked pleasure all the way through my body. Ronan turned around, walking through the courtyard and back indoors.

"Where are you going?" Mateo shouted to him.

"I'll be back."

I switched my focus to the way Santos' hands moved up and down my body, caressing me, moving over the sensitive parts of my thighs before he'd slip a finger or two inside me briefly. Always teasing, never fully committing, and driving me wild with want.

"Oh fuck, Morena. You're drenched." He lifted his fingers up to show me the proof.

"Fuck me, please," I begged through my whispers.

Mateo chuckled, stepping closer to the edge of the bench, where my cunt dripped down over the leather fabric. I was sensitive everywhere, aching to be touched and for the next release when he lowered his head between my legs and slipped his tongue inside me.

"Shit!" I gasped, my fingernails gripping tight around Santos' forearms.

They lifted my hips up into the air, Mateo's mouth staying locked around my clit even as Santo impaled me onto his thick shaft. I shuddered at him filling me up, each bar of his Jacob's ladder rubbing up against me in the most delicious way.

He thrusted into me, each time a wild spark of pleasure surging through me, threatening to bring me closer to ruin as pleasure spread throughout my body. Tremors took over me as I convulsed from pleasure around Santos' cock.

Mateo's head lifted up from between my legs just as Ronan reappeared, taking his shirt off and reaching into his pocket and pulling out a clear bottle.

"Are you ready for me to fuck your ass, Reina?" Santos whispered in my ear.

"No," Ronan answered for me, dropping his pants down and stepping out of them before he coated his cock in lube.

He threw it in our direction, barely giving Santos the heads up he needed to catch it.

"You don't want me to—" Santos started.

"I want to feel those bars against my cock while we're both inside her," Ronan explained with a smirk.

"Wait, what?" I finally understood what he was suggesting, worrying about what state they wanted to leave my poor pussy in.

Rest In Peace.

"You can handle it. You can handle anything, can't you?" He taunted me as Santos' fingers locked tighter around my hips.

He layed back on the bench, bringing me down with him so that my back was pressed to his chest. Ronan climbed over us, his hard abs against me and sandwiching me between the two of them.

"Oh fuck, you're dripping, Flower." Ronan exhaled into my ear.

Santos pulled out of me just enough to allow for Ronan to push the tip of his cock inside me, both of them in the same hole was way too much. Way too intense, and he wasn't even fully in yet.

"Oh shit. Oh fuck!" I cried, Mateo laughing from the side with his dick in his hands, stroking up and down. I licked my lips at the sight.

He walked towards me like he could read my thoughts. Each step closer Ronan pushed himself deeper inside me, coating himself in my arousal and filling me up. I reached out, wrapping my hand over Mateo's cock and earning the sound of his pleasure.

He groaned, his hands stretching over me, his fingers pinching my nipples and squeezing my breasts with a gentle touch. Santo and Ronan moved slowly at first, until they'd both found their way fully inside me, bottoming out and wrecking me with a fullness that was near maddening.

And then they moved on their own terms, uncoordinated and out of sync in a purposeful way so that Ronan would feel every single one of Santos' piercings against his cock as well. He dropped his head to my shoulder, biting down like it was nearly too much for him too. The sharp sting of his teeth piercing my flesh was just the pain I needed to push me closer to the edge.

I felt my climax building inside me again, every thrust of their hips taking me deeper into an altered state where I could feel myself losing the ability to feel anything but bliss. It erupted all around me, taking Santos with me as he held me tight against his body and emptied his release into me.

Santos pulled out and Ronan lifted off of us so he could roll out from under me. Ronan laid down on the bench and I crawled over him, sitting on his erection once more and grinding down on him. I felt Mateo's hot hand pressing onto my spine, urging me to lean forward as he settled in behind me. I opened my eyes to find Santos' cock, still covered in cum right in front of my face, almost dripping onto Ronan's forehead.

I opened my mouth to take him in just as Mateo squeezed the bottle of lube over my ass and let it drip down my crack. I hollowed my cheeks, relaxing my throat as Mateo thrusted his fingers into me from behind. First one, then two and eventually three fingers filled my ass and moved at a slow and delicious pace.

I cried out again as Ronan began to move once more, all three of them finding a new rhythm together, filling all of my holes and forcing me to fall apart again, making me come over and over until I was nothing but an empty bag of bones being handled by them.

That was the easiest part about this. How effortless it was to be in control of my world and still drop to my knees for them because I wanted to be cared for. Because they could make me feel like I didn't have to worry about only being strong.

I was theirs.

There was so much power in relinquishing everything to them.

And I always would.

Santos pumped his release down my throat just as Mateo emptied himself inside me. Ronan proved once again that his stamina had no end once the other two stepped back.

He flipped me on my stomach over the bench, holding nothing back, he moved with the ferocity of a soldier as his fingers tormented the most sensitive bits between my thighs.

We cried together as he forced one final orgasm from me, sweaty and panting from exertion and bliss. They carried me up to our room, washed me and dropped me onto the silk sheets of the bed. Ronan draped a blanket over me before sliding in next to me.

"I just need a fifteen hour nap, then we can go again." I mumbled out sleepily as the other two cuddled in around me.

"What is all this?" Santos said with marvel in his voice as my hands came off his eyes and his tia and primos shouted surprise.

"It's your... retirement party. *Officially*," I clarified.

Though he had easily slipped into a life of comfort and peace we had never actually discussed him leaving the life. Mateo, Ronan and I all knew he had long been done. He'd killed too many people for Guillermo, and he'd seen too many innocent lives snuffed out to keep going.

So had I.

But some of us were built differently. All I wanted for Santos was happiness and if I could provide it to him by taking the guns out of his hands and replacing it with a michelada instead, then I was happy to do it. I had plenty of good soldiers. I had the best of bodyguards. My man deserved for war to be over.

He deserved a way out that didn't involve a shallow grave.

More than all of that, he deserved the community and village that his family thrived on. He deserved to have them here. With Guillermo's untimely death and the family losing the financial means Los Muertos had provided them, I took it upon myself to move the Álvarez familia across the border.

There were no tears shed at the mention of her son's death, and I was sure in some way, she knew that I had been responsible. But Santos' tia thanked me regardless and within days they had made their way south and settled in like she had never left. After all she'd been a girl too when she first left. It was funny how the motherland always welcomed you back with open arms, no matter how long you'd been away.

I'd been so afraid of her judgment, of what others would think of me, and sure, there were certainly some along the way who felt I was less than for not having grown up here. But at the end of the day, my connection to my country was in my blood, it was in my eyes, and it was in my skin.

And even if I'd lost all those things, it would still be mine because Latinidad was in your soul. It was something they couldn't take from you, though they were desperate to try. But the beautiful thing about it, was that it was a lot like a fire, all you needed were a few small embers to stoke it back to life.

We stayed up too late, dancing around the fire, drinking strong drinks, and eating well seasoned food before giving up on the night. Or rather, the now early morning. Some of Santos' primos passed out on the floor of whatever rooms they could find to avoid trying to find their way home drunk despite Mateo's offer to drive them.

"What a sunrise," Taylor said from her wheelchair as we made our way back inside the house.

"Glad to share it with you." I smiled at her, Ronan squeezed her shoulder from her other side, and with a slight gesture of his head he silently asked to push her in.

She nodded, and we followed the rest of the way into the guest room she'd been making residence in. Didn't feel right to keep her any further away from us. It was probably not going to be as temporary as we all tried to make it out to be. She *was* family. Because family was more than blood, more than who you slept with, more than who you created. It was the people who were there for you unconditionally.

The ones who cheered you on, who made you believe you were worthy of love and happiness.

"When are you gonna stop milking it and get out of that chair? I was shot *twice* and was walking a week later," Ronan teased her.

"Look my ugly friend, I have absolutely *nothing* to prove. I'm gonna relax and heal on my own." She elbowed him off her chair and I chuckled.

"I think I keep you around because no one puts him in his place like you do," I told her.

"What can I say, I have a way with the assholes. Goodnight Celia."

"Buenas noches amiga." I shut her bedroom door and followed Ronan back through the hallway to find Santos and Mateo sleeping on the couch together.

Their legs entwined and Santos' head resting on Mateo's chest.

"Take a picture, this is adorable," I whispered to Ronan, knowing damn well my phone had died at least three tequila shots ago.

"Should we wake them up?" he asked, and I shook my head.

"Nah." I pointed to the other couch. "They look so comfy." Ronan walked over to the other sofa, laying down and gesturing me towards him.

I sank into his hold, melting in his embrace and smelling the lingering scent of the bonfire in his clothes.

"Te quiero," I told him.

"Te quiero mucho, mi amor," he responded. "Is this everything you wanted?"

"And more. Is this enough for you?" I asked, lifting my head up from his chest.

"Enough? You're everything." He squeezed me tighter.

"You think it's enough for them?"

"They wouldn't be here if it wasn't, Flower." He kissed the top of my head, his fingers raking gently through my hair, coaxing me into a peaceful sleep.

It was enough. Because we were together.

We were enough.

The End.

BONUS EPILOGUE

25 years later–

The following epilogue has content that could be considered spoilers for **Heartless Heathens: A why choose gothic romance :**
Be sure to read first

"Señora Presidente." A blue-eyed girl with an array of silver and black hair was led into the office by my secretary.

She couldn't have been more than twenty-five.

This was the girl that was going to change the world?

I'd heard plenty about her, how she graduated at the top of her class, the orphaned granddaughter of the multi-billionaire and rumored occultist, Arlan Black. It was a known fact when you got high enough in the chain of the world that the Black family had been responsible for discreetly placing and choosing world leaders. Something happened twenty-five years ago and that potato with arms ended up sending the country to the gutter just as we found our way back in México.

Lucky for me.

I'd heard how she was using her inheritance to try to fix the steaming heap of shit that had become The United States. Despite his dying it looked like Arlan Black wasn't going to be leaving a gap at all. My heart pained when I thought about the country I'd spent my youth in. For years I begged my brother to come home, to relocate his motorcycle club and bring Los Diablos Locos south of the border.

The US was controlled by the church now, it was no place for Devils.

But this little girl had all the answers apparently.

That's what people said.

"Miss Black." I stood from my chair and extended my hand out to her.

She gripped firmly, a glazed over look to her eyes as she stared through me blankly. She cleared her throat and let go, sitting down in the chair across from my desk.

"I'm grateful you took the time to meet me, Señora Presidente. I've heard so much about the great things you've done for your country."

"Please, you can call me Celia. And it seems our mutual friend has great respect for you, how could I turn you down?"

"Dr. Emory O'Connor is the very reason I went back to the United States after finishing school. I would have preferred to leave it all behind, to let it all burn behind me—"

"But it's not in your nature?" I asked.

"No, it very much *is*. But that's the problem isn't it? Sometimes seeing something through to the end isn't just about leaving it behind, it's about fixing the damage. Even if you weren't the one who caused it," she explained with a sentimental look on her face.

"Why do you care what happens to the Americanos?" I didn't hide the suspicion in my expression.

"Can I be frank with you? You seem like a woman who's seen it all."

I sat back into my chair and crossed my arms over my chest with a nod. She took notice of the Santa Muerte statue on my bookshelf and smiled.

"I know that you know what my family is capable of doing. And I also know what *you* are capable of Señora Presidente, because I've *seen* it. I've dreamt of your necklace made of teeth, I've dreamt of the scar on your back and your childhood villa burning down, twice."

"Excuse me?" I leaned forward, my mind running wild with thoughts of betrayal and the breach in my security that I was going to have to address.

I was too old to be killing my own men, too in the public eye. The deeper I got into politics the more I entwined the cártel into it, blending the two into one so that no one could tell them apart. It was my second term, and in my six years in office we'd fixed most of the country's violence, drugs, and poverty. México's currency stood amongst the highest in the world. I knew that when the time came for me to step down, the divide would begin once more, and that would all depend if my successor and I would see eye to eye.

After all Señora Presidente was just a temporary title, Reina del Cártel was my fucking name.

"Relax. My family has been contracted with... a deity, for generations." She looked back at La Flaquita knowing she didn't need to explain herself.

She didn't.

Where she was contracted to whatever demon held her leash, prisoner to doing their bidding, I was just a servant of death. Devoted to her, merely a child at her altar accepting whatever love she would give me in return for my offerings.

"There is a reason why we are the ones putting people in power. I've been getting glimpses of your past for the last two years, now most recently I've seen your future." She smirked.

I hardened my eyes, not trusting this overly cheery stranger who dared speak so openly like she had no secrets.

"We're going to do great things together, Celia Flores. The faster you accept it the faster we can clean up that mess."

"What do you want from me?" I asked, knowing damn well she wouldn't be here, revealing so much to me if I wasn't already involved in her own mind.

"We're going to fix the North." She smiled big, the kind of smile that still hurt my face from time to time when the old scar pulled at my skin.

"An impossible dream," I said. "What makes you think I would even want to?" she asked.

"Because it is no longer in *your* nature to leave things burning behind you." She stood up from the chair and dropped a black card with a gold outline of a horned goat on it.

There was nothing more on the card at all.

"Come find the Satanic Shrine when you are ready."

"You know my ties run deeper than politics. I can't abandon my country." I told her.

"We both know you've already trained your replacement, and that she's more than capable of taking over once you decide to step down. *Whenever* you decide to step down. This will be the first time leadership is passed without bloodshed, am I wrong?"

She knew too much, but everything she knew seemed to be the truth. I'd been training Dominico's daughter Gabriella to take my place for the last twenty years. Her father passed five years after working for me and I didn't hesitate to take her under my wing. There was something in her eyes that reminded me of everything I could have been. It made me want to give her more than the chances I was offered, just to see where she would go with them. Maybe I was projecting but my therapist didn't seem to think that was an issue.

I had broken a generational cycle.

It was enough.

She stepped out of my office, leather boots clad with buckles all the way up to her knees clinking together as she walked away from me.

So fucking typical, I couldn't even retire in peace.

The overworked Latina curse.

Payasada.

Closing Words

Hi.

We just spent a long time going through this story together and it felt right that we have a little chat about what just went down. We owe each other that. Thirteen months, that's how long Celia Flores lived in my head. There were so many alternate endings that ran through my mind while I wrote this story, and while a lot of them would have been satisfying, some even considered traditional, they weren't authentic to me, and they weren't authentic to our girl. Celia didn't want a traditional happily ever after, she didn't bleed herself dry just to walk away from it all. After everything, the happy ending that seemed to fit her best was… embracing her culture, owning her destiny, being with her men, and therapy. Because despite being loved by others, and despite them seeing past our flaws and faults, we still hold the responsibility of working on bettering ourselves.

Thanks for reading this little piece of my heart.

The Author

Santana Knox is the pen name of a Brazilian writer, neuro-divergent creative, follower of Santa Muerte and self acclaimed Witch who emerges from the foulest swamp bogs to bring you even filthier stories. Santana got tired of letting the voices in her head drive her crazy, and decided to write down the stories they were begging to tell instead. A lover of the unusual, and a hopeless romantic when it comes to toxic villains, Santana's books should always be taken with a grain of salt, specifically the kind that keeps demons away.

To enter her cult, join her facebook reading group: Santana Knox's Heathens, like her on facebook, or follow her on social media. (@Santana.knox)

Also By Santana

Heartless Heathens :
A why choose gothic romance

coming 2023:
No Place For Devils: Diablos Locos MC book 1

Acknowledgments

Amy - My friend, as always thank you for turning my trash into something worth reading. You're my rock.

Jessie K. - Thank you for giving me the courage to write this ending, thank you for the love and the encouragement you've given me every step of the way, I love you.

My beta demons: Jen, Louise, Kendall, Christian, Christina: I am so lucky to have found you, I would keep writing these crazy fucked up stories even if they were only written for you.

Siany & Mildren - Thank you for your help, for looking over this story to make sure everything was in its place and represented correctly.

Ruthie, Jessie A., Aleera, Erinne, Addy, Wanika, Mildren, Steph - My love for all of you is eternal! I'm so grateful to have you in my corner!

Brianna - My sister, bestie, my emotional support person. Thank you for everything that you do for me on a daily basis. I couldn't do this without you. Your art inspires me to write better stories deserving of your talent.

Karen – Thank you for dealing with my insane brain!

To my husband, my family, my friends - I don't know what the hell you're doing here, but I'm either grateful or mortified, take your pick.

To my ARC team - You all mean the world to me, thank you for your support and love.

To all my readers – Thank you for continuing to pick up my stories, you all hold a piece of my heart.

Made in the USA
Middletown, DE
05 December 2025

22309902R00222